FAIRY BLADE UNMADE

ALSO BY THIS AUTHOR

AND MORE AT PDWORKMAN.COM

FAIRY BLADE UNMADE

REG RAWLINS, PSYCHIC INVESTIGATOR

P.D. Workman

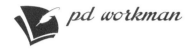

ISBN: 9781989415771 (IS Hardcover)

ISBN: 9781989415764 (IS Paperback)

ISBN: 9781989415979 (Large Print)

ISBN: 9781989415733 (KDP Paperback)

ISBN: 9781989415740 (Kindle)

ISBN: 9781989415757 (ePub)

To those willing to go above and beyond

And then beyond that

AUTHOR NOTE

Dwarfs or dwarves? The traditional English plural of dwarf is dwarfs, though dwarves was popularized by Tolkien, a fact he regretted. So please don't send me nasty-grams for choosing to use dwarfs in Fairy Blade Unmade.

"No reviewer (that I have seen), although all have carefully used the correct dwarfs themselves, has commented on the fact (which I only became conscious of through reviews) that I use throughout the 'incorrect' plural dwarves. I am afraid it is just a piece of private bad grammar, rather shocking in a philologist; but I shall have to go on with it." —J.R.R. Tolkien

CHAPTER 1

Reg looked around the cottage for some sign of the small black cat.

Starlight, her own cat, a tuxedo with mismatched eyes and a star in the third-eye position on his forehead, gazed at her, radiating irritation and displeasure. Reg looked down at the bowl Nico had knocked to the floor, scattering popcorn everywhere.

"What happened?" she asked Starlight.

He stared back at her. What did she think had happened? Did she think that <u>he</u> had somehow been involved in the incident?

Reg shook her head. "I know <u>you</u> didn't do it. But did he mean to? Or did he just—was it just an accident?"

Starlight's gaze didn't shift, nor did the emotions hanging around him like a dense cloud.

"Where did he go?"

Starlight broke her gaze and looked around. He stopped, ears pointing at the couch. Reg walked over to it, then got down to her knees to look underneath.

Nico, all black with blazing yellow eyes, crouched under the couch and, when she got down to his level, hissed at her, putting his ears back.

"I didn't threaten you, why are you hissing at me?"

He hissed again, just to make sure she understood what would happen if she reached under the couch and tried to pull him out. Reg already knew; the scenario had been repeated enough times. She had scratches all up and down both arms from previous attempts to pull him out of a hiding place, down from the drapes, or out of some situation he had gotten himself into. He was not a cat who appreciated any interference or help.

Starlight had spoiled Reg. She hadn't ever had another pet, not even a goldfish. Despite his quirks, Starlight had been a pretty easy animal to deal with. He might like to get her out of bed too early, make demands about the kind of food he wanted, and bite her ankles if he didn't like what she was doing but, dealing with Nico now, she understood what an easy cat Starlight had been. She'd had no idea how antagonistic a cat could be.

"Why did you knock down the popcorn?"

He stared at her. His aura was red, as it often was. She had trouble sorting out what he was feeling. Confusion? Anger? Fear? She sometimes had the feeling that Nico's emotions were much the same as

Reg's had been when she'd been a child in foster care. Hypervigilant, always afraid of what was going to happen next, unable to trust adults no matter how nice they might seem on the outside. Because all adults betrayed her sooner or later. If they didn't do something to hurt her, they were disappointed in her behavior, or they told her social worker that she needed more therapy. Or medication. Or hospitalization. Even the nicest foster parents were still trying to force her into a different mold, an unnatural fit. Reg had been the typical square peg people tried to jam into a round hole.

Was that what she was doing with Nico, expecting him to be like Starlight? Was she expecting his behavior and personality to be like a cat who was much older and had grown up in a different set of circumstances and had a different personality or needs from Nico's?

Before the arrival of the nine kattakyns, the magical black cats that the Witch Doctor had sent his self into, Reg had assumed that all cats were the same. People talked about them as if their natures were all the same. But she had found the nine identical black cats were not identical at all. They all had completely different personalities, some of them sleepy and some of them energetic, with different affinities for magical or psychic gifts, preferring different activities and social contact even when Nicole (pronounced NEE-cole in her owner Francesca's charming creole), the cat who had adopted them all as her own kittens, expected them to do the same thing—taking a nap, play hunting, or eating.

Nico was particularly distractible, always off doing something different from the rest of the cats. Chasing Reg's shoelaces when it was time to sleep or hunting for mice when there was food in his bowl. Then, of course, he would want to eat in the middle of the night and was very vocal and insistent that he be fed immediately.

Francesca was Nicole's owner and had taken on the job of taking care of the kittens. But Nico was getting to be too much for her and Reg had agreed to take him for a few days to see if she could do something with him. She had been pretty sure it was just a matter of persistence and paying attention to catch him being good, but he was wearing her down too. She was no longer sure that she was going to be able to do anything with him.

* * *

Officer Marta Jessup came back from the bathroom. She looked at the popcorn all over the floor and at

Reg, on her knees in front of the couch. "What happened?"

"Well, that's just what I was asking him, but he isn't in much of a mood to discuss it."

"You know he's a cat, right?" Jessup inquired.

"I know. But that's no excuse."

"Do you want me to pop some more?"

"I don't know. You can check in the cupboard to see if there is any left, but I don't think there is."

Jessup shook her head. She went to the kitchen and looked through the cupboards.

"You see?" Reg said to the cat. "You ruined our girls' night. We were going to do popcorn and a movie, but how do you do that without the popcorn?"

"We could have something else," Jessup suggested as her search petered out. "There's a bottle of wine and some pretzels."

Reg grimaced. Who knew how long they had been in the cupboard. Wine might improve with age, but that was when the bottles were properly stored in a cool cellar, on their sides and turned regularly, or whatever you were supposed to do with wine. Not when you just shoved it into a warm cupboard in Florida and hoped for the best. And the pretzels might have been there from the time she had moved in. She couldn't remember buying any. Sarah, her landlord, lived in the big house at the front of the lot. She might have purchased them, but usually, the stuff that Sarah bought for her was nutritious. Sarah tried to get Reg to eat properly instead of just snarfing down convenience foods whenever it was… convenient. But Sarah might have bought pretzels for herself and then decided she didn't want them, so she had gifted them to Reg.

"How about in the fridge? I think there might be ice cream in there."

Jessup opened the freezer door and pushed a few unidentified packages around.

"Yes, there is ice cream," she agreed, pulling out a couple of small tubs. Reg was of the opinion that if she bought the small, expensive containers, she wouldn't eat as much and wouldn't put on weight, but she had already noticed her skirts starting to get tight. She gave herself the excuse that she had been too skinny before, living hand-to-mouth and barely keeping herself off the streets, but she had a suspicion that if she were to weigh herself, she had put on a bit more weight than she hoped.

"Why don't you get the popcorn cleaned up, and I'll dish up the ice cream," Jessup suggested.

Reg sighed and got back to her feet. There was no point in dragging Nico out from under the couch. He would scratch her, and she wouldn't be able to explain to him what he had done that was wrong. He would growl and yowl and try to squirm out of her grip and, eventually, she would just let him go. He would slink off to pout in some corner. Or back under the couch.

She got out the broom and dustpan and started to sweep up the popcorn.

Starlight, who had an irrational fear of brooms and dusters, immediately bolted, running to hide in the bedroom.

Then again, Reg didn't know much of Starlight's history. His pathological fear of brooms might be totally logical. Maybe a previous owner had hit him with one. Or maybe witnessing Sarah beating down the garden with a broom as she tried to chase Nicole out of the yard had traumatized him.

Who was to say what a cat thought or why they did the things they did?

When Reg was finished cleaning up the popcorn, Jessup presented her with a large bowl of ice cream, several scoops of different flavors, complete with a spoon. Reg sat down on the wicker couch and sighed in satisfaction. She regretted the loss of the popcorn, but she couldn't deny the comfort of a bowl of ice cream.

Jessup sat down beside her, and they turned on the TV.

CHAPTER 2

While Reg was trying to train Nico to be a good kitty, Davyn was training her.

As Reg had grown up, any sign of psychic or magical gifts that Reg might have shown had been quickly beaten down. People didn't like unexplained things and, when something didn't make sense, they would alter their memories to a more logical explanation. The things that Reg heard in her head were easy to pass off as a wild imagination in the early years or psychosis as she got older and should have been leaving her imaginary friends behind. Reg being able to find lost items was easily explained; not that she had a gift for finding lost objects, but that she was the one who had stolen them in the first place.

When they saw something that wasn't easily explained, like glass breaking without anyone touching it, their memories were revised. The window hadn't just broken spontaneously, but Reg had thrown something or hit it with something. Other things that happened when she was upset were easily explained as violence originating with her temper tantrums and uncontrolled anger issues. A child obviously couldn't break things or fight someone without touching them, so she <u>had</u> touched them. And that was what everybody remembered.

Since she had arrived at Black Sands, things had been different. Instead of people denying what was going on and telling Reg that it was just her imagination, they told her that the voices in her head were the spirits of people who had passed on and that things breaking or falling down when she was angry were not just bizarre coincidences, but telekinesis. She had thought that the reason she was so good at fortune-telling was that she could cold-read people really well, but the witches and warlocks that she had met in Black Sands told her that she had actual psychic gifts.

While they had encouraged Reg to use her gifts, no one had ever trained her in any of them. They had given her bits of advice or told her that she could do things she didn't think she could, but the idea of someone training her to control and develop her innate gifts was new.

Davyn, the leader of one of the warlock covens in Black Sands, happened to be a fire caster—among other gifts—and having seen in Reg the signs that she shared this gift, he had taken her under his wing to teach her to use the gift without putting herself or others in danger.

"You don't want to be practicing fire casting without any instruction," he had told her. "That's just going to lead to injuries. Either to you or those around you. Or maybe you just burn down the cottage."

Remembering the way that the box of Yule candles had burst into flame when she had tried to send out her fire, Reg had been quick to agree. She didn't want anything like that happening without an experienced fire caster there to help her.

"You can teach me how? Is that... something that is done? Do I need to sign a contract with you or pay a retainer...?"

"Younger practitioners are traditionally mentored by those who are more experienced," Davyn assured her. "You don't have to sign in blood or mortgage your soul."

Reg had been a little worried about something along those lines, so she nodded in relief, laughing it off.

"Okay, good. But I'm not exactly that young. I mean, I'm adult, I'm not a kid."

"You are younger than me."

Reg found it difficult to assess the age of the magical practitioners around her. They all seemed to possess a youthfulness that belied their actual age. She would think that someone was fifty, only to find out that they were centuries old. She didn't think that Davyn was centuries old… but she believed that he was older than he looked, which was maybe his late thirties or early forties, like Corvin. Of course, Corvin too looked younger than his age, though she wasn't sure how old he really was. It was disconcerting.

"Besides," Davyn went on, "mentoring doesn't have anything to do with your chronological age, but with how long you have been using your gifts, or how much training you've had."

"Which is none."

He gave a grave nod. "A situation that needs to be remedied, especially with a fire caster. I'm surprised you haven't had any serious accidents in the past."

Reg nodded, frowning.

"Maybe you have, but you just haven't told me about them," Davyn suggested.

"No. I mean… not that I can remember. When I was in foster care, there were a few kids who were firebugs."

He raised his eyebrows. "Firebugs?"

"Kids who light fires. They would do it whenever they were feeling stressed or overwhelmed. Like kids who cut themselves. It's a safety release valve; helps them to feel better."

"I see."

"Not because they were fire casters; just because it made them feel in control, and to put on a show for people. They liked the attention. Seeing how much they could do without getting caught."

"You seem to be very well-versed in the situation."

"Well, yeah. You get to be if you live in the same house with one of these kids. You have to be aware of where they are at all times and what they are doing. You can't assume that just because things are quiet, you are safe. A fire can cause a lot of damage or injury before people discover it."

"Yes, it can."

"So I had to know about them. Why they did it and what to watch for. So I could help and get an adult if anything happened."

Davyn held his hands a foot or so apart, and slowly conjured a ball of fire between them. Reg watched it intently, feeling it call to her gift. She wanted to hold it and control it, to add to it.

"Are you sure that the other kids in your house were firebugs?"

"What?" She turned her attention to Davyn's face with difficulty, having a hard time prying her eyes away from the fire.

"Are you sure that it was one of the other children who was a firebug, and not you?"

Reg blinked at him. "Of course I'm sure."

"Were you ever around when they lit a fire?"

"No. Not there in the same room."

"So you never saw one of them light a fire."

"No. But why would they do it while I was there? They would hide it from me."

"Did they admit to lighting the fires?"

"No." But that was a ridiculous idea. Any kid would deny it. They didn't want to get in trouble.

"Then how can you be sure that they did it?"

"Because they were firebugs."

"Maybe you were the firebug. But you didn't light fires in the room you were in, because that would get you in trouble. So you sent it out farther away from you. And someone else took the blame."

"No…"

He squeezed the fireball into a smaller space, compressing it between his hands. Reg reached out to take it from him, eager to handle it herself.

"You went your whole life without lighting a fire?" he challenged.

"Of course I've lit fires. But just… the conventional way."

"And you never got in trouble for it? Or had one get out of control?" Davyn passed the fireball to her slowly, his movements small and deliberate.

Reg held the fire between her hands, feeling the warmth radiating from it. Not dangerously hot. She

didn't fear that she was going to burn. It just felt…
friendly and healing. Like sitting next to a fireplace on
a chilly day. Or roasting marshmallows over a
campfire. That warm, safe, welcoming feeling.

"Reg?"

Reg tried to focus on Davyn again. He had asked her a
question, but she wasn't sure what it was. "Sorry, what
was that?"

"You've never lit a fire that got out of control?"

The burning that came to Reg's cheeks didn't have
anything to do with the fire in her hands. "Well…"

Davyn chuckled. "Yeah, that's what I thought. Maybe
more than once?"

"I'm just… really good at lighting fires. If you wanted
someone who could light a campfire at a youth camp

or in a furnace that kept going out… I would be the one to call."

"Because you're really good at lighting fires."

"Yeah."

"Even with damp wood? Even when others had tried and hadn't been able to get it going?"

"Yes."

"And every now and then, maybe it's gotten a little bit larger than you intended it to?"

"Yeah, maybe. But… I was just a kid. Kids don't know…"

"I think you did know. You might have wanted to control it and keep it small, but you also wanted to burn. You wanted the fire to get bigger and bigger, and to consume all of your problems…"

The ball of fire in Reg's hands flared. She tried to keep her focus on it, to make sure that it stayed small and in control. Davyn's hands hovered around hers, not touching her, but shadowing her position and taking back some of the control over the fireball.

"Don't," Reg protested, "I can do it."

"One step at a time. You need to learn to keep your focus."

"How am I supposed to do that when you're talking about fires getting out of control?"

"I want you to feel the difference between when you have the fire under control, and when you let go."

"I didn't let go."

"You were close. You were losing control."

Reg made the ball smaller, trying to show him that she was still fully in control. The fireball quieted, letting her take back her control. Just like that. She could control it. It only took a little more focus. And Davyn not talking about how many other fires she had lost control of before.

It wasn't possible that the firebugs she had known in foster care hadn't really been firebugs. They had a history.

<u>Didn't they?</u>

It wasn't like her foster mothers had ever sat her down and told her about their history of fire setting. There had been discussions about staying safe and monitoring what was going on in the home, about everybody playing a part in keeping the family safe.

But talking about the history of another foster child would have been a breach of confidentiality.

"Stay focused. I want you to put your hands together."

Reg inched her hands closer together. The fireball stayed steady, glowing between her hands.

"All the way together."

Reg wasn't sure what would happen if she did that. Was it possible that she would get burned? Would Davyn tell her to do something that would be dangerous to her? She cast a sideways glance at him. "All the way?"

"Press them together, palm to palm."

Reg was anxious about pressing her hands into the flame, but she had seen Davyn press the fireball into Starlight when he was sick and needed healing. It hadn't hurt him. She took a deep breath and pressed her hands closer and closer together. Eventually, the flames were licking at her hands, but it just felt like the warm tickle she got when she passed her finger quickly through a flame. She had loved that trick when she was a kid, scaring the others by passing her finger right through a fire. Was that something all kids did, or just those with an affinity for fire casting?

She looked at Davyn. He nodded. She kept moving her hands closer to each other until the palms were pressed against each other, the flames disappearing. She didn't know whether she had smothered the fire, or if it was still there, inside her hands. She looked at Davyn for his next instruction.

"Good," Davyn approved. He didn't tell her to do anything else.

Reg parted her hands slightly to see if the ball of fire was still there, between her hands. Her hands glowed a little, but the flame was gone.

"You can safely take the flame within yourself, if you are properly focused," Davyn advised.

"What if I'm not focused?"

"Then it might be a little hot."

Reg grinned. It wasn't really funny, but she couldn't help smiling at his dry tone.

* * *

When the training session with Davyn was over, Reg saw him to the door. In the beginning, she hadn't been sure whether to allow him into the cottage. She'd had bad experiences with Corvin, another warlock, and was leery of inviting any others into her home. Nobody had warned her to stay away from Davyn as they had about Corvin, but what if there was some reason they wouldn't tell her he was dangerous? Sarah and others had neglected to inform her that Corvin could take away her powers if she allowed him to because it was a taboo in the community. What good did it do to tell her to stay away from him without telling her why?

Maybe other women would have heeded the warning without knowing the reason, but Reg had never been one for blind obedience. She liked to make her own choices based on what she knew and experienced for herself.

And nothing had prepared her for what she would face with Corvin.

"I'll see you next Wednesday, then," Davyn confirmed.

"Right." Reg had made sure to write it down in the appointment book on her kitchen island so that she wouldn't forget about it or schedule a psychic reading for the same time. "See you then."

"No practicing on your own."

Reg hesitated. How was she supposed to get better if she didn't practice? If she only practiced once or twice a week when Davyn was there, her progress would be at a snail's pace. She could advance much further if she could put what she learned into practice during the week and be ready to learn new things when she met with Davyn instead of going over the old ground.

Davyn raised one eyebrow and gave her a hard look. "No practicing on your own," he repeated. "You are not to do this without another fire caster present. You want to burn the whole place down?"

"I wouldn't. I can control it. I did really well today."

"You did well. But you needed to be reminded to focus, and you needed extra control more than once. You are not ready to practice solo."

Reg felt deflated. She thought she had done well.

Davyn patted her on the shoulder. "You will be able to in time," he promised. "Just not yet. You're still a toddler. You're not ready to go running races and climbing the monkey bars."

"Toddlers still get to practice toddling. Walking."

"Give it time. This is a safety issue, Reg. Promise me you won't."

What would he do if she refused to promise? Or promised but then broke her word? He couldn't exactly stop her from doing what she liked once he was gone. She stared past him, not meeting his eyes. "Fine."

"You will not play with fire until I come Wednesday?"

"What constitutes playing with fire?"

"Reg!" His voice was exasperated.

"Can I light candles?"

"No."

"Not even with matches?"

"No."

Reg rolled her eyes and folded her arms.

"Not even matches, Reg."

"Fine."

"What you can work on is meditation. The better you control your thoughts, the easier it will be to keep your fire under control."

"I don't like meditating."

"Use your crystal ball. Get Starlight to help you. If your mind is going every which way, you will not be able to keep your focus on your fire."

"Okay. I'll try."

"Good. See you Wednesday."

He finally walked out the door. Reg stood there, watching him take the pathway up past the big house to the street where his car was parked.

A shadow darted across the yard toward her. With a yelp, Reg jumped back, slamming the door before it could reach her.

CHAPTER 3

Reg wasn't fast enough. Something caught the door before it could latch properly, making it bounce open, back toward Reg.

She was prepared for Corvin or even a draugr or the Witch Doctor. She didn't have time to think, and the pictures that jumped into her mind were not all logical. She feared Norma Jean or Weston or some other shadow from her past. There were too many possibilities, too many dangers she had discovered since moving to Black Sands.

The peril that she faced when the door bounced back open was a boy, rosy-cheeked and short, with unruly brown hair and clothes that were dirty and patched, topped off with a dark hoodie that was new since she'd last seen him in person.

"Ruan!"

Despite his youthful appearance, the pixie was an adult, maybe even Reg's senior, though he looked about ten. Reg immediately looked past him for Calliopia, the fairy Reg had helped to rescue from the pixies, only to have her run off with one of them by choice. Since pixies and fairies were enemies, they were now outcasts from both of their communities.

But Calliopia was not behind Ruan. There was no sign of her. Had they broken up, then? Maybe Ruan had come after Reg for vengeance, somehow blaming her for whatever had happened between them.

"You are a powerful mage," Ruan said to her, bowing his head slightly. His hands in his pockets, he slouched there, not trying to enter the cottage, not making any accusations or trying to lay a curse on her.

Reg took a deep breath and tried to relax. Maybe there was a good reason for him being there. Maybe he wasn't there to hurt her.

But maybe the reason that he hadn't tried to enter was that he could feel the wards that kept enemies and uninvited guests from crossing the threshold. If she invited him in, then the wards would be defeated and Reg would be vulnerable.

"What are you doing here?"

"I seek my love."

"Your love?" Reg repeated stupidly.

He stood there, saying nothing, waiting.

Of course, Reg knew who his love was. "Calliopia is not here."

He nodded his agreement. "But you can seek her."

"I can't seek." She hadn't been able to psychically find an object reliably since she had been injured by the dagger currently in Calliopia's possession.

"You can seek <u>her</u>."

It was true that Reg had been able to seek and even call Calliopia in the past because they were magically bound together by the dagger. But Calliopia had severed that connection, or at least had tried to, the last time Reg had called her.

"How exactly did you lose her?" Reg asked, wondering whether they'd had a fight or whether Calliopia's eye had been caught by a taller and more handsome suitor.

"Do you invite me in," Ruan said, and his tone told her it was an instruction rather than a question. So he did know that the wards would prevent him from entering.

"No. I don't know your intentions."

"I will answer your questions. Tell you what happened."

"And then what? I don't trust you, Ruan. You've lied to me before."

Her words reminded her that she must not look in his eyes, or he might ensorcel her. He was, despite his childlike appearance, a predator. One who had managed to get control of her once before. She didn't think he could do anything while she was inside and he was out but, if he could still bewitch her in spite of the wards, he might be able to get her to walk out to him rather than needing her to invite him in.

She had found the pixies and fairies challenging to read. Their feelings were not as clear to Reg as human feelings were. While she could feel some emotions from them, it was an effort, and she often wasn't able to get anything from them. But as she studied Ruan, she started to feel emotions from him, bleeding off at the edges, as if he were trying to keep them contained, but couldn't quite manage it.

It was darkness. Not despair, but more than sadness. Mourning, helplessness, longing. Reg hesitated, wondering what to do.

"Why don't we sit in the garden?" she asked eventually.

He looked at her speculatively, but she didn't sense any anger or malice from him. He made another little bow. "It is your domicile."

Reg motioned toward the path that led to the garden. He turned toward it, and she stepped out her door and followed him. He didn't turn and attack her. Despite their small size, she knew pixies were very strong.

Reg looked around the garden. There were a few places to sit and, thanks to the ministrations of Forst, the garden gnome, everything was lush and blooming and beautiful. Ruan looked around, seeming unimpressed. He found a bench under the shadow of a tree and nodded to it. Reg walked over to it with him, and they sat side-by-side. At least that way, she could avoid his wide, childlike eyes. Ruan shrank his body as far into the shadow of the tree as he could and pulled the hood down over to shade his face. Reg looked up at the midday sun.

"Sorry about that."

Ruan shrugged. "I can withstand the sun," he said flatly. Pixies normally lived in the dark underground. The sun was something to be tolerated rather than appreciated.

"So... tell me what happened to Calliopia. The two of you... broke up?"

"No." He shook his head firmly, sending the brown curls bouncing. "She is mine. We do not break apart."

Reg waited for him to answer the question. He had said that he would explain what had happened. Ruan tugged at the hoodie once more and shifted uneasily. No doubt, he would have been more comfortable indoors, but she wasn't ready to open her house to a potential enemy. Not again.

"On rising, I entered Callie's bedchamber to greet her. She was not there."

He stopped, and Reg wondered whether that was the extent of the explanation. She waited, letting the silence grow, allowing Ruan to think about what he wanted to tell her. She was going to need to know more than that.

"Her sheets were in disarray as if a struggle. And there was blood." He swallowed audibly. "Much blood."

Reg's breathing became restricted. She put her hand over her heart, trying to calm the pounding. It was not a mere break-up or even a lover's quarrel. Calliopia had been injured. Or someone had been injured in her bedroom.

"And you don't know where she is? There was no sign of which way she had gone?" Reg hesitated to suggest it. "A blood trail?"

"No. She had not left the room on foot."

"No? How had she gone, then? Where could she go if she was injured?"

She could feel him looking at her, studying her from beneath the dark shadow of his hood.

"You will tell me."

"You have no idea?"

"It was fairy magic." Ruan shook his head. "I have not fairy magic. I could not read it."

"Do you think she was kidnapped? Taken by force?"

He nodded. "She would not choose to leave me."

Reg doubted that. She didn't know much about fairy relationships. Maybe fairies mated for life and it was rare for them to break up. But Calliopia was not mated to another fairy. She was mated to a pixie, and that had to be a problematic relationship. Calliopia, no matter how old she was, was still an adolescent, barely 'come into her own' as a fairy. Like the adolescents in many species, a teenage fairy's behavior was unpredictable, her magic difficult to control.

But blood in Calliopia's bed did not suggest that she had just decided to leave Ruan. There had been violence.

"You shall seek her," Ruan said firmly.

Reg conceded. She needed more information than she had. If she could seek Calliopia, she could decide whether to share that information with Ruan.

If it turned out that he was the one who had hurt Calliopia and he was trying to deceive Reg, she would know.

She closed her eyes and thought about Calliopia. It helped that she had just been working on focusing and training her mind with Davyn. Her mind was still close to a meditative state.

Calliopia.

She envisioned Calliopia's face, transformed from the rather homely visage of the pixie race she had been born into to the glowing beauty of a fairy as the magic of her adoptive parents had come to fruition. Reg tried to remember the bewitching melody Calliopia had sung when the pixies had kidnapped her in an effort to prevent her final transformation. Karol said that Calliopia meant beautiful voice, and Callie definitely had that. When she sang, all movement around her ceased while every soul listened. Reg hummed to herself, trying to find the notes and the melody.

It had been too long since she had heard Calliopia's song.

Beside her, Ruan sang a few of the notes in a voice like a choirboy's. Reg picked it up immediately. She pressed her fingers to her temples, humming the song and picturing Calliopia, trying to reach out with her mind to touch Calliopia. They had been connected once.

All at once, she was doubled over with pain.

CHAPTER 4

It was excruciating.

Reg clutched at her side, trying to find the wound and put pressure on it, hoping that her touch would dull or mediate the pain.

Her breath came in short, panicked pants, and she cried out as another stab of pain lightninged through her. She tried to find something to hold on to, aware that she had fallen to her knees, unable to see through the blinding pain.

There was a touch on her shoulder, a small, warm hand, which eased some of the pain. Reg tried to focus on her surroundings.

She was no longer seeing through her own eyes. One wall of the room was filled with floor-to-ceiling windows. The last time Reg had been there, the blue velvet drapes had been closed and the room had been only dimly lit. This time, despite it being a sick room, the draperies had been pulled open, and sun streamed into the room. There were several plants arranged around the bed that Reg didn't remember being there before.

The pain was a steady throbbing in her side, better controlled, but still nearly overwhelming. She pressed both hands to it, breathing shallowly.

"Where is she?" Ruan asked. "Show me where."

Reg wanted to know more first. She needed confirmation that Ruan hadn't been the one to hurt Callie. It was horrible to think of Ruan intentionally hurting her, but Reg was only too aware of domestic violence. Even a man who seemed devoted to his partner could hurt or kill her.

It was Ruan's hand on her shoulder, somehow lessening the pain to allow her to focus on her—or Calliopia' s—surroundings.

"What happened?" Reg asked, barely able to raise her voice above a whisper.

Gentle hands changed the damp cloths on Calliopia's forehead, attempting to cool her fever.

"Shh, Callie. Rest thyself," a woman's voice murmured.

"What happened? Who did this?"

"It is a mortal wound. You must be still and allow us to work healing magic."

Reg's mouth formed a name, and she forced herself to still it, not to voice it aloud to Ruan and give Calliopia's location away.

"A mortal wound," she repeated.

Ruan gave a strangled cry. "Take me to her," he insisted. "I must be at her side."

"No. I need to know what happened."

Reg pulled her consciousness away from Calliopia's mind, the pain slowly falling away until she was able to breathe and to look around and see her own surroundings again.

She was on her knees, hands clawing at the ground. She slowly climbed back onto the bench and rested there, feeling weak all over.

"Where is she?" Ruan demanded. "You saw."

"I can't tell you yet. Not until I know what happened to her."

"I will find out. Show me where she is. I will discover what happened."

Reg shook her head.

"It is a mortal wound," Ruan repeated, his voice taking on panic. "I must be at her side."

"Not until I know what happened."

He grasped her arm with fingers as strong as iron. "Tell me! Take me to her!"

"No."

CHAPTER 5

The emotions Reg had seen coming off of Ruan were now not just seeping out from Ruan's carefully composed demeanor. They billowed out like clouds of steam—rage, despair, alarm. Reg had no doubt that he loved Callie, but love could lead to violence just as surely as hate.

"You must not refuse me!"

"I want to find out more. But I can't do that with you here. You need to go away. Let me investigate further."

"Take me with you. Do you go to her?"

"I don't know. But I can't take you. Not until I know what happened."

He stamped his foot, fear transforming to anger. "You must take me to her."

Reg got to her feet, knowing how strong and violent pixies could be. She didn't want to have to defend herself against him alone. She didn't even have the cats with her; they were both shut in the house, where they could not help. Reg started back toward the cottage. Ruan jumped to his feet and grabbed at her once, but missed, Reg's arm slipping out of his grasp as she pulled quickly away.

"Leave here," Reg commanded, hoping that he would heed her if she were stern. If he wanted her help, then he would have to do what she said, even if he didn't like it.

Ruan stood still for a moment, scowling at her, then slunk off without a backward glance. Reg kept on eye on him as she went back to the cottage and let herself in, not wanting to be tricked into allowing him to enter with her.

* * *

The last time Reg had gone to the Papillon estate, she had been with Jessup. Detective Jessup had been the one who had involved her in the case of the missing fairy daughter in the first place, hoping that Reg's psychic gifts would allow her to guide the investigation in the right direction. Reg had succeeded in seeing Calliopia in her prison room, and they had eventually been able to unravel what had happened and to rescue her.

This time, Reg didn't know if she should recruit someone else to go with her or to just go on her own. She didn't exactly have a great relationship with fairies, and knew very little about their protocols and traditions. They seemed to be very rigid people, and if Reg did anything wrong, they might not allow her in the house or let her help. They would probably deny that Calliopia was there.

Reg considered her options. Sarah might know some of the fairy traditions. She had known some of the folk at the ball she and Reg had attended together. But Sarah had said that she had something to go to out of town. Reg hadn't paid much attention and wasn't sure if it was a witching conference or a singles event. Either way, it would be a couple of days until Sarah would be back.

Davyn had already been there to help Reg out and would undoubtedly have other things to get done.

She couldn't be alone with Corvin.

Damon, then? Or was she overlooking someone who might be of help? Francesca? Another witch or medium that Reg got along with? She could try asking Harrison, but he had a habit of wandering off or disappearing when she needed him.

Eventually, Reg decided that Damon was the best bet. She pulled out her phone to give him a call.

* * *

Damon accepted Reg's invitation to go out with her, despite the fact that she didn't expand on where she was going or why she wanted him. She met him at the cottage door.

"Do you know much about fairies?"

Damon pursed his lips and considered. "Aside from what I learned in school, not much. We covered general fairy history and treaties. I know some of the traditions and practices."

"Enough to keep me out of trouble?"

The corner of his mouth went up. "I don't know about that."

"Well, you're not likely to make it much worse, anyway. Are you?"

"I haven't caused any riots while providing security services. I deal with the kin and many other peoples in that work. You know that one of my gifts is in calming emotions."

"And that works with fairies too?"

"Just because they don't show their emotions easily, that doesn't mean that they don't feel just as deeply. In fact, sometimes I wonder if those who mask their feelings better actually feel things _more_ deeply."

It might have been helpful to have had Damon there while she was dealing with Ruan. Reg looked around as she and Damon walked out to his truck, squinting in the falling light.

"What are you looking for?"

"I just think…" There was a shifting shape in the trees beside the pathway, and Reg focused in on it. "I knew it. Ruan."

Damon frowned at her like she'd lost her mind. Reg had seen that look often enough before.

"Ruan," Reg repeated sternly.

The shadowy figure made a motion like pulling back a curtain, and became visible to both of them, making Damon jump. Ruan's expression was not a happy one.

"You have not gone to see Callie. Where is my love?"

"I will go see her. You need to stay away, or I won't."

"Not acceptable."

Reg folded her arms stubbornly. "Really? How are you going to make me go?"

He glared at her, his pupils wide pools of blackness that almost obliterated the blue irises. Reg looked quickly away before he could ensorcel her. She bumped Damon's arm to make sure that he was not taken in either. "I guess we'll just go inside."

"No!" Ruan moved toward her at a lightning-fast pace.

Reg's hand went up automatically to defend herself. She had been working hard at defensive spells, and Ruan stopped in his tracks. She was not as good as Corvin, and not even in Harrison's league, but she was pleased with how far she had come in a short period. It was the first time that she'd been successful in stopping an attack from anyone other than Corvin.

Damon looked at Reg, raising an eyebrow. He wasn't sure what she wanted him to do next. Reg let out her breath slowly, concentrating on the spell. She wasn't confident about holding a conversation and maintaining the protection at the same time.

"Do you want me to go see her or not?" she asked Ruan.

"You must see her."

"Then you'd better make yourself scarce."

He didn't move, looking at her. "What is scarce?"

"You need to leave. Stop trying to follow me or convince me to take you with me to see her. Otherwise, I'm just not going to go. I'm not going to do anything that might put Callie in danger."

"I would not put my sweet in danger."

"I've heard that line from too many men. I don't believe it. Not until I know for sure who attacked her and how she was injured."

"Not I!"

"I'm just going to go back into the house if you're not going to let me pass and agree not to follow."

He fell back a couple of paces, face like a thundercloud. He clearly did not appreciate being told what to do.

"And no following me," Reg repeated.

"I cannot follow human cars."

"I'm not so sure. You have magic. How do I know you don't have a magical way to transport to where I am?"

He looked offended by the question. "I have no such magic."

Reg looked at Damon, trying to hold her concentration on the spell, the threat from Ruan, and her conversation with him all at the same time. Not an easy task. "Can he?"

"Not that I know of."

"This is not piskie magic," Ruan insisted. "We do not magically transport."

"Or track?"

He blinked slowly. "No."

"He's lying," Damon advised.

Ruan hissed. "Unwelcome Diviner! You are not wanted here!"

"No tracking me," Reg repeated.

Ruan looked at Damon, then back at Reg, weighing his response. Finally, he stepped back again, giving Reg a bow.

"I will not track," he agreed.

Reg waited for Damon to tell her that Ruan was lying about that too, but he did not. He stayed silent at her side.

"Okay," Reg said. "You keep your word, and I will see what I can find out about Calliopia. If it was someone else who hurt her… I will see about you being able to visit her and be by her side. But I cannot promise that you will be allowed."

Ruan shifted from one foot to the other. "You can call her here. To you. Then I can be by her side."

"I don't know if I can call her if she is not conscious or strong enough for travel," Reg said. She didn't know nearly enough about calling. She had only done it once before, and she hadn't known at the time what she was doing.

Ruan considered this and gave a nod of acceptance. Apparently, it at least made sense.

She started walking down the path to the front of the house. Damon walked beside her. Reg focused on keeping the protective force around them. It was like walking and chewing gum at the same time. Something that should have been easy enough to do, but which required a lot more concentration than one would think.

They reached Damon's truck. Reg turned to look behind her to see whether Ruan had followed him, and could not see him, either in visible form or as a shadow. She looked for a long minute before deciding he had not followed that far and let the spell go.

Damon's shoulders tensed. He looked around and opened the truck door for her.

"Do you need a hand?"

Reg had been able to climb into his truck before, as high off the ground as it was. But she had been wearing pants that time, and had forgotten about that complication when she had called him to drive her to the Papillon estate. She had tried to dress in a way that would be respectful to the fairies, who tended toward traditional, old-world dress. Women in long gowns. Her skirt didn't quite meet the standard of a gown, but it at least was traditionally feminine.

She looked at the running board of the truck, trying to figure out whether she would be able to step up that far with the long skirt, which was a slim fit rather than her usual flowing skirt.

"Turn around," she told Damon.

He looked at her for a moment, eyebrow raised. Reg gave him a hard look. "I'd like to get out of here before Ruan changes his mind. So if you don't mind."

Damon smirked and turned around. Reg hiked her skirt up almost to her hips, managed to plant one foot on the running board, then used both arms to haul herself up. She let her skirt fall back into its natural position and scooted onto the seat.

"There."

Damon turned back around and closed the door for her, grinning. She suspected he had peeked. Without another word, he went around to the driver's side and easily stepped up into his seat. Long legs and no skirts; it wasn't a challenge for him. He turned his key in the ignition and the engine roared to life.

"So, where are we going?"

"I'll tell you when we're away from here. I don't want to worry about eavesdroppers."

He shrugged and pulled away. Reg waited until they were a few blocks away.

"Don't you think you're being a little paranoid?" Damon suggested.

"Was I being paranoid when I told you something evil was following me before?"

"No," he admitted. The draugrs had been only too real.

"I don't know all of the magical abilities that the pixies have, do you?"

"Can't say I do," he admitted. "We tend to know only general things about the other magical races, not specifics. Except for people like Corvin who might have made a scholarly study of such things."

That made Reg wonder if she should have called Corvin instead. But she couldn't deal with him on her own. She would have to call Corvin and… everybody else she knew who might be able to stand up to him. Not just Damon, but also Harrison. The three of them together would hopefully be able to control Corvin together. Maybe. Unless he'd learned how to manage all of the new powers he had acquired recently. If he knew how to exercise all of the Witch Doctor's capabilities, she didn't know if any of them would be able to withstand him, even together.

"So, where are we going?" Damon prompted.

"Do you know where the Papillon estate is?"

"The fairies? I know the general area, but I haven't been there before. Can you guide me when I get close?"

"Yeah, I think so. I've only been there a few times."

"Do they know that you are coming?"

"No."

"Fairies don't often entertain uninvited guests."

Reg shrugged. "I helped them with Calliopia once before. Hopefully... they're still grateful."

"And if they're not?"

"I don't know. I need to get in to see Calliopia and find out what happened to her. Ruan wants to be with her, and he is her mate. I assume the fairies would allow a mate to sit with her."

"When it's a pixie? I wouldn't be so sure. They are not on good terms."

"I know. But one step at a time. Right now, I don't even know whether Ruan is the one who hurt her."

"What did he tell you? Who did he say it was?"

"He said he woke up to find her missing from her bed, with blood all over the sheets. He doesn't know that she's at the estate. He asked me to find her."

"He didn't wake up when she was taken? If she was taken?"

"It didn't sound like they sleep in the same room."

"Ah." Damon's brows went up. "But he claims they are a couple?"

"I know they are," Reg confirmed. But she didn't tell him any of the details of how she knew. It wasn't her place to tell him what she might have seen in her crystal ball or within her mind. "Not all couples sleep in the same bed."

"I suppose not. But with youngsters... you would sort of expect it."

"They come from two different environments," Reg reminded him. "The pixies live under the ground in burrows, where it is dark and damp. The fairies like light and space and nature around them. I imagine they like... different sleeping conditions."

Damon looked suitably impressed at this line of reasoning. "When you put it that way, I suppose it makes sense. Ruan will want to regenerate somewhere cold and slimy, but Calliopia would want first light."

"As far as I can tell, he's spending most of the day aboveground. Probably enough to drive a pixie crazy if he can't get some burrow time."

"Crazy enough to kill his lover?"

"Or at least to attack her? Who knows? Do you know any stories about fairy-pixie matches?"

Damon shook his head. "I've never heard of such a thing."

CHAPTER 6

The long lane to the Papillon estate was just as Reg remembered it, so lush and green that there had to be fairy magic involved. She expected to see little Tinkerbells flying in and out of the trees and flowers, even though she knew that the Papillons were not that kind of fairy, if that kind of fairy even existed. The Elves, she had found, could make themselves tiny or fly through the air as twinkling lights, but not, it would appear, the fairies. They were a tall people, like the fairies from Tolkien's tales.

Damon's eyes were wide and interested as they drove down the lane, taking it more slowly than he had on the highway. He had never been there before, maybe never been to a fairy house before, so he was all eyes.

They reached the castle-like mansion at the end of the road, and Damon pulled carefully onto a gravel pad and turned off the engine.

"Now… you want me to go in with you? Or to wait out here?"

"Come in with me. I might need your… calming skills. I don't know how they're going to feel about me sticking my nose in when I wasn't invited. Like you were saying."

"Okay. I'm just not sure whether they will be happier about there being yet another person who wasn't invited to be here."

"We'll have to chance that."

He nodded and stepped down from the truck. Reg moved quickly to get out of the truck before he could get around to her side to watch how ungracefully she dismounted. She smoothed her skirts and walked sedately to the door.

She couldn't hear the chimes ring as she pressed the doorbell at the front door but, in a few minutes, the wide door was opened by a tall fairy Reg recognized. Not Mr. Papillon, but a fairy who seemed to be a servant there. The butler or manservant. He looked at Reg without expression and said nothing.

"I'm here to see Calliopia," Reg told him.

"Miss Calliopia is not receiving guests."

"I know. But I need to see her and to find out if there is anything I can do for her. Do her parents know? How did she get here?"

"This house is in mourning. Please leave and do not return without an invitation."

Ouch. That was harsh. Reg looked at him, frowning. "In mourning? That doesn't mean Callie is dead, does it? She was okay this afternoon…"

"She was not 'okay' this afternoon."

"Well, not okay," Reg amended. "But she was still alive. Is she… still alive?"

How awkward would it be if Calliopia had died in the interval between Reg seeing her psychically and making it to the mansion? How would she explain to them how she had known that Calliopia was mortally wounded, but she had not made it there in better time? If she had left right away, would she have been able to do anything for her? Maybe she would have been able to help… somehow. Reg didn't have the power of healing that Corvin did. Maybe if she had sent him over on his own, he would have been able to do something. Or maybe Sarah, with some potion she had whipped up in her kitchen. But Sarah was away, and the Papillons had not been eager to accept Corvin the last time he had gone to the estate. He would be even less welcome since his hearing and shunning by his coven.

"She lives yet," the butler informed Reg stiffly, but made no move to get out of the doorway and invite her in.

"I need to know what happened. What can I do?"

"You cannot enter. You are not invited."

"I've been here before. Tell Mrs. Papillon that it is me. I know Callie is injured, I saw earlier today... but I need to know more. I need to talk with her."

She wasn't about to tell the butler that Ruan wanted to come. She knew very well what his reaction would be to suggesting that a pixie be allowed into the house.

She'd be lucky if they didn't put some kind of curse on her and the generations to follow.

"Mrs. Papillon is engaged. She cannot take visitors at the moment."

"I might be able to help."

"There is nothing you can do." He looked down at her. "The Papillons are far more powerful than a human being. There is nothing you can do here."

Reg looked for an argument. Damon, beside her, was faster, coming up with an excuse as the butler started to close the door.

"Regina is more than just a human being. She has both immortal and siren blood. And she has been bound to Calliopia. She has already viewed Calliopia remotely today. She believes that she can be of assistance."

The butler hesitated, eyeing Damon, looking down his nose at the warlock as if he were a piece of something smelly that had been tracked in on someone's shoe. But eventually, he conceded.

"You will wait here," he told them. "You are not invited in... but I shall talk to the masters and see what they say."

"Make sure they know everything," Damon warned. "Don't just tell them you have unexpected guests."

The butler shook his head slightly and closed the door. Reg turned away from it in case there was some camera or remote surveillance, speaking quietly to Damon without moving her lips.

"What do you think? Do you think there's any chance they will let me in?"

Damon gave a small shake of his head. "Doesn't look promising. Fairies are not well-known for welcoming strangers or being talked into anything they don't want to do."

"I'm kind of stubborn too."

"Really?" His eyebrows went up. "I never would have guessed."

Reg laughed quietly, then felt guilty. They were standing on the doorstep joking, and Calliopia was inside, her life ebbing away. If they would only let Reg in to see her.

It seemed like forever before the door opened again. Reg was beginning to think that they weren't going to bother to give her a final answer. They would just leave the door closed and eventually, she would have to give up and walk away.

Then finally, the door opened, and it wasn't the butler, but Mr. Papillon, Calliopia's father. He looked down at Reg, considering her.

"I need to see her," Reg said firmly. "I don't understand the problem. You expect me to make an appointment or wait for an invitation when your daughter is on her deathbed?"

Fairies weren't easily shocked or surprised, but it wasn't the first time Reg had caused the Papillon family consternation. Mr. Papillon frowned, his brows drawing down, forming deep furrows.

"What know you about Calliopia?" he demanded.

"She has been injured. She's here. Her mother said it is a mortal wound. I want to see."

"Why?"

"Maybe I or one of my friends can help her. Maybe there's something we can do to heal her."

She thought about Corvin's healing powers. Davyn's fire casting. Harrison's powers were great if he could be talked into interfering with human lives. Into fairy lives. She knew that the immortals found humans entertaining, but didn't usually do anything to change the course of their lives. Except maybe for their favorites. Reg had benefited from Harrison's protection in the past. Possibly. But she had no idea how the immortals felt about fairies. Were they friendly with each other? Enemies? Indifferent?

"We are already treating Callie. There is nothing you can do."

"Fairy magic is good," Reg countered, "but it isn't the only magic."

Even the gnomes had specialized knowledge of what they called physic. Maybe they knew a few herbs or remedies that the fairies didn't. One race couldn't have all of the knowledge.

Mr. Papillon cocked his head, looking at Reg with a faintly puzzled expression. Finally, he drew the door back to admit Reg and Damon. He looked Damon over as he walked in, but did not object to his coming in with Reg. After entering the house, Reg turned and looked behind her, searching for the shadowy form of Ruan. Did he have the ability to follow them there? He had given his word, but did pixies have any honor? Did an oath mean anything to them? Or would Ruan decide that finding Calliopia was more important than any strictures Reg had put on him?

"Did you see something?" Damon asked.

"No… just checking." Reg turned back to Mr. Papillon, a little uneasy. "You have wards that would prevent… uninvited guests, right?"

"Of course." Mr. Papillon didn't seem to be in any hurry to take them to Calliopia, perhaps doubting his own decision. "Who, exactly, would intrude here? You do not mean yourself."

"No… I was more worried about Ruan."

"Ruan." Mr. Papillon said it as if he had no idea who she meant.

Reg had assumed that he would know more than she did about the pixie that Calliopia had run away with.

But perhaps Calliopia had managed to keep that a secret from him, and he knew only that she had run away.

"Ruan... Rosdew."

Mr. Papillon sucked in a quick breath between his teeth. "Rosdew. A pixie name."

"Yes. He's a pixie. That's who... that's where Calliopia went..."

"She did not return to the pixie burrows. She would not. Not when she had come into her powers. Spending her time underground... she would die."

"She didn't go back to the pixie community here. The two of them stayed together. Just on their own." The fairy and pixie communities were sworn enemies, so how could the two of them ever be part of either one again?

"A Rosdew." Mr. Papillon still seemed stunned by the development. He put his hand on the doorway he was about to walk through, as if he needed the support. "That is… that was…"

Reg nodded. "That's the family you stole her from."

He did not demur to her use of the word stole, as if it meant nothing to him. Reg knew that it probably didn't. Fairies had a low birth rate and supplementing it by taking infants of other races and over time magically transforming them into fairies seemed to be no different to them from legal adoption among humans.

"Then… to answer your question… no, our wards could not keep Ruan Rosdew away from this place. Not with the blood magic Calliopia did. He is… of her blood."

"Even now, when she's been transformed into a full fairy? Doesn't that change her DNA?"

He frowned at her, nonplussed. "DNA?"

"The… stuff that makes her unique? That makes one fairy different from another and fairies different from pixies." Reg looked at Damon, hoping that he could answer the question or contribute to the conversation. "Hasn't… that all changed?"

Damon shrugged widely. "It is hard to know how science and magic intersect. I don't know how their magic affects a person biologically."

"But she isn't a pixie anymore. She isn't a Rosdew. She's a fairy. You changed her to be like you, part of your line," Reg addressed Mr. Papillon again.

"They sprang from the same source," he said firmly. "I cannot protect her and bar him."

"Dang it. Then you'd better keep an eye out. I did everything I could to keep him from following me here. But if he figures out this is where I was going... he could show up at any time."

Mr. Papillon moved out of the doorway he had been standing in, back into the large hall that they had entered through, and picked up a small silver bell. He shook it, letting the clear tinkling sound reach through the house. In a moment, the butler was back again. Mr. Papillon leaned close to him and spoke in a voice too quiet for Reg to hear. But it was obvious he was explaining to the butler about how he needed to guard against further unwanted guests. The manservant glared at Reg, then eventually withdrew, disappearing into another wing of the house. Reg watched him go.

"I need to see Calliopia."

Mr. Papillon did not begin the argument again, but gave a small nod and led them toward the stairs.

CHAPTER 7

Even if Reg hadn't been in the house before, she would have known that she was getting closer to Calliopia. She wasn't trying to connect with the fairy psychically again, but she could feel how close Calliopia was, and how much pain she was in. She stumbled on the stairs, and she had to stop partway up to breathe and get the strength to make it the rest of the way. Damon stood by her, looking concerned. But he knew enough to stay quiet and wait for her to either get herself together or to tell him what she needed him to do.

Reg breathed a few more times and continued to climb the stairs.

Mr. Papillon stood at the top of the stairs, watching her. His skin was so pale it was like moonlight, and she tried to remember if it had been that white the last time she had seen him. He looked like he might fade right away. Did fairies do that? Just give up on life and evaporate into nothingness? She thought she might have seen something like that in a movie. But movies didn't reflect real life. Not even close where the paranormal was concerned.

Mr. Papillon reached to her when she was three steps below him, and Reg reached out her hand to take his automatically, not even thinking about it. His touch was cool, but even so, strength flowed into her. He didn't ask her what was wrong with her. Maybe he already understood what was going on.

Reg took a deep breath and made it up the last three stairs a little more easily. "Thank you."

"It's just along here."

She remembered which door it was. Mr. Papillon led them into Calliopia's bedroom.

Calliopia's mother sat beside the bed. Reg remembered the lovely, fresh-faced woman, who looked like she couldn't possibly be old enough to have a child Callie's age. But Jessup had told her that the fairies were probably centuries old. Even Calliopia was not likely a teen by human standards, but Reg's senior by several decades. Which explained why so many of the fairies insisted on calling Reg a child.

The last time Reg had seen Mrs. Papillon, or the last time before Reg and Jessup took Callie home, Mrs. Papillon had been exhausted and weighed down with a burden the pixies had left on her. Physically drained to the point where she was aging rapidly and felt as if she might drop at any moment. She was more energetic this time. Reg could feel her restless energy, her desire to be up and doing something for her daughter instead of just sitting there watching the life fade out of her. But emotionally, she was like Ruan, already in mourning, having lost hope that Callie could return to them whole.

Mrs. Papillon lifted her head as her husband came in. She saw Reg and straightened, forcing a smile. She rose gracefully to her feet and stretched out her hand to greet Reg.

"Miss Rawlins, a pleasure to see you again."

Reg squeezed her hand lightly, pain slicing like a knife through her heart. "I'm so sorry. I had to come." Reg didn't explain further, but approached Calliopia's bedside, dreading what she would see and feel. "Do you know how it happened? How did she get here? I don't understand how, if she was so badly injured, she managed to make it back."

"It is a homing spell," Mrs. Papillon explained. "Most fairies have one. If she is badly injured or sick, the homing spell brings her back here. Where she can be cared for."

"Oh. So ‚you brought her back."

The fairy woman shrugged her lovely shoulders. "In essence."

"And do you know... can you tell from the spell or her condition when she arrived here... what happened? What injured her? Or... who?"

Calliopia's mother sat on the edge of the girl's bed and readjusted the chair she had been sitting in, indicating that Reg was to take it. She stroked Calliopia's hand. Reg couldn't feel it. Whether because Calliopia's pain was too great for her to be able to be soothed by her mother's touch, or because Reg wasn't connected with her deeply enough, she wasn't sure.

"She has a dreadful wound," Mrs. Papillon whispered. She reached out and pulled the sheets back from Calliopia's body, and Reg flinched away, not wanting to see the bloody wound. She knew how much it hurt. It had to be terrible. But she couldn't look away for long, and in a minute she looked back, needing to see just how bad it really was.

But all she could see were thick, white bandages tied around Calliopia's waist, without a spot of blood. Calliopia's skin was the same color as the bandages, not a shade darker. Reg swore under her breath, shaking her head. Tears sprang to her eyes.

"Was she in a fight? Did somebody attack her? Try to kidnap her? Or was it with... someone close to her? A betrayal from a loved one."

Mrs. Papillon's eyes widened. "A fairy would not hurt another this way."

Reg was pretty sure there were fairy wars. And surely they were just as bloody as human wars. But she didn't try to argue the point. The important thing was to find out how Calliopia had been hurt. Reg grimaced, trying to figure out how to say what she needed to. She glanced over at Damon for help.

Damon closed his eyes, breathing out. In an instant, Reg's mind was filled with vibrant images. Reg talking comfortably with the fairies, helping them, finding a way to help Calliopia.

She blinked and glanced back over at Damon. She had told him before not to put images into her mind, but this time he had done it when she had looked to him for help. She had to accept that visions were his gift, and that was how he was going to help her.

His visions were intended to make her more comfortable, to make her see how she could help Calliopia, if she would relax and let it happen. Reg squared her shoulders and pressed forward. She didn't know the best way to tell them what she needed to, but she didn't need to know the best way, she just needed to do it.

"Mrs.... Mrs. Papillon..."

"Yes...?" The fairy nodded to her, encouraging her to go ahead.

"This wound... you can't tell if it was someone she loved? Her mate, for instance?"

"Her mate?" Mrs. Papillon shook her head. "Calliopia was not mated."

"She had… I don't know what you would call the relationship. I don't know your ways. When she left here, she didn't go alone."

Mrs. Papillon stared out the window. There was a faint crease across her forehead. Just barely visible.

"Fairies who have just come into their own… they often take time to learn about their magic and to come to know themselves. It is not unusual for a new fairy to go off on her own."

"But that's not what happened. She wasn't just exploring her powers. Maybe she was doing that too, but there was a boy. She didn't leave to be on her own. She left to be with him."

Mrs. Papillon shook her head slightly, but she didn't argue the point. She seemed to accept that things might have happened to Calliopia of which she was unaware.

"If she had taken a mate… she did not inform us. The kin have important ceremonies and traditions. They are not like humans, who just… move from one relationship to another from one day to the next."

"She might not have felt like she could have told you about him."

"It is an important part of our tradition. And fairy children… they do not pick their own mates, like humans and other animals. Their parents and other close kin, they make the appropriate arrangements."

Reg looked at her, trying to find a way to explain Ruan.

Calliopia's father spoke. "The child said that Calliopia had taken... a Rosdew."

Mrs. Papillon's hand flew to her mouth, covering up the open 'O' of dismay. She shook her head wordlessly. Reg covered her eyes, unable to look at either of them, embarrassed and awkward.

"A piskie. No."

Reg nodded her head without uncovering her eyes. "Yes. Ruan Rosdew. He was... from her family. Her pixie family." To Reg, that was the worst part of all. Not that Calliopia had taken a mate from another species, or had broken the feud between the pixies and the fairies, but that Ruan was part of her own family, among humans one of the most grievous taboos.

But to the fairies, that didn't seem to matter at all. Callie was a fairy, part of the Papillon family, and Ruan was a pixie, part of the Rosdew family, and their relationship was taboo for much different reasons.

"Could he have been the one who hurt her?"

Reg uncovered her eyes to look at Mrs. Papillon. She didn't want to meet her eyes, didn't want Mrs. Papillon to take out her anger on Reg, for being the bearer of bad news. She just wanted to work through it and help Calliopia.

"He?" Mrs. Papillon looked at her daughter. "Could he do such a thing? Attack his own mate unaware?"

"I don't know." Reg thought it was a rhetorical question, but she didn't know the answer to it. She didn't know enough about fairy or pixie lore to know whether that was something that happened. "I was hoping you would tell me. He came to me, asking after Calliopia, begging me to find her for him. He was afraid of what might have happened to her, had no idea where she had gone. I guess he didn't know about homing spells or didn't know that she had one on her."

"A Rosdew came to you?"

Reg nodded. "Yes. I'm sorry. I didn't ask him. I don't… I don't even like pixies. But he showed up at my house, begging me to connect to Calliopia and find out where she was."

"He knows you are here? That she is here? This magic is not known to piskies."

"No. I didn't tell him. And I told him he couldn't follow me or track me to find out where she was. I tried to protect her until I could find out if he did this."

"Why would he?" Mrs. Papillon asked blankly. "And if he did… he would not be asking you where she was."

Unless he wanted a chance to finish the job he had started. Or maybe he was remorseful. Abusive partners were often remorseful. For a while. Until they got angry again.

Reg gathered from the answers that Mrs. Papillon was giving her that Calliopia's family knew even less than Reg did. And that meant that Reg would have to find out the answer herself.

CHAPTER 8

"Mrs. Papillon…"

"Yes, child?"

"Can I… touch her? Connect with her?"

Mrs. Papillon started to shake her head. "Humans are very frail. I cannot say what would happen to you if you were to join with her while she is in this state."

"I… did earlier. Today. When I was looking for her. That's how I knew she was here."

"This is not a light thing. It is very dangerous."

"I don't know how else to help her. I think… we need to find out how she got hurt. If it was not Ruan, then she would want him at her side, wouldn't she?"

Mrs. Papillon's eyes widened in alarm. "That would not be done."

"If he is her mate, then shouldn't he be at her side when she's in such a bad state? Shouldn't he stay with her until... the end?"

"If he were of our kin... of course. But he is not. He does not have that right."

"You have to let him. If he wasn't the one who hurt her. He is... in a great deal of pain. Like you are. I can feel it."

"Piskies." Mrs. Papillon shook her head in disbelief. "It is not done."

"There have never been fairy-pixie pairings in all of your history?"

She looked uncomfortable at that and didn't answer. "If you can change pixies to fairies, then there must be some compatibility between the species. I know that pairings are possible between other races who are… even less alike." Reg thought about what she had learned about the immortals. She couldn't even begin to wrap her mind around that one. The stories in ancient mythologies about gods coming to earth and pairing with mortals or even with other parts of nature were beyond her comprehension. Fairies and pixies she could understand. They had the same basic human-like form.

Mrs. Papillon looked down at her daughter. She touched Calliopia's cheek. Changed the cold cloth on her forehead.

"Isn't there anything else you can do for her?" Reg asked. Their medicine seemed primitive. "No fairy doctors? Spells? Potions?"

"We have done all in our power. It… is not enough."

"Then maybe me, or one of my friends… if I can figure it out, maybe one of us can help to heal her. I know several healers. We might be able to do something."

Mrs. Papillon stroked Calliopia's hair. Callie's father stepped closer to the bed so that he and his wife were side by side.

"If you wish it," Mr. Papillon said finally. "What will happen to you when you join with her, I do not know. It is your own choice. If you choose death… that is upon your head, not the kin."

Reg nodded. She didn't dare look at Damon. She was sure that he hadn't had any intention, when she had asked him to go with her, of letting her die from joining with Calliopia. But he didn't put any vision into her head to dissuade her. Reg had to give the guy that. He hadn't tried to interfere with her business. However crazy or dangerous it might be.

Reg rose from her chair. She wasn't sure exactly what she was going to do and had no idea what she would find. She wished that Starlight were there with her. He was good at helping to focus her psychic energy and guiding her to the right choice. But fairies didn't like cats, and they wouldn't have allowed him in the house. Reg remembered Calliopia and Starlight hissing at each other, and couldn't help smiling at the memory.

Not appropriate. Not when Calliopia was on her deathbed.

Reg didn't want to waste any more time. She motioned for Mrs. Papillon to relinquish her spot on the bed at

Calliopia's side. Mrs. Papillon moved from the bed to the chair, moving it back a little so that it would not impede Reg's movements.

Reg sat on the bed beside Calliopia, dreading the moment when they would connect and Calliopia's pain would overwhelm her. She didn't want to go too deep. If she could connect just enough to find out what it was that had happened to Calliopia. That was all she needed. Then she would know whether she could allow Ruan at her bedside or not, if the fairies would allow it. And maybe, just maybe, someone would be able to tell her what she needed to do to heal Calliopia. There had to be a way to overcome the wound she had been given. If she had been a human, she would have been in intensive care, not just lying on a bed at home with a cold compress on her head, hoping that she would heal by herself. It seemed the height of foolishness that they were not able to treat her medically.

Then again, Reg herself had once had a magical wound that no amount of allopathic medicine had been able to heal. And Starlight had received a magical curse that had kept him from recovering from being poisoned. There were magical spells that could make injuries worse or prevent them from being healed.

"Callie. Calliopia, do you know who this is?"

She didn't touch Calliopia at first. Not physically and not psychically. She just sat beside her, reaching out with her voice. "It's Reg Rawlins, Callie. Do you remember me? Do you remember how I rescued you from that dungeon? My friends and I? We helped you once before."

There was no sign of movement or understanding from Calliopia. She lay there as if she were asleep, oblivious to everything going on around her. But Reg knew when she had joined with Callie before, she had been able to see and hear everything. Calliopia knew that Reg was sitting there, could hear every word she was saying. But did she care? Did she understand that Reg was trying to help her? And was there any possibility Reg could do something for her?

"Callie. Talk to me."

Calliopia's lips moved. Otherwise, she lay still as a statue, and just as pale as marble. She looked like something that had been carved by a great artist, and then left there to lie on the bed until someone could, somehow, magick it to life.

Reg reluctantly reached out toward Calliopia, and let the very tips of their fingers touch. Almost as soon as she did, she felt a rush of movement, the roar of waves, and was nearly overwhelmed with pain in her side. She tried to stay sitting up, tried to pretend that it wasn't affecting her like it was.

"Calliopia, what happened? Show me what happened."

There was too much pain. Reg couldn't see anything through it. She opened her eyes wide enough to see the bandages on Calliopia's side, and she touched them gently, trying to soothe the pain. She didn't have a gift for healing, but she had helped to give Starlight strength when he had been sick, and she tried to dig down deep into that part of herself and to ease it just a little.

"Reg?" She could hear Damon speaking to her, but he was far away. "It's too much, Reg. You're going to lose yourself."

Reg shook her head. She knew she could do it. If they would just let her, she could give Callie the strength that she needed, find out what had happened to her, and find the way to heal her wound. Reg could do all of that if she just focused hard enough and had all of the skills. But she worried she didn't have any gift but psychic ability, and all too often, even that failed her. She had figured out where Calliopia was, but was that just a good guess? Where else was she going to go if she were injured?

Reg poured all of the energy she could into the wound, trying to envision it, to explore it even though it was covered. She tried to knit together the flesh, to stanch the leaking blood, to encourage Calliopia's body to heal itself, the way it was meant to.

What had happened to her? How did a fairy get attacked in the middle of the night? Surely she had protections around her room and her bedchamber. She would have done whatever she could to avoid being harmed by an enemy.

Unless Ruan were the enemy.

CHAPTER 9

"No!"

Reg was nearly thrown back by the emphatic denial. She wasn't sure where it had come from at first, then realized that it had come from Calliopia herself. It had not been a verbal reply, though it had been so powerful in Reg's head that it had felt like a shout.

Calliopia could do and say nothing else, but she had given Reg the one answer she needed. It was not Ruan who had harmed Calliopia. Or at least, Calliopia would never believe that it was.

"Then who?" Reg whispered. "Who could get into your bedroom at night to harm you? Did you not weave protections? Didn't you guard yourself?"

There were no more answers from Callie. Reg tried to picture every detail she could. Calliopia preparing herself for sleep. Saying goodnight to Ruan. Weaving protective spells around herself and Ruan before they separated and went to bed. Callie in a nightgown, a white lacy thing, looking like an ageless queen.

She had sung her song. That was how she had initiated the spells that would protect her. The spells helped to keep away enemies. They provided her with protection of the innermost parts of who she was. It was more than just physical protection; it was something that would help her regenerate and retain her identity and grow and learn more about the magic she held.

"I am a fairy." Reg could hear Calliopia's exultant joy when she had become a full fairy and come into her powers. She had been so proud to be a fairy and to have the magic she did. Reg meditated on those words. The pain still pulsed in her side, threatening to make her black out, but Reg did the best she could.

She hung on to all of Calliopia's words. All of the things she had ever said to Reg.

And then instead of hearing Callie, she heard Ruan's voice.

"It is an evil blade. It will cause pain to both of you."

She was so startled that she opened her eyes and looked around, sure she was going to find Ruan standing right next to her.

Reg felt a chill like ice water rush over her. It was like she'd been dumped into a dunk tank.

"Ruan."

She looked around, again making sure that he wasn't there. She looked at Mr. and Mrs. Papillon, their pale faces worried.

"It was not Ruan who hurt her. But he might... know something about it. He might be able to help."

Mr. and Mrs. Papillon looked at each other, checking to see what the other thought.

"A piskie cannot help." Mr. Papillon asserted.

"There was a dagger. Did Calliopia have her dagger when she came back here?" Reg had no idea whether the homing spell would bring Calliopia and whatever else was with her, or just the girl herself.

"A dagger." Mrs. Papillon shook her head. "That evil dagger."

"It was... Ruan said before that it should be unmade." Reg struggled to remember what else she had heard about the dagger. Others had given her warnings about it as well. Reg wasn't likely to forget that it had harmed her at one point. It had been used to torture her and had cut into her hand, causing a wound that would not heal. Calliopia had used it to draw blood for a spell. Maybe the magic from keeping the knife at her side was preventing her from healing now, just as it had prevented Reg's healing.

"A blade that has imbibed fairy blood should never be allowed to exist," Mr. Papillon agreed. "It cannot be so."

"But it still exists. How do you… unmake it? Can you do that?"

"Can we unmake fairy steel?" Mr. Papillon demanded. "Here? No. That cannot be done."

"It must be done, but it cannot be done?"

"Fairy steel cannot be forged in our home. It needs to be smithed. We have not the tools nor the skill."

"Who can do it, then? We need to find out who can unmake the blade?"

The two fairies shook their heads at each other and looked at Reg with wide eyes.

"No one here can do this thing."

"No one here. In this house, you mean? Or... in Black Sands?"

"No one in this kingdom," Mr. Papillon said slowly. "It is a skill that is only had by dwarfs."

Reg put her hands to her head as the world tilted. She had assumed that when she came to Calliopia's side, she would be able to understand what had happened to the girl and would know something about what she needed to do to help her. But the one idea she'd had was impossible.

She still had no idea how Calliopia had been injured, who had been in that bedroom with her and inflicted such a horrible wound, but now she had another thing to worry about. She needed to unmake the fairy dagger if Calliopia were to heal.

But there was no way for her to do that. She couldn't just smash the knife with a hammer and achieve her ends. They needed to take it to the dwarfs. And how long would that take? Where were they? Sarah had told her before that there were no dwarfs living nearby. They probably lived halfway around the world, in Germany or Russia.

"It needs to be unmade," she repeated.

Mr. Papillon nodded his agreement, but did not appear to have the same level of concern about it as Reg did. His daughter was fading away on the bed. He didn't understand that the existence of the dagger might be what was preventing her from healing.

Reg took Calliopia's hand in her own and tried to connect again, but her energy was flagging and she wasn't sure that she could maintain it even if she managed to connect again. She might lose herself in the connection, as Damon had warned.

"Callie, stay strong. We'll figure this out. If you can just hang on… we'll figure out how to help you."

Reg was too mentally exhausted to hear any stirrings of Calliopia's consciousness. She looked at Mrs. Papillon.

"I need to go… recharge. If I come back, will you allow me in?"

It would be much easier if she could come back with an invitation the next time. Having to fight her way in was a waste of precious time and energy.

Mrs. Papillon nodded. "Of course. You are welcome here any time." She looked at her husband and at Calliopia lying in the bed. "If there is anything at all that you can do for her."

Reg shifted uncomfortably. "What if she wants her mate at her side?"

They both looked at her, eyes wide. Mr. Papillon's lips tightened. His expression changed only microscopically, but it was like a thundercloud had rolled across his face.

"She needs healing," Reg urged. "She needs her loved ones around her. She ran away from here with him. That means he is important to her. The magic that brought her back here—this homing magic—was that her magic or yours? Did she choose to return here?"

"It is… something she has had since she was a child. Any fairy, if she received a mortal wound, would want to return home."

Reg wondered briefly why this homing magic hadn't returned Calliopia to her family when she had been kidnapped by the pixies. Maybe because they _were_ her family. Or maybe something about the pixie magic or being held underground had countered the magic of the fairy spell. Or because she hadn't been harmed physically.

"So it is your magic, something you put on her, without her permission."

"Every fairy…"

"But she wasn't every fairy. She left here, knowing that you would not approve of her choice, ready to live separate from the rest of the fairies forever."

"This is who she is. A fairy. Loved by fairies."

"She is a girl who is in love with a pixie. You might not like that, but that doesn't make it not true. She is in love with who she is in love with, and he should be here at her side to give her strength and so that she knows her loved ones are all close by." Reg looked at them. "All of her loved ones."

"It is not done."

"So?"

Damon opened his mouth, trying to say something to her, but apparently unable to get it out or put it into words. Reg knew that confronting Calliopia's parents with reality might not be the best course of action, but she couldn't think of how else to convince them that Ruan had just as much right to be there as they did.

"You do not understand the ways of the kin," Mr. Papillon said.

"Those ways change. They can't stay the same for thousands of years. There are things that are different now than they were a hundred years ago, right? Look at the way technology has changed even in just the last decade. You can't expect everything to always stay the same. You make adaptations."

"Fairies do not mate with piskies. He has no place here."

"Fairies do mate with pixies."

His look told her that he would undo his wife's invitation if he could. But a promise had already been made.

"Denying what happened does not undo it," Reg pointed out. "It doesn't matter how many times you say it can't happen, that doesn't change the fact that it did. She is partnered with Ruan. He needs to be here with her. That's why he came to me."

"You may associate with piskies, but we do not."

"If Calliopia survives, don't you want to be a part of her life?"

Mr. Papillon shook his head slightly, and Reg knew that he meant that he didn't think Calliopia would survive, not that he would not want her to be a part of his life if she did.

"If she survives, you want her to feel like she can come back here. You can't do that if you tell her that she can't love the person she loves."

"If she wants to come back here, it has to be without him."

"Would she do that?"

It was Mrs. Papillon that shook her head this time. "Fairies do not leave their mates."

"Then he needs to be here with her."

Mrs. Papillon looked at her husband. He shook his head adamantly. "A piskie can never come into our home."

"What if you forget about the fact that he is a pixie and a Rosdew and just remember that he is Calliopia's mate?"

"It is not done."

"Does your household have to be the same as everyone else's? Can't you make decisions on your own instead of based on what everyone else has done?"

He seemed to have difficulty with this suggestion. Reg felt walls around him. Walls of tradition and taboo at war with his feelings for his daughter. Even though they were not a demonstrative folk, Reg had no doubt that they loved Calliopia. They just didn't know how to deal with her breaking their social rules.

"It's just like in the real world—the human world," Reg explained. "Parents might not like it when their kid brings home someone they don't approve of, whether they are gay or black or just a big jerk. But if they don't allow her to bring her mate home… then they lose that relationship with their child. So if the relationship is important to them, they do their best to accept their child's boyfriend or girlfriend the best they can. So they can keep seeing their child. And grandchildren."

He blinked at her. "This is what humans do?"

Reg nodded. "Some of them, yeah. The ones who want to keep seeing their kids."

He shook his head as if trying to clear away the cobwebs. "Humans are not the kinfolk."

"No. But they deal with similar problems. I can't tell you what they would do about pixies."

Mr. Papillon scratched his temple with one long, slender finger. He exchanged another puzzled look with his wife.

"Allowing a piskie in the house..."

"You told me yourself that you couldn't keep him out. He's of her blood," Reg pointed out.

"I cannot prevent him with a ward. That is not the same as not being able to keep him out."

She pictured him challenging Ruan to a sword fight, skewering him rather than letting him in to see Calliopia. She shuddered. "He has a right to see her. Calliopia took him as her mate."

Mrs. Papillon reached over and turned the cold compress on Calliopia's forehead over. "Perhaps... if it would give Callie the strength..."

"It is not done," Mr. Papillon repeated, but it wasn't a command overriding her suggestion; it was a question, uncertainty.

"It <u>could</u> be done," Reg appealed to his ego. "You are not an automaton, just doing whatever the other fairies tell you to. You have your own mind. You have not lived this many years without gaining wisdom."

Damon flashed Reg a grin of approval. It was apparently a good approach to use on a fairy.

Mr. Papillon nodded slowly. Reg waited. Was that a yes? Would he consent to Ruan's presence? After seeing the animosity between the two species, it was hard to believe that he would even consider it. But so was Callie pairing up with Ruan in the first place.

"We... have need to discuss this privately," he said finally.

Reg nodded and waited for them to leave the room. They stood looking at her for a minute, but Reg wasn't going to be kicked out. Eventually, Mr. and Mrs. Papillon left the room together. Reg was left there with Calliopia on the bed and Damon keeping watch.

"You've made progress," Damon said. "I wouldn't have thought it possible."

"Shh." Reg waved him to silence. "Do you want to stand outside and give me some warning when they are coming back?"

He raised a brow, then moved to obey. Reg was alone in the room with Calliopia. No other consciousnesses or emotions to distract her, just her and Callie.

"Calliopia..." Reg put her hand over the bandage. She was beyond tired, but she wasn't likely to get a chance like this again. "You must stay strong. Ruan is coming. He will need to see you. You can't leave him."

She could feel Calliopia's agreement. Her certitude that Ruan would come and that she needed to see him. Reg tried to focus on the wound to Calliopia's side.

"How did it happen? Can you tell me? Can you show me?"

The pain came again. Wrenching, burrowing its way into her like a screw was being rotated, deeper and deeper into her side. Reg wasn't just adjacent to Calliopia; she was inside her body and inside her mind. She tried to sift through the memories.

It had been a relief for Calliopia to find herself back in her parents' home, but at the same time, heart-wrenching, because she wanted her mate to be there at her side. She didn't want to die so far away from him. She had made her life with him, not the kin. Despite what she was, despite no longer being a piskie, life within the fairy community was not what she longed for.

She hated the burrows of the piskies. She was grateful to Reg Rawlins for rescuing her from them.

What she wanted was Ruan at her side.

From the time she had first seen him across the classroom at school, she had been entranced.

By a piskie? Dirty, earth-dwelling creatures? She had been raised to hate them. She had not liked the sun in the days before she had come into her own, but she would never have willingly entered a piskie burrow. She made her own shelters, pulling the heavy drapes closed, hiding under the blankets of her bed in order to escape the brightness of the sun. But she had never wanted to be a piskie. Never thought about that being her source.

Ruan's eyes. His laughing face. The wild, unruly brown curls and freckles sprinkled over his pale skin. He looked so childlike, but that hadn't put her off. The adult fairies and other species she met through school looked so old, their faces pinched and angular. Something inside Calliopia had predisposed her to Ruan's apple cheeks and puckish face.

My boy. My boy.

Even before she had formally met him, he had been 'my boy' in her head. And when they had met, quietly, away from everyone else, she lapped up every word he spoke. And she did the blood magic, mixing their blood, breaking the protections between Calliopia and the piskies. Without doing so, she never would have been able to be with him.

She held the dagger in her hand, enjoying the weight of it, studying the sharp point and the intricate carvings in the handle. The blade had opened the doorway between them. Had made their joining possible.

It did not matter that fairy lore said it should be unmade after having imbibed the blood of the kin. It didn't matter that Ruan said it was evil. It was hers, and she intended to keep it with her all her days.

CHAPTER 10

Reg knew that she had been asleep for a long time, but she didn't know where she was. She looked around the unfamiliar room, trying to construct a timeline that would tell her where she was and what had happened. She patted the bed beside her, calling Starlight. But he didn't jump up beside her and start nuzzling and purring.

"Star?" Reg called softly. "Where are you?"

There was movement, and then a shape beside her. "Reg? Are you okay?"

Reg tried to focus on the bearer of the voice. "You…"

"It's Damon, Reg. Are you alright? I thought you were a goner!"

"A goner?"

Reg's mind drifted for a long time, trying to put all of the pieces of the puzzle together. She opened her eyes abruptly.

"Callie!"

If Calliopia had died while Reg slept, she would never forgive herself. She was supposed to be completing a mission, not sleeping while her client faded into nothing.

"Shh. It's okay."

"Calliopia. Is she all right?"

"As far as I know, there has been no change. I haven't… heard anything." He shrugged. "Wailing or any preparations. It's been quiet."

Reg wasn't sure how comforted she was by this. "I need to see. And to get Ruan. We need to bring him here."

"I don't think you should go anywhere right now. You need to get your strength back."

"You're the one who will be driving. I can close my eyes and sleep all the way back." Reg sat up. Doing so caused a wave of dizziness and nausea. She held her stomach and closed her eyes. "Ugh."

"You see? I don't know what you were doing, but you expended a lot of energy. You had collapsed when I came back in."

"I can't just sit around here. Help me up."

"I think you should wait."

Reg braced herself to rise under her own power. If she showed him that she was able to get around on her own and didn't need to be coddled and get another twelve hours of sleep, he would be more likely to agree to drive her home. Then they could collect Ruan, and then… Reg couldn't think ahead any farther than that. When Ruan got to Calliopia's bedside, would that be the end? Would she let go at that point because her mate had made it there? Or would she hang on for longer, wanting to be with him for a few more hours or days?

The door opened quietly and light from the hall spilled into the room. Mrs. Papillon glided in with a tray of tea things, which she set down on a bureau.

"She is awake?"

Reg felt instantly assailed by guilt. Mrs. Papillon should be sitting next to her daughter again, seeing to her needs and providing her comfort, not making tea for Reg.

"I'm okay. You should go be with Callie."

"We treat our guests with respect. I have a restorative for you."

"I'm sorry. I don't want to take you away from her. Just leave it here, and I'll have the tea, and then go get Ruan."

Damon's brows drew down.

Reg shook her head, not understanding. "What?"

"They didn't say whether they would allow Ruan to come."

"But…" Reg turned her eyes back to Mrs. Papillon. "That's what you decided, isn't it? You are going to let him come see her, sit by her? Because that is what she wants. She needs him here."

Mrs. Papillon gave a single nod, a slight smile on her face. Her eyes shone in the dimness of the room. "The child is correct. We have decided... we will break with the tradition of the kin and allow this thing." She shook her head slowly. "It is difficult to believe that we would choose such a thing. But it is what Calliopia would want."

"What she _does_ want," Reg insisted.

Mrs. Papillon poured Reg's tea. "What she does want. You know this? She has told you?"

Reg nodded. "She wants him here."

"Then he shall come, to be with her in the end."

Reg took the teacup that Mrs. Papillon handed her, trying not to let it shake too much. She tasted it, dreading the bitterness that was bound to accompany the remedy. But it was sweet and light and didn't taste medicinal at all. Better than Sarah's potions, which always seemed to taste horrible. Even the sleepy tea tasted like she had scraped grass clippings from the bottom of an oily lawnmower and brewed them. Reg licked her lips.

"Is there... isn't there any hope? We have to be able to do something for her. She can't just... die."

"Fairies are hardy folk, and we live many years naturally. But we can be killed by knife or poison, or many other ways. We are not immune to violence and intentional harm."

"But you must be able to do something. Corvin, he's good at healing. He could try to heal her wound…"

"Corvin Hunter?" Mrs. Papillon gave a shudder. "I would not let such a creature near my daughter."

"Well, not normally, no. But he can treat her. He can try to heal her. If there's any hope, wouldn't you want him to try?"

"A drinker of powers? No. He shall not be allowed near my child."

"Well… someone else then. A fire caster or an immortal. Even a witch might know some remedy that you don't… or a powerful gem, like some of the pixies have. Every time I turn around, I'm learning of some other kind of magic."

Mrs. Papillon put her hand on Reg's arm, her touch as light as a butterfly. "You must not worry. If this is what is meant to happen…"

"How can you say that?" Reg challenged. "You can't just let your daughter die without trying everything within your power. You need to do everything you can, try every possible avenue."

"No. That is not our way. Some powers are best not accessed. We will do what we can do, as fairies, and if that is not enough, and the maker wishes Calliopia to return to her rest, then it shall be so."

Reg took a few more swallows of the tea. She was starting to feel less wobbly, her stomach settling down and the room slowing in its revolutions. "I have talked to spirits that have gone on," she said. "It isn't a very restful state."

"Your spirits may not be. But Calliopia shall find her rest."

Reg suppressed a 'not if I can help it,' and sipped the tea instead, keeping her eyes down. The fairies were not psychic, as far as she knew, but they could surely read her face if she gave away that she intended to go against their wishes.

"You can go back to sit with Callie. I'm feeling much better now. Damon is going to take me back to Ruan so we can bring him here."

"Thank you," Mrs. Papillon said softly. "This second time, you have helped my Callie. It will be the last. It is good to know that she will be happy, at the end."

Reg tried to swallow the lump that threatened to block her breathing. She put her hand on Damon, who was standing nearby. "Let's go."

CHAPTER 11

It took Reg longer to get down to the truck than she had expected. Going down the stairs after funneling so much energy into Calliopia and feeling her pain made it just as hard for her to get down the stairs as it initially had to go up. When they arrived at the truck, Reg stared up at it. It suddenly seemed much taller than it had been. It had been awkward to get into it with her skirt. It was going to be nearly impossible to do so again without any physical strength.

"Will you let me help you?" Damon asked.

Reg stared up at her seat, which could have been on the moon, it seemed so inaccessible.

"Reg?"

"Um… yes, I guess. But I don't quite know how I'm going to be able to get up there." Reg shook her head.

"Are you sure they didn't swap out the tires while we were in there?"

He swept her up in his arms without warning, making Reg gasp in shock. Before she could arrange herself or decide how to proceed, he gave her a little toss, and she ended up scrambling into the seat. She looked back down at him. "Hey, that wasn't…"

She wasn't sure what complaint to give. He had asked first. He just hadn't waited for her to work out the best thing for him to do. An independent thinker. Reg shook her head, at a loss for words, and pulled her seatbelt around her.

Damon slammed the door shut and then went around to his side of the truck. In a few minutes, they were on their way.

* * *

She had said that she would sleep all the way home, but the restorative tea had swept all sleepiness from her mind and she couldn't even close her eyes for five seconds. She felt the need to act, and sitting in the truck without anything to do was excruciating.

Eventually, they were pulling back in front of the house. Reg was out of the truck almost before Damon stopped, though she didn't have the strength she had hoped and nearly fell flat when she hit the ground.

"Ruan?" She called out as she approached the sidewalk around the big house, not willing to wait until she spotted him or was in the yard. If she knew him, he would be right there, waiting for her and her news.

"You have been a very long time," Ruan complained, his voice grieved. He was in shadow form in the side garden, but when she looked in his direction, divested of the veil and faced her, in the visible plane. "Did you not know I would wait?"

"I know. I got back here as quickly as I could."

She could see the gears turning as he tried to calculate how far she could have gone, where he was going to have to look for Calliopia. The task was enormous, but he faced it head-on, knowing that he had to find his Callie. Failure was not an option.

"Come with us. Get in the truck. We will take you there."

His eyes widened in surprise. She had never seen them so round and large. She looked away from him, not wanting to give him the chance to mesmerize her.

"You will take me to my love?" he repeated stupidly.

"Yes. And you should get ready and come as quickly as you can. I don't know how long she will be able to hang on, but she wants you there. She needs you at her side."

"Yes," Ruan nodded vigorously. "It is my place. I must be with her."

"It is…" Reg tried to tell him in a way that would not cause him too much pain. "It doesn't look good, Ruan. Her parents say there is nothing else they can do. They can't do anything more to heal her wound."

"Her parents? She is at home?"

"Yes. With her fairy parents. The Papillons."

"How came she there?"

"They have something called a homing spell. When she was so gravely wounded, it automatically returned her home, where she could be cared for."

"And her people..." Ruan frowned deeply. "You will not be able to convince them to let me be with her. They will not do this thing."

"They have agreed. It took some talking, believe me, but I managed to get them to agree to let you be there... in the end."

Ruan's eyes got even bigger, his brows going up and disappearing into his mop of curly brown hair. "Reg Rawlins is a sorceress."

Reg laughed. "Come on. Let's get on the way so that you can see her before she gets any worse."

Ruan followed her to the truck. Damon climbed down and opened the small door to the back of the extended cab, showing it to Ruan.

"Do you need a hand getting up there, it's pretty—"

Ruan scrambled up into the seat like a squirrel, and sat perched there, looking around at the strange place. Reg thought at first that he had probably never been in a motor vehicle before, then remembered the station wagon she had seen him drive to Callie's house to pick her up and spirit her away after they had gotten her away from her kidnappers. So maybe rather than being baffled by the strange device, he was well-versed in cars and was admiring the many luxuries in Damon's truck.

Damon motioned to Reg. "Help you up again?"

"No, I think I've recovered enough."

He stood there to watch. "Fine, if you think you'll be okay."

"I'll be fine. Go around to your own side." She was regretting again that she hadn't worn something more practical for the errand to go see the Papillons.

Damon reluctantly obeyed, and Reg did her best to imitate Ruan and scramble up into the seat. She did not have his squirrel speed or grace, and it took a couple of slips and bangs before she managed to get herself back into her seat. On her own and without help this time. She settled herself in her seat and pulled on the seatbelt while Damon watched her. He shrugged, deciding that she must be okay, and looked into the back at Ruan.

"Seatbelt."

"Piskies do not wear seatbelts."

"It's the law."

"Not for Piskies."

"Pixies don't usually even ride in cars. But when they do, they have to follow the same laws of the road as anyone else does. So put it on."

Ruan stared at Damon, perhaps weighing whether he could get away with arguing with the big warlock. Then he looked at Reg, and came to the conclusion that it was more important to see Calliopia as soon as he could and pulled the seatbelt across his body.

"Good," Reg approved. "Thank you."

He nodded to her and sat up as high as he could in order to look out the window of the truck. He really did need a booster seat, but Reg didn't tell him so.

CHAPTER 12

There was no need for Reg to argue her way past the butler at the door this time. He was apparently watching for their return and Reg didn't even need to ring the doorbell. The door opened of its own accord. It wasn't until she was inside the big hall that she saw the butler behind it. He said nothing to stop them, and Reg led the way this time, showing Ruan the way up the stairs. He swarmed past her and up to the hall that led to Calliopia's room. Callie's door stood open and he was able to find her without any further direction. Reg lagged behind, both because she was too tired and in too much pain to go up the stairs quickly, and because she wanted to give him time to be with Calliopia without too big of an audience. Callie's parents were already there. Ruan didn't need Reg and Damon both hanging over his shoulder as he greeted his injured mate.

But they did eventually get there, Reg with a little help from Damon. He put his arm around her waist and allowed her to lean on him as she climbed the long flight of stairs. It seemed like a mountain this time. Damon looked into her face as sweat ran off of it in rivulets.

"Are you okay?"

"There's no point in you asking me that over and over again. I don't think I'm going to be 'okay' for a while."

"But… I mean… is there anything else I can do? Are you going to make it?"

"I'll make it. Somehow."

When she reached the top, Damon half-carried her into the bedroom. Mrs. Papillon immediately vacated her chair for Reg. The tea service was now in Callie's bedroom, and the fairy poured Reg another cup and gave it to her, helping her to hold the cup steady to drink a few sips.

Ruan was on the bed beside Calliopia. Not sitting beside her as Reg and Mrs. Papillon had done, but lying down with her, one hand behind her neck and one on her cheek, his face wet with tears. He whispered to her, but Reg couldn't tell what he was saying. Was it a spell or chant? Or was he telling her everything he could about how much he loved her before she left the mortal world?

Tears dripped down Reg's own face. She tried to get the tea past the lump in her throat, but her chest hurt as well as her side and she couldn't seem to get any more down.

Ruan stroked Callie's hair. He pressed his forehead against hers, still whispering. He put his hand over the bandage on her side and groaned. It might not hurt him physically as it did Reg, but Reg could feel the agony rolling off of him. If anyone ever tried to tell her again that a pixie and a fairy could not love each other, she would have more than a few choice words for him.

"My love," Ruan whispered. "My love, my love, my love."

Reg wiped at the tears flooding her own eyes. It was a private moment that she shouldn't be intruding on, but she couldn't help herself. She was connected to Calliopia and she couldn't have been anywhere else at that moment. Without trying to, she slid into a trance, entering Calliopia's mind once more.

The pain was less. Maybe something that Ruan had done. Maybe just having him there, distracting her from it.

"I do not want to go," Calliopia whispered.

"No," Reg agreed with her. "Tell me what I can do. How can I help you? Isn't there anything I can do?"

"How are you here?"

"Where else would I be?" Reg asked her. "How could I not be here at this moment?"

"I am home." Calliopia's thoughts were broken, disparate. "Here with my loved ones."

Reg nodded. "Yes."

"Is it time?"

"No." Reg didn't want her to go. She had feared this. That once Ruan got there, Callie would give up. "It is time to fight."

There was no answer from Callie for a long time. Finally, she roused herself.

"To fight?"

"You must fight."

* * *

It was difficult for Calliopia to raise any energy. She had been lying there in pain for days, and Reg had been wiped out by her few brief touches of Calliopia's pain. Reg tried to help her to stay focused, to think about the fact that she was with Ruan and her mother and father. That seemed to help a little.

She again tried to do something about the open wound, using all of the skill she could to knit the injury together. It was dreadful, so deep and long. Reg didn't have much experience in giving strength or healing, so she didn't know if it did any good. Once Davyn had taught her more about fire casting, she might be able to do more. Would he give her some emergency lessons? Or try to heal Calliopia himself?

Ruan kissed Calliopia's forehead once more. "Goodbye, my love." It took a few seconds of stunned silence before Reg realized that Ruan had drawn Calliopia's dagger from somewhere beneath his coat. "The blade that did not protect thy life shall end it."

Reg tore herself from the trance and lunged at Ruan. "No!" She had wrestled a pixie before, and they were unbelievably strong and tough. She had thought that her strength was spent, but the adrenaline renewed it, giving her new life. "No! What are you doing?"

Ruan's palms were cut as Reg wrestled the knife away from him. She knew that he hadn't fought her with all his strength. She thought fleetingly that he didn't want to complete the task any more than Reg wanted it done. She looked at Mr. and Mrs. Papillon, expecting help, but they stood there looking at her, not moving.

Reg looked at Damon. "What's going on? Why are you all just standing there? He was going to kill her!"

"It's their way, Reg."

"Their way? Stabbing someone to death?"

"She is suffering," Ruan choked out. "She is in great pain."

"It's not over. You can't just kill someone because they're in pain."

"The fairy craft cannot heal her," Ruan pointed out, motioning to Callie's parents. "We have no healing stone. You have not the power to make her whole."

"We don't know what might work," Reg insisted. Sarah had a gem that could be used for healing, but Reg knew from experience that she would not or could not share it. But they hadn't exhausted every avenue open to them. The others in the room all had more experience in magical healing than she did, and were all ready to give up, but Reg couldn't accept that. Calliopia was young and vital and there had to be a way to help her. "We can get her something for the pain, can't we? Don't drugs work on fairies?"

Damon looked at Mr. and Mrs. Papillon and shrugged. "I have no idea. I assume they've tried their own forms of pain remedies."

"We can get her narcotics. Dull the pain so she can rest and heal."

"Human healing!" Ruan rolled his eyes. "The feeble efforts of the most short-lived race." He stared down at his cut hands, eyes wide and unblinking.

"Maybe the most short-lived race has figured out some tricks to extend the few years we have," Reg snapped. "How do you know it won't work if you don't try it? Isn't it better to try a human drug than to kill her outright?"

Ruan tenderly touched Calliopia's hair, his fingertips barely brushing her tangled tresses. "My love."

"Let her live. Give her a chance."

Ruan looked at Callie's parents. "What think you? Be there hope from human remedies?"

Mr. Papillon's expression was not promising. Reg felt the weight of the dagger in her hand. She stroked the carved handle. She had told Callie to fight when the fairy girl was ready to give up. Was she just extending the fairy's suffering needlessly? The thought of euthanasia by stabbing was repellent to her, but was the quick release of a blade really any worse than some concoction prepared by a doctor and injected into her veins? Reg was interfering with the traditions of people who were far older and more experienced than she was.

But Callie's parents hadn't dispatched her themselves, nor had they reproached Reg for what she had done or tried to take the dagger back away from her. Even

Ruan had not fought very hard to keep it. The blood on his hands testified to the fact that he had been reluctant to let it go, but he had not fought her with all of his strength. Not unless living in the sun or mourning for Callie had drained all of his pixie power away.

Mrs. Papillon was studying Reg. "You are connected to her. You can hear her and feel her."

"Yes."

"Does she not desire death? An end to the pain?"

"No." Reg knew she was fudging her answer. Calliopia hadn't asked for death. She had been willing for her life to end, but she had accepted Reg's suggestion that it was still time to fight.

Reg had never enjoyed English classes in school, especially when analyzing obscure passages in archaic language. Poetry was almost as bad as Shakespeare. But two lines of a Dylan Thomas poem had wormed their way into her brain and came back to her as she sat there with the knife in her hand, fighting to preserve Calliopia's life, however long that might be.

Do not go gentle into that good night

Rage, rage against the dying of the light.

"She will fight. If we will help her, she will continue to fight."

"To fight?" Mrs. Papillon repeated, as if Reg had said something incomprehensible. "To fight what?" She looked at the dagger in Reg's hand. "There is no enemy here." She avoided looking in Ruan's direction.

"To fight death," Reg explained. "To fight for her life."

"Our people do not fight death when it comes for us."

"It isn't her time."

"Is it not?" Mrs. Papillon looked at her husband and at Ruan.

They all considered the question, not speaking to one another telepathically, but considering their own feelings and trying to read each other's faces and body language.

Ruan looked at the dagger in Reg's hand. "Perhaps it is not. Perhaps the one to whom Calliopia is connected is meant to be here to preserve her life and give us hope."

Reg nodded. "Please."

There was silence for some time. Then Mr. Papillon motioned to the knife. "You hold her fate in your hand. It is your choice."

There was no way that Reg could thrust the knife into the fairy who felt like a part of her. But if she handed it back to Ruan, she knew he would do the deed.

She shook her head.

"We can do more. We must."

CHAPTER 13

Reg remembered little of the next few hours. Talking the options over with Damon long into the night, falling asleep in his truck, at some point changing into worn sweats and falling asleep in her own bed, dead to the world. She kept the dagger with her. Not because that in itself would prevent Calliopia's loved ones from taking her life, but because it seemed the only thing to do.

When she awoke, she was fuzzy and disoriented, but she remembered that Damon was supposed to be taking care of things. He could find a doctor who would work with the fairies. They would find a way to get her the painkillers that would ease her physical pain and allow her to sleep and heal. But that wasn't a solution. Her wound was dire, and just giving her painkillers, particularly ones that would depress her nervous system, was not the answer. It was only one piece of the puzzle, helping to keep Calliopia comfortable.

The question of how to heal her was much more complex.

Reg and Damon had talked about it and agreed that they were unlikely to get any other humans, practitioners or not, into the Papillon house. The Papillons were about at the end of their hospitality with allowing two humans and a pixie access to their daughter. They had made it clear that they would not even consider Corvin Hunter, no matter how great his healing powers. Reg really couldn't blame them. He had proven himself to be completely untrustworthy and a predator in the past. And since he had increased his powers by consuming them from the Witch Doctor and his horde, who knew what his abilities were. Reg wouldn't want to trust him around her daughter either. But he was very skilled, and if it were the only way...

Reg sat up and scrubbed at her eyes, knowing that doing so would only make them redder and more swollen. But they were so gritty and blurred that she couldn't help herself. Starlight was sleeping on the bed and sat up at her movements. He made a low, questioning meow and approached to rub against her.

"Hi, Star," Reg whispered. "How's my kitty? How long have I been asleep?" She clawed at her phone on the side table to see what time it was. Even if Starlight could communicate with her with human language, she was sure he would still have had no interest in what the time was on the clock. If it were time to eat, that was one thing. But cats did not run their lives by clocks.

She had a headache, the result of either her psychic exhaustion or sleeping too long or not long enough. She shook her head, trying to clear her brain. It was time for her to begin the next phase of their plan, however unpalatable that was. She started with a call to Davyn.

The phone rang too many times, and she was afraid it was going to go to voicemail. Davyn had a day job and probably a lot of other warlocky things to do too. He wasn't exactly at her beck and call.

"Davyn, answer your phone," she moaned, trying to transmit the message to him telepathically, but she knew she didn't have a connection to him. He was too far away and her powers were too depleted for that to work. But after another ring, there was a click. She waited for the voicemail message.

"Dave Smith," he said briskly.

"Davyn, it's Reg Rawlins."

His voice was vague, thoughts on something else. "Mmm, Reg. Hi."

"I know this is last minute, but... I wonder if you could help me with something."

"Help you with what?"

"Well... it's about an injured fairy."

There was only silence in response. Eventually, Reg spoke again.

"I need help with... if you could show me a couple of things on healing with fire."

"You're not that advanced in your training."

"I know. That's why I'm wondering. If you would show me a couple of things. I'll be really careful."

"Fairies have their own ways of healing. Where is her family? You should take her to them."

"She's with them… but they've done everything they can and have given up hope. I was hoping that we could try a few other things, work together to heal her."

"You're not likely to even get close to her. You need to leave it to the fairy community, Reg. They don't like interference."

"They've agreed to let me help. I'm not calling you for advice whether to do it, I'm calling to find out if you would show me what to do, so I can try to help her when I go back there."

"You don't have the skills. You need to continue with your training and, in a few months or years, you'll reach the point where you can learn about healing."

"Years?" Reg's voice rose despite her intention to be calm and persuasive. "I can't wait for years; she needs to be healed now!"

"And you can't do it. You need to accept that."

"I'm going to go there, and I'm going to do whatever I can. If you don't at least give me some tips and I end up lighting her on fire…"

She thought from the choking noise on the other end of the line that Davyn was going to have a stroke. She might have pushed a little too hard. But the idea that she would have to wait for years before she could attempt healing with fire was infuriating. She had been able to strengthen Starlight when he had been sick.

Corvin had said that it had helped. Starlight might have died without that. So why couldn't Davyn just give her some help when she asked for it?

"You can't threaten me," Davyn finally choked out.

"I'm not threatening you. I'm just telling you. I'm going to do whatever I can. If you're not going to help me, I guess you'll have to live with the consequences."

"When are you going to do this?"

Reg considered the timing. "She's in pretty bad shape, so I can't wait very long. Damon is trying to get a doctor who will prescribe something for the pain. And then... as soon as I can get there to do something for her."

"A doctor?"

"Yes, a doctor. Why is it such an unbelievable thing that a doctor might be able to do something for her?"

"Fairies are not known for being accepting of human medicine. And their magic is very strong. If they can't heal her... I can't see what good a doctor is going to do."

"Everybody is prejudiced against the humans. What's up with that?"

"Well, we are not the longest-lived of species. Which tells you that we're not exactly getting everything right."

"Or that we have lots of practice in extending our lifespan. It's like comparing an elephant's lifespan to a mouse's. They're two different creatures; it doesn't mean that the mice are doing something wrong."

Davyn was quiet. Reg heard him take a few deep breaths. "All right," he said finally. "I'll come to see you at your house as soon as I can. Will you wait for me?"

"Depends how long you are. If it's going to be hours... I don't think I can. I don't think she'll make it through another night if we can't find something to do for her."

"I have to tie up a couple of loose ends here. I can't just rush off in the middle of the afternoon without any warning. I'll be there as soon as I can, so please wait."

"I'll wait as long as I can. But if you had a heart attack or your kid was hit by a car, you'd leave without tying up loose ends and giving them any notice. It's an emergency."

"It isn't an emergency for me. And I'm not going to try to explain to them about a sick fairy. I'll get there as soon as I can."

"See you soon," Reg said curtly, and hung up.

* * *

Davyn was there in just over an hour. Reg met him at the door. He was in his office clothes rather than his cloak, so she knew he had come directly from work and hadn't bothered to go home or change first. She looked around.

"Can we work outside today?"

His brows drew down. "Why?"

"It's just... such a nice day, I don't want to be cooped up inside."

It was pretty much always nice weather in Black Sands, so the excuse was pretty lame, but Reg didn't need a good excuse. It didn't matter if he thought she was crazy or being dramatic or had something to hide. She just wanted to work outside with him.

"I'm worried you might be more distracted outside. And it's a little harder to put out wildfires if vegetation catches fire."

"It's not like it's dry. Everything is green and well-watered. It's not going to catch fire easily."

Davyn rolled his eyes, not looking pleased at the new development. Of course, he hadn't looked pleased when he had arrived anyway. She was going to have to be really nice and make a fuss over him in the future so that he would keep training her. No one wanted to have to deal with a prima donna.

"Sorry. I'm... not having the greatest day," Reg apologized. "Or... couple of days. This whole thing has been really stressful and it has taken a lot out of me."

His expression softened slightly. The kind of guy who felt more kindly toward those who were less fortunate than he was. "This… fairy. Exactly how did you become mixed up in this? And what happened?"

"She's someone… that I was involved with in a case. And she and I were… sort of on the same wavelength. I didn't exactly keep in touch afterward, but when she was hurt… her mate asked me to help out, so, I'm back in it again…"

"Fairies don't ask humans for help."

Reg didn't know if he was talking about the initial case or Ruan asking her to find Cassie after she was injured. She didn't plan to fill him in on the details about Ruan. That just complicated things and wouldn't help her to help Callie, and that had to be where her focus was for what time she had with Davyn.

She led the way around the cottage to the garden. As Davyn took a look around, she sent a quick text from her phone.

"I know. It's an unusual case. Anyway... she's been hurt... very badly, and I'm trying to help. Did you know that they..." Reg grimaced, trying to figure out the best way to put her question. "They don't like their loved ones to suffer, so if they don't think there's hope for recovery..."

Davyn's lips pressed together. "I'm not very familiar with their customs. But I can imagine."

"No, I don't think you can." She saw again Ruan pulling out the dagger and preparing to stab Calliopia through the heart. She still had the dagger, back in its sheath, heavy in the hidden pocket of the skirt she had put on while she was waiting for Davyn's arrival. It seemed to grow heavier the more she thought about Callie and her dire situation. "I really need to get over there to help her. Can you show me how to do what you did with Starlight? When you put the fire into him, to help with his healing? It seemed to make a difference. Maybe if I can do that for Calliopia, it will help. Maybe it will magnify whatever the fairies have done for her so that it can work."

"That's pretty advanced magic. I can't teach you to do that in one afternoon."

"What can you teach me? You need to show me something. I don't know what else to do."

He shook his head slowly. He didn't answer her, but started to rub his hands together briskly to prepare to form a fireball. Reg mimicked his movements, reaching deep down to gather her fire. But she had so little energy even after her sleep, that she was having trouble even warming her palms with the friction.

Davyn's fireball began to form between his hands, and he grew and manipulated it. Reg watched in fascination. Even though she was tired, she still wanted to do what he was doing. Corvin had said that Davyn's fire called to her. That was a good description. She put her hands out toward Davyn, waiting for him to pass the fireball to her.

"How are you going to do anything if you can't even conjure fire?" Davyn asked. "I'm not going to be there with you."

"I'll be able to. I just need a bit of a rest."

He looked at her dubiously and passed the fire over to her. Reg held it between her hands, feeling the warm buzz. It was comforting, not like holding on to something too hot to handle, but a warmth that radiated from her hands and spread over her like a blanket. She encouraged it to grow and looked at Davyn to see what she was supposed to do next.

"How did she get sick or hurt?" Davyn asked. "What is it that needs to be healed?"

"She was stabbed in the side," Reg touched her own side, demonstrating. "It's very long and deep. It has bled a lot."

"Do you remember this?" Davyn nearly touched the scar of the wound on Reg's palm. The one she had received from the dagger.

"Yes."

"It's recent. So you remember how you got it? How it felt?"

"Yes."

"I want you to look at your scar and feel the fire going down into it. Can you do that?"

"Okay." Reg breathed slowly and imagined the fire going down into it, heating it up and burning away any impurities left by the cursed blade. It was a nasty magical wound but it had connected her to Calliopia. Maybe it still did connect her to Calliopia. And maybe that connection could be used while Davyn was there to help her.

"Can I—"

He held up his hand to stop her from speaking. Reg was quiet. She tried to focus on the job he had given her. She clearly hadn't completed it to his satisfaction and was letting her mind jump from one thing to another. She focused on her scar, sending the heat of the fire there with her mind. It seemed like a very long time had passed before Davyn decided she had done what he asked.

"You didn't physically push the fire into the wound, like you saw me do," he pointed out. "You can work on healing without getting the fire against the wound or inside her body. I don't want you getting so close that it will be uncomfortable for her or risk setting the bed on fire."

Reg nodded. "Okay. I can do that." She studied the scar on her hand. She thought it might be a little lighter, but it was still very clear on her palm.

Davyn took her by the wrist and bent it toward himself, studying it. "Give the fire back to me," he instructed.

Reg passed it back to him and waited. He closed his eyes and concentrated, and she could feel him doing as she had done, manipulating the fire with his mind and sending the heat into her scar. He was stronger than she was, and the scar heated up quickly. It was not so hot that she cried out or tried to push it away from her, but just on the edge of pain. After a minute to two, Davyn withdrew the heat again. He looked down at her palm. Reg studied the scar, trying to discern any difference from when she had been working on it. Davyn frowned.

"That's a very stubborn scar. Tell me what happened."

"I don't really want to… it was… torture."

"Torture." He nodded slowly. "Magical?"

"Umm… I don't know if it was intended to be. But the blade was… contaminated."

"With what?"

"Uh…" she looked down at the scar, "fairy blood."

He blinked at her. "You lead a curious life, Reg Rawlins."

"Yeah. Curious."

"The blade that did this, has it been cleansed?"

"No. And I know it should be destroyed, that's what I keep hearing."

"I could, perhaps, do that for you. And then I could heal this scar."

"It's not that important. It doesn't hurt anymore. It's Calliopia I need to heal." Reg pondered on what he had said. "Does that mean that if I found the blade that injured Callie, that maybe if you cleansed it, she could be healed?"

"Well… possibly. If it was somehow contaminated and that was preventing her from healing. But that's not a very common occurrence. Fairy magic is strong and, despite what you might have read or seen in the movies, cursed swords are not terribly common."

Reg tucked this away for future reference. Maybe the next time she connected to Calliopia, she could find out more about the blade she had been injured with. Maybe Reg was missing out on an important step to healing Calliopia.

"Okay. What else. Is that all I can do? Make it hot?"

"It may not seem like much, but it can help. It is stronger magic than you think, despite the lack of results here." He tapped her hand, then let it go.

Reg nodded. She was disappointed that it wasn't more, but she had to be satisfied with what she got. She might have gotten nothing at all from Davyn, if he had not responded to her pleas.

She turned at the sound of footsteps crunching down the pathway toward them. Davyn turned as well.

Reg felt a different kind of heat spreading over her. It was Corvin. He was smiling until he saw Davyn, then the expression fled and he looked at Reg with bitterness.

"What is this? What are you trying to do, witch?"

CHAPTER 14

Corvin always called Regina by name and he knew that she didn't consider herself a witch, so the appellation stung. She had known he wouldn't be happy to find another warlock there. Especially Davyn, his old friend and leader of his coven. The coven currently shunning him.

"You just both happened to get here at the same time," Reg said casually. "I needed help for Calliopia, and…"

"What has the fairy girl gotten herself into now?" Corvin demanded. "I knew I shouldn't have gotten involved in that affair. Now we're going to be called in anytime an adolescent fairy needs to be taken in hand."

Reg shook her head. "No… it's just Calliopia. And it wasn't her parents who wanted help. It was Ruan."

"So she decided to go back to her parents, leaving him behind? Fickle child. He should have known better than to get together with her in the first place. Such mixed pairings never work."

Reg raised her hand, trying to stop him. "No. She was injured. She was returned by what her parents called a homing spell. So that they could treat her. Ruan didn't know where she had gone, so he came to me to see if I could find her."

"And so you're up to your knees in it again. Tell them that you don't want anything more to do with it. And don't get involved in fairy-pixie relations." He turned as if to leave. "I'll see you another time. When it can be just the two of us. Doing something more… pleasant."

"Corvin."

He stopped.

"I need your help. Please."

"I don't heal fairies. Even if they would allow me in their home. You know they won't."

"I know that. I've already tried to get them to give in, but they won't. I know you can't heal her. But I thought... you might be able to help me to heal her."

He raised one eyebrow, giving her a sardonic grin. "You are going to heal her?"

"You know I helped with Starlight. I couldn't heal him by myself, but I helped a little bit. And maybe that little bit would be enough to put Callie over the edge. So that everything together would work."

"Maybe." He shrugged. "And are you taking the fire caster with you as well?"

"No. I was just..."

"Trying to get him to help you to heal her. Oh, I see how this works. You call everybody you think will be able to give you the instruction you need to heal a fairy."

Reg shrugged. She couldn't deny it. But he made it sound like it was a bad thing. Like she'd been cheating on him by calling Davyn. "I'm… so tired. From connecting with her. Every time I do, it takes so much out of me. Especially when she is in so much pain."

"Then don't do it again. You are putting your life in danger. You can't withstand the same level of pain as a fairy."

"I need to do it. I need to find out exactly how she got injured. By who, with what blade. Then maybe I can figure out how to… reverse whatever magic is preventing her from healing."

"You'll end up killing yourself."

"I have to try. Can you… help me out?"

He folded his arms. "How about an exchange?"

"Corvin," Davyn warned.

"You are not supposed to be acknowledging my existence," Corvin pointed out with a smirk, reminding him of the shunning. "You can't see or hear me. Well, what about it, Regina?"

She felt his pull, smelled the scent of roses on the air, and was drawn toward him, wanting to touch him. To walk into his arms and stay with him forever.

Davyn put a hand on her arm. His fingers were hot and made Reg jolt back in pain, remembering herself.

"Not an exchange," she told Corvin. "You can't take my powers. How could I heal Calliopia if I gave them to you?"

"I'm sure we could work something out. A little agreement."

"No. I am not giving you my powers."

"Just something little. You don't need to give me everything. I could take... maybe... something of your siren nature."

Reg recoiled at the mention of her mother's heritage. Reg had not inherited any of that nature. She was nothing like Norma Jean. She had no desire to prey on men or to destroy them. That was Norma Jean alone.

"I don't have—"

"You can't deny that you do. You may try not to give in to it, but it is still there, in your body and your mind."

"No."

"I could take it away, then you wouldn't have to worry about that anymore," he coaxed.

"Corvin!" Davyn protested again.

"If you can hear me," Corvin said poisonously, "then you hear me negotiating, not taking. Wasn't that your whole point? That I must get _real_ consent? Not just the words?"

Davyn looked away, falling silent.

"You expect me to just give you strength and instruction on healing without anything in return?" Corvin asked Reg.

"I… I just thought, we've worked together in the past, and I thought you could help me out. Give me a boost so that I can help Calliopia."

"You think it's okay to drain my strength on a whim? All you need to do is ask? Until now, you've just taken, and I don't see how that is any different than what you've accused me of."

She'd certainly caught him in a bad mood. Usually, Corvin was happy to do whatever he thought might help him to get closer to her. It was probably due to finding Davyn there. She hadn't exactly told him that she would have backup in case he tried anything. Davyn might not be strong compared to Corvin, but if Corvin wanted to get back into good standing with his coven, he had to have Davyn on his side.

"Okay. I thought you would help. If you don't want to, that's your right. I'm not willing to give up powers in return. I don't know what else to offer you. Money? Something else I could do for you?"

"She did rescue you from a siren," Davyn pointed out, still looking away from Corvin, studiously pretending that he didn't know Corvin was there. "Voluntarily, without any promise of payment, at great risk to herself, when no one else would help you."

Corvin rubbed his chin, nodding.

"And drove you home by herself when I told her not to," Davyn reminded him. "And claimed you when the siren tried to take you a second time."

His words had a definite effect on Corvin. "Of course you're right," he agreed, sounding abashed. He looked back at Reg. "Forgive a warlock's short memory... my only excuse is that I can't remember most of what happened while I was under her power. I know what you did, but it's not accessible to me."

Reg nodded, hoping this meant he would help her without her having to give him something more.

Corvin still seemed reluctant. He shrugged and sighed, then motioned to the cottage. "Why don't we go inside? You have an escort, so we don't need to stay out here."

"I don't think so," Reg countered. "Sarah reset all of the wards after Yule, and you want to find a way past them. Not gonna happen."

"Inviting me in one time wouldn't mean that I could come in any time I wanted to," he coaxed.

"Yeah, unless you left something behind so you could come back for it, or there's some other loophole that I don't know about yet. That one with my keys was good. You're just going to have to get used to the idea that you're in the doghouse. You're not allowed to come inside. Be glad that we have such nice weather."

"Not very kind words for someone you want a favor from."

"Those aren't words for the warlock I want a favor from. They're for the warlock who is trying at every turn to charm me into giving him my gifts."

"It's the same warlock."

"I wish it wasn't."

Corvin snorted. He glanced around the garden. "This might be easier if you were sitting down. Do you want to pick a comfortable seat?"

Reg selected a white wooden swinging couch with a padded seat and tried to make herself comfortable.

She looked into the green of the garden and focused on a reflective blue gazing ball. The wind chimes Forst had put up to echo the bells of the elves tinkled quietly in the breeze. Corvin positioned himself in front of Reg, not on the swing beside her. He raised his hands and held them toward her, like he was warming himself by the fire. Only he wasn't the one who was getting warm. The energy was flowing off of him, a warm, comfortable, exhilarating feeling.

Reg leaned into it. It felt so good. She could feel the strength returning to her body, feeling stronger and more energetic than she had in a long time. She hadn't realized how run-down she was getting, even before connecting with Calliopia again.

Reg inhaled the fragrances of the garden. All of the different flowers blending almost as if they were drawing a picture. Reg felt like she was in a warm embrace. So soft and gentle and undemanding.

"Mmm…" she sighed, letting herself relax and float in the warmth and power.

Corvin's hand was on her arm, buzzing with energy. Reg put her hand over it, marveling at how they fit together. When he touched her, she felt like she was home. This was what she was made for.

"That's enough, Corvin. No touching."

His hand pulled away from hers, and Reg reached back toward him, wanting it back.

"No…"

"Reg," a voice that was not Corvin's warned.

"I need him."

"No. He's charming you, just like before."

"It's okay."

"Reg!" A hand shook her shoulder. Reg knew it wasn't Corvin, because when Corvin touched her, it was electric. She blinked, looking at Davyn's face in front of her.

"You."

"Yes, me. Time to wake up."

Reg stretched, luxuriating in the feeling of well-being. It had been too long since she had felt like that. Calm and focused and energized. Everything seemed crystal-clear. She looked around and saw Corvin, watching her with a half-smile. Why was he smiling? She still had her gifts. The voices in her head. The fire. A sense of purpose. He hadn't taken anything away from her. Maybe he was just exulting in the fact that he could still charm her, thinking that someday, Davyn would not be there, and he would be able to do what he wanted to.

Davyn was apparently thinking the same thing. "I see you charming her when she clearly had not made an agreement with you."

Corvin chuckled. "I didn't take anything from her. Ask her yourself."

"She's too starry-eyed to know the difference."

"No, she's not. She would know."

Reg nodded her agreement. "I would know."

"How can you be sure he didn't... skim off the cream."

"I would know," she repeated firmly.

"Walk me to my car," Corvin suggested.

Reg hesitated. She had plenty of energy. She felt like she could do anything she set her mind to. Blocking Corvin wouldn't be a problem if he tried anything. And he wouldn't with Davyn right there, waiting for her return.

Corvin made a gesture of invitation to encourage her, and Reg accepted.

"I'll be right back. If I'm not here in five minutes, send out the dogs."

Davyn watched her go without a word.

They got down the path to the side of the big house before Corvin spoke.

"You didn't tell me you'd stolen Calliopia's blade."

CHAPTER 15

Reg looked at him. "I didn't steal it!" she declared.

"No? How exactly did you manage to get your hands on it, then? You just borrowed it?"

"I…" Reg shook her head. Did he really think she would steal Calliopia's knife while she was on her deathbed?

Well, there had been times…

But never someone who was on their deathbed.

Not actually on their deathbed.

"I didn't steal or borrow it. I… took it away from Ruan, to keep him from killing Calliopia."

"Sure." He gave his head a little shake as they continued to walk toward his car. "You took it from a pixie."

"I don't think he tried too hard to stop me from taking it," Reg admitted. "Although, he did get his hands cut in the process."

"And he just let you? Why? Why would he let you injure him and take the knife away?"

"Because he doesn't really want Callie to die. He would have done it, to put her out of her pain, but he didn't want to. So when I stopped him... well, he didn't want to, so he let me take it."

"And you just hung on to it for safekeeping."

"I don't want him to change his mind and decide that he can't wait for me to get back. So, yeah, I took it for safekeeping."

"It's very valuable."

"Fairy steel, I know."

"More than just fairy steel. It is a powerful artifact."

"Yes." Reg knew that too. "Fairy blood, and my blood, and pixie blood. Who knows about the rest."

"It must have been forged for a great sorcerer."

"Why?"

"Because only a great sorcerer could have control over that kind of a blade. You don't think that it only became evil because of the blood it drew, do you? It was already evil. It already had magic on it."

"A spell that made it… evil? An inanimate object can't be evil."

But Reg remembered the key that Weston had left for her. It had called to her. It had been something that she wanted to hold in her hand, wanted to turn in its lock. It wasn't just a key; it was a key that spoke to her. Was the blade the same? Had she taken it from the Papillon home because it called to her too?

She didn't like to think of what it might want from her. A key, of course, wanted to be turned. But a dagger? One that had already imbibed the blood of at least three races? It clearly wanted blood and violence. Not just to be used to cut a block of cheese.

"What should I do with it?"

"What you do with it is your business. I would recommend... giving it to someone powerful enough to master it."

Reg looked at him as he unlocked his car using the key fob, standing there very casually, talking about something that he clearly wanted.

"Someone who could suck the power right out of it?" she suggested.

He gave a satisfied smile, like a fat cat. "Yes, that sounds like the perfect solution," he agreed. "I could dispose of it for you."

"You are not getting Calliopia's dagger. If she gets better... she's going to want it back. So I'm going to keep it safe for her until she's able to tell me what she wants to be done with it."

But she remembered how Calliopia had responded when Ruan told her the blade should be unmade. She had been drawn to its power and had been adamant that she was going to keep it, that she would not allow it to be unmade just because it had tasted of fairy blood. Calliopia had chosen to go against the traditions of the fairies in more ways than one.

"Thank you for giving me a boost."

"You're welcome." He was still smiling. "And just between you and me, I think that a dinner date would be a suitable recompense for me making the trip all the way over here just to give you a bit of energy to approach an impossible task. If you don't kill yourself trying to heal the girl, that is."

"I'm not going to kill myself. And you don't know; I might be successful."

"When everybody else has told you it's impossible? You're just that kind of girl, aren't you?"

Reg shrugged. She couldn't deny it. She knew very well that the way to persuade her to do a thing was to say that it couldn't be done. Or to forbid her from doing it. It worked on her just as surely as it worked on Erin. The two of them were as different as could be, but in that one thing, they were sisters. Neither one liked to be told no.

"So, it's a date?" Corvin asked.

"We'll talk later. If I survive."

Corvin snickered and got into his car.

* * *

Reg went back to see Davyn, thoughtful. He looked relieved to see her coming back down the pathway, his shoulders relaxing. He gave a nod and an attempt at a smile.

"Good. You're okay then." He hesitated to say anything further. "You do… seem to take risks, don't you?"

Reg shrugged uncomfortably. Davyn had already pointed out to her that her behavior with Corvin was reckless. But she couldn't help being drawn to him. That was part of who he was. He attracted her like a flower attracted bees.

Or like a Venus fly-trap attracted insects.

"I'm fine. In fact, I'm better than fine. I'm feeling pretty good."

"Well, I don't want to deplete your strength too much with practicing, but do you think that you could give me a quick demonstration, show me that you can do what we covered?"

Reg nodded, confident in her ability to replicate what they had done already. It would be harder when she was working on a live patient, but it was a snap when she was just showing Davyn.

She held her hands apart, and almost before she had considered what she wanted to do, a fire started to form, shivering and rotating between her palms. She felt the warmth and manipulated it as if it were a ball of clay, enjoying the sensation of handling something insubstantial and dangerous with just her hands and her mind.

"See?"

"Very good," Davyn agreed. His eyes were narrow. "Keep your focus."

Reg nodded. She stared into the fire. "Do you want me to send the heat into you, or back into my scar, like last time?"

He held his hand in front of himself, palm up, like a child asking for a candy. "Go ahead."

She focused the heat on his hand. She switched between watching his hand and watching his eyes, looking for any sign of pain or discomfort. If she made it too hot, she supposed he could just put it out, but she didn't want him to have to protect himself. She wanted him to see that she could do it, and it would be safe for her to go to the Papillon castle and to see Calliopia, without the risk of burning the whole place down around them.

At least it was made of stone.

Mostly.

When Davyn's expression changed infinitesimally, she stopped, held, and then withdrew a little of the heat. They both stayed there for a few minutes, looking at Davyn's hand, Davyn evaluating Reg's skill and focus. Finally, he nodded.

"You did well. That was much better."

"I told you I was just tired. That's why I asked Corvin to come."

"You need to be careful of calling on him like that. He isn't a safe person. You know how dangerous he is."

"I think I know that better than anyone else."

"Then why do you continue to court him?"

"I'm not courting him," Reg protested, her face heating up. "I'm just... friendly, I guess. Who else is going to help me like that? I don't know of anyone else in the community who can do that, do you? I mean, you know the people who live here. Can any of them give me energy like that? Can any of them heal?"

"There are other healers. But probably none as skilled and, at the moment, his powers are very... potent."

"I wish the fairies would let him see Calliopia. I bet he could heal her. Instead, they're going to have to rely on me, with my little bit of heat and extra energy. And the painkillers that Damon is going to get."

"You know you are fighting a losing battle."

"Other people had fought against worse odds."

"I suppose so," he agreed, but he did not sound convinced.

"Well... wish me luck. There's no point in me waiting around here while I start to lose my energy boost."

"Good luck," he said sincerely. "I hope that... things work out well. Please be careful. Realize that you cannot expend all of your energy on this fairy, or take on all her pain."

"I know."

Davyn gave a little salute and walked away. Reg took a deep breath to galvanize herself and went back into the guest cottage.

CHAPTER 16

Almost the instant she was in the cottage door, a shadow streaked across the room, and Reg was almost knocked over when it hit her in the leg.

"Ow! What?" She followed the black streak. "Nico! What are you doing? What was that for?"

Nico dashed to the other side of the room and crouched, watching her to see how she would respond.

"It isn't time to play! I have to go out to see if I can make someone feel better. You need to stay here and practice... practice sitting quietly and concentrating."

He stared at her with his yellow eyes, and Reg knew that his answer was something along the lines of 'just who do you think you're talking to?' She had to laugh at his expression and the rebellious feelings that bounced back at her whenever she corrected or lectured him. It was as bad as having a teenager, all of that attitude that showed up the instant she tried to talk him into behaving better.

"Well, ask Starlight what you should do, then. Maybe you'll listen to a cat better than to a two-legged human."

But she remembered that he hadn't behaved for Nicole, his adoptive mother, either. That was why Francesca had eventually broken down and brought him over to Reg's to see if she could whip him into shape.

"You have the gift," Francesca had said. "You know and understand him better than anyone else. If there is anyone who can take him in hand, it is you, Regina."

Thanks for nothing.

So far, all Reg had gotten out of the assignment were scratches and bite marks up both legs, just joined by another bruise from Nico's dash-and-nip maneuver, some broken dishes, and twice as much litter cleaning to do.

"Look," she told Nico seriously. "I need you to settle down. You can't attack me whenever I walk into the room. That hurts. I'm not your enemy. If you want to cuddle or want me to feed you, just tell me. But I don't understand why you're always scratching and biting."

He was just a kitten. Or just a young kattakyn. Reg had never had one before, so she couldn't be sure how they were supposed to behave. But she knew it wasn't how the other kattakyns behaved.

Nico stood up on his back legs and scratched the wicker couch.

"Stop that."

He didn't.

"I got you a scratching post. Use the scratching post."

She had an idea that she should pick him up whenever he scratched and relocate him to the scratching post, until he got the idea, but whenever he was scratching and she tried to interrupt him, he used _her_ as a scratching post.

"Scratch scratch," she told him, "use your scratching post."

He stared at her for a moment, then resumed his scratching.

"Oh brother. Cats. I don't know how we're ever going to find a home that will put up with your antics."

Reg gathered together her purse, phone, and anything else she might need when she got to the Papillon mansion, kissed her very well-behaved tuxedo cat goodbye, and left him to deal with the young ruffian.

* * *

She called Damon on her way to the castle to make sure that he'd been successful with his mission.

"I have narcotics," he told her. "You'd be surprised how easy that actually is."

"No, I don't think so." Reg laughed. She'd been on the streets for long enough to know just how easy it was to get a bottle of whatever you needed to take away your pain. She was lucky to have had a biological mother who was an addict, because it had convinced Reg never to touch any narcotics or illegal drugs. She had managed to stay away from cigarettes, as well.

Alcohol was another story, but she prided herself on the fact that she only had the occasional drink. She could have allowed herself to become a raging alcoholic. But she hadn't. She had self-control.

"Well, maybe you wouldn't," Damon said, disgruntled.

"How about antibiotics?"

"I got those too. But I'm less sure about whether that is a good idea."

"We don't know why she isn't healing. If it's because of an infection, I want to boot it out before it can get established any more."

"But we don't know that is the case. Or that fairies even get infections. I suspect that they don't. I've never seen a fairy that was sick that way."

"Have you seen a lot of sick fairies?"

"Well… no."

Reg laughed. The nose of her car was pointed toward Calliopia's house and, provided she didn't get pulled over by any cops, she would be able to be back at the mansion in another half hour. Then she could get to the work of healing Calliopia.

"It's just that I don't know…" Damon said uncomfortably. "What if we give her antibiotics and her body rejects it? What if they burn her or make things worse?"

"Why would they do that?"

"I don't know. I don't think it's an infection. I think that if it were, her parents would have been able to heal her with their treatment. But they didn't."

"What do you think it is, then? A spell or curse?"

"Yes. Of course. They're fairies."

"Then shouldn't they have some kind of... anti-curse?"

"Reg, I'm driving. I'll see you there."

His call ended. Reg rolled her eyes. She could drive and talk at the same time. But she had a sneaking suspicion it was more than just an inability to drive and talk at the same time that had made him hang up.

She turned on the radio and zipped through the saved channels, looking for something to keep her spirits up.

* * *

Back at the Papillon mansion again, Reg spent a few seconds just staring at the side of the building before she finally got out of her car. Much easier with a wider skirt and her own low vehicle. She felt much more graceful and prepared, instead of being embarrassed by her entrance.

Damon was waiting nearby in his truck. He descended and walked with her. He had a bag of goodies with him. Reg was grateful to him for splitting the errands with her. While everybody else had argued and put up roadblocks, Damon had been willing to help.

"How are you doing?" he asked seriously.

"I'm good." Reg turned her face up toward him so that he would be able to see that she was calm and refreshed. No more raccoon eyes. No anxiety over what they were about to do, breaking all of the rules and traditions of Calliopia's family in an attempt to help her.

"Good. Let's do this, then."

Maybe the difference was that he had seen how much Calliopia was suffering and how much her family was grieving for her. It was different when all of that raw emotion was right there. The others hadn't been there. It was just an academic question for them.

For Reg and Damon and Calliopia's family, it was not all academic.

It was all too real.

The butler was watching for them again and opened the door as they approached. Reg nodded at him, trying to be polite and respectful to make up for the way she had treated him earlier.

The stairs hardly even raised her heart rate this time. She was prepared. She was strong, bursting with energy, and ready to put it to work.

The sun was going down, so the sick room was much darker than it had been. Reg hoped that Callie's spirit wouldn't go out with the tide, something that she remembered from an old book they had read at school. That spirits always went out with the tide. And that was at night, when the darkness was falling.

"Hi," Reg nodded to everyone. She tried to be solemn and to keep her movements slow and calm, as if this were something she did every day. Not something that would upset anyone.

Maybe if she actually were a doctor or healer, her heart would not be pounding so fast.

Damon's bag crinkled as he opened it up. He handed Reg a vial and a syringe with a wicked-looking needle. They had agreed that the best method of administration would be intravenous. Trying to get anything down Calliopia's throat, even if they dissolved it in liquid, would be too difficult.

"You looked up dosages?" Reg asked.

He nodded and pulled a paper out of his pocket. "We'll start with a low dose. Make sure that she doesn't have a weird reaction to it. Then increase it incrementally, until she's more comfortable. Even if we can't eliminate all of the pain, we can still do something."

Reg nodded. She looked at the markings on the syringe and the first dosage he had marked, and pulled liquid into it.

"I really hope this works. If it turns out that fairies are allergic to morphine, I'm going to be in real trouble."

Damon didn't say anything to encourage her. But he didn't stop her from what she was doing. He pulled a length of rubber sheeting out of the bag. "For a tourniquet, if you need one. I wasn't sure how comfortable you were with injections."

Both more and less comfortable than she would like to admit. "Thanks."

Reg tied the bit of rubber around Calliopia's slender arm and tapped her arm, waiting for the vein to pop. It was very cooperative, and Reg was able to jab a needle into it the first try. She slowly pushed the plunger down. Calliopia didn't show any change.

That was good, though. They hadn't given her what she would need to kill the pain yet. But she hadn't gone through the roof or melted into the sheets in a pool of green liquid, either.

"Okay." Reg nodded. "Let's give that ten minutes, just to be sure, and then we'll give her another dose."

"Do you want to try one of the other things you were planning, or we just want to do the painkillers right now?"

"Let's do the painkillers first. Then hopefully... I'll be able to strengthen her and start the healing process. And get her to tell me what happened."

"You think she'll be able to?"

"I don't know. When Warren was in a coma... he didn't really understand what was going on or what had happened to him. But I'm hoping she'll be able to give me some indication of who did this to her. If we can understand just what happened, we'll know more about what we need to do to heal her."

Ruan moved around the room, barely visible in the shadows. Reg looked at him.

"You are helping Callie?" Ruan inquired. "You have begun your physic?"

"Yes. Just starting, though; it will be a while before it will start to work. We're just making sure it doesn't hurt her first."

Ruan leaned close to examine the liquid in the vial. "What is this? Water?"

"No. It's made from poppies. Very special poppies. Distilled down to… this medicine."

"And you put it in her blood?" Ruan examined the mark where Reg had injected the morphine into Calliopia's arm.

"Yes. She can't eat right now, so we thought it best…"

He tried to take the syringe from her, but Reg did not release it. Ruan had to be satisfied with merely studying the needle.

"This is very cunning work. Putting medicine directly into blood." He shook his head. "Humans do indeed come up with many clever ideas."

"Uh… thank you." It was a little strange to hear him complimenting human ingenuity rather than badmouthing them and their strange ways.

Damon kept an eye on the time and nodded to Reg when it was time for another injection. Reg gave Calliopia a larger dose and stayed very still, her hand on Callie's arm, trying to discern whether it was making any difference to her pain.

CHAPTER 17

It was some time before they reached the point that, although all of the pain had not been dulled, it was reduced enough that Reg could get some response to her questions. Not answers, exactly, but noises and movement that indicated Calliopia was aware of her. Her breathing eased and she was less restless.

"Next stage," Reg told Damon, and took a deep breath. None of the spectators asked her what she was going to do or tried to stop her. They all just stood, silent and still, waiting.

Damon gave an encouraging smile.

Reg decided to try fire first. She conjured a fireball between her hands as she had done for Davyn. It quickly flared larger. Reg focused on the flame and she tried to manipulate it with her mind. She had to keep the movements small and to keep the fire small and compact. No flares. No lighting the bedsheets on fire.

Everyone watched her. Reg held the fireball near Calliopia's bandaged side. She concentrated on the injury, and tried to work the heat of the fire into it. She slipped more than once, causing Calliopia to moan and move away from or toward her. She was glad that Davyn hadn't shown her how to put the fire directly into Calliopia. If she couldn't handle just the heat without making mistakes, how would she have managed sending her fire into Callie?

She closed her eyes, concentrating hard, visualizing the wound under the bandage and how she wanted it to knit together and to begin to heal.

She was aware of the dagger in her skirt pocket, pressing against her leg, heavier than it ought to be. She tried to ignore it. She was not going to follow the pixie or fairy tradition and put Calliopia out of her misery. There were still things she could do. She had already made a difference with her inexpert administration of morphine and magical heat. She could do more. She could heal Calliopia's dreadful wound, or strengthen her enough that her own body could heal it.

Eventually, she felt that she had done all she could with the fire, and folded it back gently away between her palms. She opened her eyes and looked at Calliopia, who finally seemed to be sleeping peacefully. Reg could feel the dull ache in her side, but it was so much better than it had been, Calliopia would be able to sleep. She would be able to heal.

Reg sat down on the chair beside the bed. She looked around the room at the others.

"You cast fire," Mr. Papillon observed, brows raised. He and his wife exchanged looks.

"Yes. I'm just a beginner. But…"

"This is a very rare gift among humans."

Reg nodded. "I guess. I didn't know I had it before."

They all looked at Calliopia, lying so still, only her breath moving the sheets.

"She is healing?" Ruan asked.

"I hope so. She isn't in so much pain anymore. Hopefully, that will mean that she can rest and regenerate."

They all looked at her gravely. She had expected more cheer, expected them to be happier about what she had been able to do so far. She had made progress.

"It is still a dire wound," Ruan said. He approached and sat on the edge of the bed, reaching out to touch Calliopia. He put his hand lightly over the bandage. He shook his head. "It is not good."

"I'm helping, though. I'm working on it. Whatever you can do, plus the things that Damon and I can do. Maybe together, we can help her to turn the corner. She's already doing better."

He grunted. "Maybe."

"What do you know about what happened to her? More than you told me?"

"No more," he said flatly.

"You just went into her bedroom, and found a bed soaked in blood and no more clues."

He shook his head.

"And her dagger," Reg pointed out. "You didn't tell me that her dagger was still there. Was it on her dresser? Or were you keeping it safe? Where was it?"

Ruan considered the question, looking suspicious. He looked over at Calliopia's parents, not answering right away.

"It was on her bed. She slept with it."

"She slept with her dagger?"

He nodded.

"Why?"

Ruan's answers were slow and carefully-considered. He didn't rush into anything. "She was afraid."

"Afraid of what?" Reg leaned toward him.

Ruan stared at Calliopia's face. He looked so young and vulnerable that Reg wanted to pat him on the back or give him a hug. But despite those apple cheeks and the messy mop of brown curls, she knew that he was not a child, but a man, and would probably not appreciate her attempts to console him.

"She was kidnapped," Ruan reminded her. "She feared… the dark. Of… enemies coming in the night."

Reg could understand Callie being traumatized after having been taken from her bed in the middle of the night. She had been held in the cold, dark, damp hole in the ground. After the completion of her transformation into a fairy, she craved the sun instead of dark burrows. She slept with a light on and her dagger with her to guard against a nocturnal attack.

"Who could get in to attack her? Did somebody break through her spells? Or was it someone she knew?"

"It was not I," Ruan said resentfully.

"I didn't say it was." It was clear that Ruan loved Callie and hoped for her recovery. And Calliopia herself had said that it was not Ruan. But who else could have gotten past any magical protections? Her family? Her parents had said she was brought home by a spell, but what if that were not true? What if they had gone to force her to return, and there had been a fight?

Had Calliopia's protections failed? Or had she decided to do something more reckless? Had she been too tired and forgotten to renew her spells? Or had someone exploited a weakness in the magical protections, as the pixies had when they had stolen Sarah's emerald? Reg was still learning all the ways there were to get past magical spells. Relying solely on magic for protection did not seem to be a wise thing to do.

Reg put her hand over Ruan's, still pressed to Calliopia's side, and tried to reach out to touch her mind. Calliopia was more comfortable; it should be easier for her to communicate.

"Callie. Calliopia. Can you hear me? Do you know me?"

Calliopia's response was slow in coming, murky, difficult to hear or read in all of the muddle of pain, drugs, and sleepiness.

"I know Reg Rawlins."

"You're feeling a little better now. I need to talk with you."

"The pain… is better."

"Yes. We gave you something for the pain. So that you could rest and heal."

Calliopia shifted, trying to find a more comfortable position. But rolling onto her other side or her stomach was impossible. She was too sore and weak to get off of her back.

"Callie. Do you remember what happened? Who came to you?"

"Who?"

"Yes. Was it another fairy? Some other race? What happened? Why did they want to hurt you?"

Reg sensed a roiling blackness and then she was in the midst of it. It was a thick, misty darkness she could practically feel. She tried to see anyone's approach, or perhaps sense an entity in the fog itself. She couldn't assume that an enemy would be corporeal. It had been able to take some physical form or it would not have been able to stab Calliopia.

There were whispers in the dark.

Reg was used to voices. She'd heard many of them in her life. She listened carefully. Living? Dead? Reg couldn't understand the language. Did Calliopia? Or was it another race and Callie didn't know their language either? Reg listened attentively and analyzed Calliopia's reaction.

Fear. Terror at being taken again, at the thought of being taken back under the ground.

The darkness made her think of the darkness of the tunnel. She tried to swim through it, to get out of the nightmarish unreality and find the light she had left on. The light was there for just that reason.

It wasn't the first time the voices had come for her in the night.

Reg felt her skirt, found the pocket that dagger was in and wrapped her hand around it. If she had to protect herself, she would. Just like Calliopia had. She knew this without asking. Callie had fought and so would Reg.

"Who are they?" Her voice was inside Calliopia's head, not for everyone in the room to hear.

"I won't go," Calliopia cried out. "Don't let them take me."

Reg's hand pressed harder to the wound on the fairy's side, pressing Ruan's hand down. He resisted, not wanting to hurt Calliopia.

"They won't take you," Reg promised. They hadn't taken Callie from that room. Calliopia had only left the room by magic when she was injured badly enough to trigger the homing spell.

Then she had left it all behind.

The blood-soaked sheets. The dagger she had protected herself with. The dark room with the lamp left on to reveal any threats.

CHAPTER 18

Reg was jolted back to the outside world, pain in her hand. She was confused as she opened her eyes, looking to Calliopia's hand to see if it had been injured in her fight with the unknown assailants. But neither of Callie's hands was bandaged. Reg realized that the dagger was hot in her hand and released it. She shook her hand, trying to cool it off quickly to determine if she were injured or not.

"What happened?" Damon asked, moving quickly to her side and grasping her hand to have a look.

"Ouch." Reg pulled it away from him and shook it some more. "That really smarts! I burned it."

"How did you burn it? Did you... not put out your fire correctly?"

Reg thought about her fire casting and whether she could identify anything that she had done wrong. Her lessons with Davyn had been pretty basic but had, of course, begun with how to conjure fire and how to put it back out. She'd never had any trouble with that before.

"No, I don't think I did anything wrong."

Reg realized that her leg was starting to get uncomfortably hot as well, and realized that the dagger was pressing against it. She reached into her pocket and tried to quickly jerk it out without burning herself any further. It took a few tries to get it out, and it lay on Calliopia's bed in front of her. It looked the same as it always had, but even when Reg got her hand near it, she could feel its heat.

"What's going on? Why did it get so hot?"

Ruan bent close to study the blade. Reg wondered whether he could see anything she couldn't. Did the pixies, with their ability to exist in the shadow realm as well as the visible world, have a different kind of vision? One that allowed them to see things that were not on the visible spectrum for humans?

"What did you?" he asked, brows drawn down.

"I didn't do anything with the dagger. It was just in my pocket. I was talking with Calliopia, trying to understand what happened to her that night. She was showing me what she could remember. I still couldn't see her attackers. I could hear their voices… but then the dagger got hot, it started to burn me, and I was pulled out."

"You took it in your hand."

"Yes."

"Why?"

Reg looked at him, shaking her head. "I just…" She thought about it, trying to reconstruct the steps in her mind. "I wanted to protect myself against… whatever was in the darkness. I took it to protect myself… to protect Calliopia."

"That is what Callie did?"

"Uh… I don't know. I would guess so. If she slept with the light on and the dagger with her, then she must have planned to protect herself. If she saw this darkness and heard the voices, then she would take it in hand, like I did, waiting for the moment when she would have to fight."

Ruan was nodding his agreement. He had been on the road with her for some time, so he had undoubtedly witnessed similar behavior. She wouldn't have been able to hide it from him. He knew that she slept with the dagger. He knew that she was afraid of the dark. Even if they slept separately when they could, there had surely been nights when it hadn't been practical to separate and he had seen all of her night preparations and activities.

"And then when they attacked, she must have fought back," Reg said, taking the next logical step. "They injured her, but she might have been able to hurt one of them. Can you tell, when you look at the blade, whose blood is on it?"

Letticia had been able to tell that it was contaminated with fairy blood. Maybe Ruan too would be able to tell, if not who, then at least _what_ had attacked Calliopia.

Ruan inched the blade carefully out of its sheath, protecting his hand with a fold of the blanket. He moved back and forth, his eyes close to the blade and following the length of it, studying it minutely from hilt to tip. Eventually, he shook his head.

"If there be blood of others, I do not know. Fairy, human, pixie… but I do not see others."

"So then whoever attacked her must have been one of those three? Is that right?"

"Perhaps."

They all sat in silence. Reg sucked on her fingers, trying to cool them without looking too obvious about it. Mrs. Papillon moved without a word to the basin of water that she had been using for the compresses on Calliopia's forehead, and soaked a piece of fabric for Reg. Reg wrapped it around her stinging fingers, and it soothed the burn.

"Thank you."

"You are doing much," Mrs. Papillon said. "You are trying to help our Calliopia... whether you succeed or not."

"I will. I'll find a way to help her."

"She is at least no longer in pain. That is good."

Reg nodded. She was happy that her thought of using human pharmaceuticals had not backfired. If it had burned Calliopia or made the pain worse, she didn't know how she could have forgiven herself.

"I want to do more. I'll find a way."

They sat and considered Calliopia and the knife on the bed in front of Reg.

"What if there wasn't anyone else?" Damon suggested. "What if it was just Calliopia, alone in the room?"

"How could that be?" Ruan demanded.

"I don't know. I'm thinking… if Reg didn't see anyone, and there is no other blood on the dagger, then maybe Calliopia was injured with her own knife. Maybe there wasn't anyone else."

Reg shook her head. "That doesn't make any sense. Of course there was someone else. I saw the darkness. I heard their voices. She didn't stab herself."

Damon shrugged his shoulders. "Didn't she?"

Reg opened her mouth to argue with him, then stopped and thought about it. She hadn't seen anyone else, even though she had asked Calliopia several times who she had fought, who had hurt her. She knew it wasn't Ruan, Calliopia's only traveling companion. Who else even knew where they were? Had someone tracked her? Was she just targeted by a stranger?

She hadn't been set upon by thieves; Reg was pretty sure about that. If they had been thieves... they had been well-trained in knife or swordplay. That didn't sound like a non-magical human thief. And would a practitioner have attacked a fairy? Especially one who had just come into her powers? Reg had heard more than once how powerful and unpredictable an adolescent fairy was.

Reg hadn't seen anyone. But she had seen the fog of darkness. It had collected around Calliopia and blotted out the light from her lamp.

Why?

Where had it come from?

Calliopia knew about the darkness. That was why she had left the lamp turned on.

"Maybe when she saw the darkness and heard the voices… she was just remembering." Reg suggested. "Maybe it's a memory of when the pixies captured her."

She avoided looking at Ruan. She didn't know if he had been part of the company that had taken her, but she wouldn't have been surprised. He had been aware of it, even if he hadn't taken part in the capture.

He was the one who had convinced her to break the protective spell, allowing the pixies to locate Calliopia, break into her room, and take her. Up until then, Calliopia had been hidden from them by fairy spells.

Ruan reached for the knife, then changed his mind and left it there. Reg glanced sideways at him, just a quick look, trying to assess what he was thinking.

Was it possible that Damon was right and there was no one else? That Calliopia had been having a nightmare or the fairy equivalent of PTSD? Had she been fighting an entity that was not even there?

"I don't know," she said aloud. "Is it possible? Does a fairy hear and see things when she is sick? Or is that... just... a human thing?"

Calliopia's parents looked at each other and didn't say anything. Calliopia had not stayed with them after her safe return from the realm of the pixies, so they wouldn't know what kind of aftereffects the trauma might have had on her. They would have to consult fairy lore to see whether it was something that happened to fairies. Unless they already knew of cases where it had happened. Perhaps like humans, fairies knew that war or trauma could change a person's brain. Whether they were human of fairy.

"Ruan... can you tell me what she was like? After the two of you left? The times I saw her... she seemed to be happy. But this fear of the dark… that's different. Did she have… emotional problems?"

Ruan scratched his ear, considering. It couldn't have been a difficult question. He would know whether she had been behaving normally or not. But he wasn't necessarily willing to divulge anything.

"Callie… she fought demons."

CHAPTER 19

Reg looked around the room at the others. She looked at Damon, raising her eyebrows, hoping he would enlighten her. Did Ruan mean that Calliopia literally fought demons? Were they yet another species that she hadn't had the pleasure of meeting? A black-fog-producing race that could defeat a fairy or turn her wound poisonous so that she could not be healed and saved? Or was Ruan using it figuratively, like a human might, to characterize her fight with mental illness?

"What was that like?" Damon asked.

Reg thought that was a good way for him to fudge that he didn't know what Ruan was talking about. At least it wasn't something that Reg should have known about. Damon had grown up in a magical home, and if demons were a species that he didn't know about, then Reg couldn't be faulted for not knowing about them.

Ruan got up and paced across the room. He rubbed his eyes. He must have been tired after his long journey and worrying over his love. He must have been as exhausted as Reg was before Corvin had boosted her strength. Though pixies were a hardy lot. Maybe they could go long periods without sleep.

Ruan was definitely looking worse for wear. There were bags under his eyes.

"Callie was happy," Ruan insisted. "She was happy to get away from this place and be on her own. With her mate. It was comforting. She did not want to stay in one place. Did not want to rest under roof or underground. For a long time, we slept above ground, in woods, in fields. No roof overhead."

"That must have been hard on you, as a pixie," Reg contributed.

"I would do all to make her happy."

Reg nodded her understanding.

"After some time… she decided… Maybe she could rest under roof. That nothing was going to come in after her." He paused. "No one knew where she was. She could be happy. Rest in a bed, better on her bones."

Sleeping outside on the hard ground, even if they had stayed in a warm climate, couldn't have been comfortable on anyone's bones. Reg knew how she ached when she had to sleep rough.

"So she was starting to get better."

Ruan paced back and forth across the room. His face was not cheerful. He didn't like sharing what he knew about Calliopia's mental state with the people she had run away from. But he wanted Reg to understand what had happened. Reg was the only one who was really trying to help Callie.

"She slept inside, but she was troubled." He walked back and forth, falling into a restless rhythm. "More than when she was outside. Yet she wanted to rest. And wanted… me to rest."

Reg nodded encouragingly. "You two were partners. She was concerned with you, too. With you having to be in the sun all day, and overground all night."

He stopped and looked at her for a moment, then nodded.

"As you say… it was difficult. Piskies… are not meant for always being in the sun."

"And it was making you sick or weak?"

He shrugged. He shoved his hands into his pockets, walking in a hunched-over position. How he must have wished that he had been able to continue to sleep outside all the time, where Calliopia was safer or happier. Thinking that she had moved inside mostly for him, and then been injured because of it, must be eating him up.

"She had many dreams. Many dark, dreadful dreams."

Dark, dreadful dreams.

Reg nodded, seeing the darkness again. Calliopia must have had to face the fear, however remote, that someday they might come for her again. Strangers in the night, binding her and stealing her away to a place where she couldn't live and be happy, could never escape from, where she had begun to waste away in body and spirit.

"Did she try to do anything about the nightmares? A potion or meditation? Is it normal for fairies to have nightmares?"

Ruan shook his head. Reg had asked too many questions and she didn't know which he was answering, or if he was just shaking off the questions themselves.

"There were many remedies, many attempts at protection spells... but no matter how many... the dreams were relentless."

Ruan reached over and touched the blade. He didn't immediately jerk back from it, so Reg assumed that it had cooled down. She didn't like him touching it and wanted to put it back into its sheath and slide it into her pocket out of sight.

Ruan looked sideways at Reg, studying her. "I told you the blade is evil."

"You said that it should be unmade. But Calliopia didn't want it to be."

"No. She kept it with her. Always. It was not good to have its darkness over her all the time."

"You think the dagger was causing her nightmares? Then why didn't she get rid of it? Why did she want to keep it with her?"

He raised his hands helplessly. "Why? No one can tell why. Why do things call to us? Gems call to piskies. Plants call to fairies and garden gnomes. Metal and rock call to dwarfs. Why?"

Reg couldn't answer that question either. She remembered how drawn she had felt to Weston's key. She now knew why she had been attracted to that. Because Weston had intended for her to find it and to set him free.

"I guess… it is our natures," she said.

"The dagger was hers… it… meant something to her. She wanted it close, did not want it unmade."

"And you think it gave her nightmares because it was evil."

"Your blood," he said, motioning to her scarred hand. "Your connection with her. Do you not feel an attraction to it?"

Reg resisted thinking about how she wanted to just put it back in her pocket. She had been relieved to have it in her possession, even knowing it had been used to torture her. She didn't feel threatened by it. She felt the need to protect it. And be protected by it. She swallowed.

"I guess so. I want it near me." She looked at it lying on the bed in front of her. <u>Near her</u> didn't quite express the feeling. "I want it... in my possession. In my hand."

Ruan nodded, as if he had heard these words before.

"It is an accursed thing. It has taken your blood and yet you want it."

"Yeah. I guess so."

"It will not be satisfied with just a taste."

Reg looked at the innocent blade. It was just a knife. Just a tool. It wasn't good or bad and it didn't have feelings, wants, or needs. She had heard a lot of weird things since she had arrived in Black Sands.

She could believe that Forst could sense the feelings of the plants he cared for, but she wasn't sure she could go as far as to believe that a weapon, an implement, could have feelings and wants or needs.

It didn't want her blood or her life. It was just a tool.

CHAPTER 20

"Do you think there was someone else?" Damon prompted, bringing them back on track. "Or do you think maybe... it was an accident with the knife?"

Reg closed her eyes and reached out to Calliopia. She tried to be as relaxed as possible. If Calliopia had injured herself with the knife, either on purpose or by accident, then she would not be eager to reveal that fact. And maybe that was why she hadn't given Reg a proper answer before. Better everyone think that she had been attacked in the night by some unknown foe.

She entered Calliopia's thoughts gently. Callie was relaxed and restful, trying to regenerate. It wasn't really fair of Reg to re-enter her mind when she was having her first rest in days.

"Callie."

Calliopia stirred. She didn't answer.

"Calliopia. Just a little longer. Your loved ones are here, and they need to understand in order to help you."

Calliopia mentally pushed her away. But she was weak, and the effort of even that minor act was too much for her.

"Sleep."

"I know. I'll let you sleep in just a minute. But we want to help you. We don't want to have to wait until you are awake again. We want to start now, while you are sleeping."

"Sleep now."

"Calliopia. Your mom and dad are here."

"Yes."

"They love you very much. They weren't there, and they want to know what happened to you."

"No. Sleep."

"Ruan is here."

There was no response.

"Ruan is here. You don't want people to think that he was the one who hurt you."

"No!"

"He is the only one who was with you. The only one you would allow in the room with you. So it is logical that he is the one who attacked you. Your own mate tried to kill you."

"No." Calliopia reacted violently to the suggestion, again trying to push Reg out of her thoughts.

"Was it an accident? Or did someone attack you?"

There was no answer at first. Reg gave her some time to think about it. She had offered the explanation of an accident. Would Callie take it? If she didn't have to be the one to suggest it, would it be easier for her?

"There was a darkness," Callie said softly.

"Yes," Reg agreed. She waited, not offering anything else at first. "Did the darkness come from inside you?" She waited a few seconds for an answer. "From the knife?"

Calliopia's hand opened and clenched on the bedsheet beside her. She was inches from the blade, and she was aware of its presence. She wanted it in her hand, just like Reg did. Reg resisted touching it.

"Did it come from the dagger?" Reg asked again.

Calliopia keened, a long, lonely sound, a cry without words. Reg felt a lump in her throat at the mental anguish Calliopia felt. How could she go on feeling that way? She needed the knife. She needed peace. She needed her loved ones near. No matter what she did, the pain was still there. The darkness still followed her.

The fear still plagued her every night.

Even when she held her dagger close.

Calliopia's hand opened and closed, questing for the knife. Reg wanted to hold the knife. But as they unwound Calliopia's story, she was loath to touch it again, no matter how tempting it was.

"Callie. It's okay. We're here. We're all here, and no one is going to let anything happen to you. You can sleep without worrying about them coming to get you. You can sleep without being afraid of the dark. Ruan is near. Your mom and dad are near. You are protected here."

Calliopia's head moved back and forth, as she rose close to consciousness.

"You can go back to sleep in a minute. Just tell me. The knife. Was it the dagger that harmed you?"

She felt the confirmation. <u>Yes</u>.

Reg felt sick. The knife that almost killed Calliopia, that might still kill her, was in her possession. And rather than wanting to destroy it, Reg wanted to protect it.

"Did you want to harm yourself? Was it on purpose?"

"No."

"What happened?"

Calliopia reached, trying to share the feelings with Reg, but all Reg got was a confused muddle of emotions.

Fear and anger and pain.

The darkness had come. The voices had spoken.

Calliopia had tried to stop them.

And then the pain.

The horrible, piercing pain as the dagger bit into her.

Knowing that she was going to die.

Finding herself back in her childhood home, back with her parents, but separated from Ruan.

Knowing she was going to die.

"It's okay," Reg soothed her. "We're going to make you better. We're going to help you to get better again. Keep fighting. We are not going to let you die."

Calliopia's feelings became more distant. They started to fade. Calliopia gradually drifted back off again, away from Reg, away from the world.

And she slept.

CHAPTER 21

Reg sat back again, trying to relax her body. Everything had changed. Calliopia had not been attacked in her bed. No one had come to kidnap her or to steal her fairy power. No one had intended to kill her.

Except the dagger.

Could a knife have intent? It didn't make any sense.

"What found you?" Ruan demanded.

Reg looked at him. He probably already knew or had guessed.

"It wasn't an intruder. She stabbed herself with her own knife."

There was silence in the room. No one denied it or said that it couldn't be. Had they all guessed it before Reg?

"What do we do?" Reg looked at the fairies. "Now we know she was cut with the dagger. The blade needs to be cleansed, right? For the cut to be healed completely. That's what Davyn said. The scarring can't be healed unless the blade that caused it is cleansed."

"It needs to be unmade," Ruan advised. "It cannot be made clean of her blood."

"Unmade. So if we do that, Calliopia can be healed."

"Perhaps."

No one seemed to be too excited about this prospect. Reg couldn't figure out why they wouldn't be jumping all over it. It was the first time any of them had admitted that they might be able to do something to heal Calliopia, so Reg was pumped. Why weren't they?

"Then let's do that."

No one moved. They didn't agree or disagree; they just looked at her.

"What?" Reg demanded. "I don't see the problem. Why don't we unmake the blade so that she can get better?"

"We cannot," Mrs. Papillon reminded her, spreading her hands. "It is not a skill we have."

"You need dwarfs," Reg remembered what he'd told her before. "So let's do that. Let's go find the dwarfs and get it unmade."

"There are no dwarfs here."

"None?"

Mrs. Papillon shook her head. "No. We are too close to the water. The nearest dwarfs are many days' journey away."

"Many days' journey? You can fly around the world in a couple of days. How far away can they be?"

Ruan's eyes widened. "You can fly?"

Reg laughed. "Well, in a plane, yes. Where are these dwarfs?"

Ruan looked at the Papillons.

"The Great Mountains. There be smithies there."

"The Great Mountains." Reg remembered the drive from Tennessee to Florida. "Is that in the Appalachians?"

Mr. Papillon nodded. "A very old trail. The Great Blue Mountains."

"Blue Ridge Mountains?" Reg guessed. "I know where they are."

"Many days' journey. A difficult climb even for our kin."

"Not so bad if you have a car." Reg knew that fairies sometimes used coaches, and witches and warlocks used cars, so why would they have to go on foot?

"It is a pilgrimage," Mr. Papillon explained. "Not to be taken lightly."

"We want to have the blade destroyed before it's too late. We can't afford to walk."

Mrs. Papillon nodded her agreement, but her words contradicted the motion. "It is not done that way."

"This time, it will be."

They just looked at her. If there were one excuse that Reg hated, it was that it was tradition. What kind of nonsense was that? Just because you had always done something the same way, that meant that you then had to always do it that way? Rules based on risks of harm, she could at least understand. 'We've always done it that way,' was the lamest excuse she'd ever heard.

"This will be my journey," Reg told them firmly, looking from one face to the other. "This is my quest. What did you call it? Pilgrimage? I'm in charge of this adventure, and I say we're driving. Not walking."

No one argued. Reg nodded once, decisive. "So who's coming along? I'll need directions to the place the dwarfs live and how to get them to unmake the blade. Do I need to give them gold?" It seemed to Reg that dwarfs in movies were always collecting gold or gems. She would have to find some way to pay them for the work that they were asked to perform.

"We cannot come," Mrs. Papillon said. "We must care for Calliopia."

Reg couldn't see any way around that. "Someone needs to stay here with her. But all of you? Someone could come with me."

Mr. Papillon looked from his wife to Ruan. "We will discuss it."

Reg felt his dismissal. She stood up. "Okay. I'm going to take a break." She walked toward the door, then realized she didn't have anywhere to go. "Uh... is there somewhere you want me to wait? Where I slept before?"

"You require refreshment," Mrs. Papillon offered. "Allow me to see you to the kitchens."

"I'm okay, really."

"You require respite."

Reg followed the fairy out of the bedroom into the hall, where the air was cooler. Damon joined her. They stuck close to Mrs. Papillon and, in a few minutes, were in a space filled with tables and trees, with baskets laden with bread and fruit and vegetables, smelling sweet and pungent, their colors bright and riotous. Reg looked around, eyes wide. Mrs. Papillon gestured to a row of cupboards. "The larders are filled if you require milk or honey or other sustenance," she advised. "We eat no flesh here, but whatever else you desire, you shall find."

"Thank you. This looks great." Reg shook her head. "I didn't think I was hungry, but now…"

Damon nodded his agreement. "This looks amazing. Thank you."

"If you have need, you have only to ask."

Before Reg had a chance to ask who they would ask for anything more, Mrs. Papillon turned and swept away. She looked at Damon and shrugged. "I don't think I'm going to need to ask for anything else, do you?"

Damon shook his head, grinning. He pulled out a chair and sat at the nearest table, pulling a basket of fruit toward him. He began to eat. Reg stood there for a moment, unsure what to do. She hadn't been hungry, but the food looked appetizing.

"If we're starting out on a quest, we need to eat," he pointed out.

"Yeah, I guess so." Reg sat down. She pulled out her phone. "Do you think it would be rude of me to make calls from here?"

"Who are you going to call?" Damon asked around a mouthful of peach.

"I don't know. I'm trying to think of who should come with us. It will have to be more than just you and me, right? On TV, you always need a big company, so that you have everyone whose skills you might need. And when we fought the Witch Doctor, we had to make sure we had all of the assets we would need."

"I don't think TV and literature exactly reflect the needs of a real-life quest. And we're not going to fight like with the Witch Doctor. We're getting some smithing work done."

"Do you know how to talk to dwarfs?"

"I assume just the same as anyone else."

"Do they speak English? Are there special protocols? And aren't there... things in the mountains? Dragons and orcs and trolls?"

Damon just looked at her.

"You're the one with a magical upbringing," Reg pointed out. "This is all new to me."

"I don't think we're going to run into modern-day dragons."

"Did you think we were going to have to fight immortals?"

"Well, no," Damon admitted.

"Do you know for a fact whether there are dragons in the mountains?"

"I don't think there are."

"Are they extinct?"

"I assume so."

"I never would have thought there were sirens and mermaids. Or even pixies and fairies. Or witches."

"You knew there were witches," he protested.

"I knew there were people who called themselves witches. But I thought it was just a religious thing. Or kooks. Or cons. I didn't know… that there were actual witches."

He raised an eyebrow at her. Reg looked down at her phone and started to call her contacts.

CHAPTER 22

The composition of Reg's quest company wasn't quite what Reg had expected. She'd figured she would have difficulty convincing Corvin to do anything, considering the problems she'd had in talking him into giving her a boost in strength for Calliopia's healing. She didn't have any way to convince him that he should come with her. No way to bribe or blackmail him into going. But it turned out that was the easiest part of the project.

"Would I like to meet some dwarfs?" he asked, falling into his professorial tone, "There are no dwarfs within miles of here and I've never had the opportunity to see them in their natural habitat. One or two here and there at a sideshow, but never an actual colony!"

"I wouldn't have thought that traveling was a problem for you," Reg said, surprised. "Couldn't you have gone and seen some whenever you wanted to?"

"Oh, no. They are a very private people. You rarely see any without an invitation. They keep themselves to themselves."

Reg's stomach tensed. She pictured herself knocking on the side of a mountain, calling out to them, trying to figure out the password to gain entrance. She hadn't arranged ahead of time for an invitation or appointment. She had just assumed that if she had a job for them, they would let her in. She wouldn't be there just to gawk, after all, she would be there with a job that only they could do.

"How am I going to pay them? I don't exactly have a lot of gold lying around here."

"Hmm." Corvin pondered this. "I have a few trinkets they might like. Not much use to me after I have drained what powers they once held."

"Do you think it will be enough?" She had a feeling that when he said 'trinkets,' he wasn't talking about a few children's rings and bracelets out of a vending machine. But that didn't mean that they would be considered valuable by the dwarfs.

"Won't know until we offer," Corvin advised, without concern. "Just be aware that they will want to negotiate. They will turn down the first deal no matter what it is. So take heart and don't believe them. Bartering is an important part of the process, and if you don't fight over every last cent, they'll think that they aren't getting a good deal."

"Okay." She'd done enough bartering on the street to be comfortable with the process. Most people expected just to pay the price on the price tag, unless it was a used car lot, but Reg had learned that most prices were negotiable, if you worked for it.

"Do you know... who else might be helpful for us to have along? I'm afraid that if we don't have enough people, we won't be able to... accomplish the quest."

It sounded silly and juvenile when she said it to Corvin. Especially after Damon had said she'd watched too much TV. But Corvin didn't laugh. He was silent on the phone, but Reg could still hear him breathing, and waited for him to tell her what he thought.

"I assume you've already talked to Davyn."

"No, not yet. I wasn't sure... if he would be interested. I don't have anything to offer him."

"Davyn Smithy?" Corvin said pointedly.

Reg frowned and shook her head. "What? I knew that's who you meant."

"Smithy."

"Yes."

"His family were silversmiths. I would think that he'd have an inherent interest in meeting dwarfs. Especially on the matter of unmaking a magical blade."

"Oh. Well, good. I'll give him a call too. I was thinking about Harrison, but I don't suppose he would be interested. Or he might be to start with, but then he'd get bored and wander off."

Corvin chuckled. "Yes, you're probably right. Immortals don't make great traveling companions."

"Even if we only have to drive for ten hours?"

"Time is such a mortal concept," Corvin said in a dramatic, pained tone. He didn't do Harrison very well, but it was still funny. Reg could picture him saying that.

"I tried Sarah, but she isn't answering. I guess I'll ask her when I get to the house."

"She might not be around."

"Really? Where is she?"

"A bunch of the witches in her coven are going on some kind of retreat. I didn't get any details, but..."

"Oh, that's right. I don't want to be the only woman in the group."

"You could always try Marian."

Reg reacted viscerally to the thought of inviting the older medium along. "Ugh. No."

"You might have to be creative, then."

"I'll ask Francesca… well, except I need someone to take care of the cats. If Sarah isn't around, then I need Francesca to feed them."

"They'll be fine by themselves for a day or two, as long as you leave them some food."

"I can't just leave them without anyone to look after them if we run into problems and are longer than we need to be. I know from movies how these quests can go. It could last a lot longer than we think."

"I'll leave it to you, then." Corvin didn't care for cats, so he didn't care who she had take care of them. But he did seem to be eager to go on the trip, and Reg was happy about that. She'd been afraid she would have to twist arms to get everyone to join in.

"Okay. We'll want to leave pretty quickly. Can you be at the cottage in a couple of hours, ready to go?"

"Yes. I'll need to make a few arrangements, but it won't be hard."

"Okay, see you then."

* * *

Davyn Smithy. Reg forgot that a lot of the names in the magical community meant something. Or had meant something far more recently than in the non-magical world. Reg Rawlins? She had no idea what Rawlins might mean. She had an idea that Regina had something to do with being a queen, but wasn't sure. So Smithy actually meant that Davyn's family had been smiths. She called him next and tried to think of how to introduce the idea of the quest. He already knew that she was trying to help Calliopia, so she didn't have to start right at the beginning. But how did she float the idea of going on a quest to someone she barely knew? Although she had taken Davyn on as a mentor to help her learn fire casting, that wasn't the same as actually being friends.

"Dave Smith."

"Hi, Davyn… it's Reg."

"Well, good to hear your voice. That means you didn't manage to kill yourself trying to heal your fairy. Unless I'm hearing from you beyond the grave, which I suppose I can't discount, you being a medium."

"I'm good," Reg said, ignoring his teasing, "Things actually went pretty well. Calliopia is resting comfortably… she can start to heal and get some strength back. But there's one thing that we do need to do to help her…"

"I get the feeling I might not want to know this."

"Well… I hope you do. She was injured by a blade… well, the same dagger that I got my scar from."

"Oh, yes?" He answered quickly, sounding interested.

"So it needs to be unmade. For her to start healing."

"I see."

"Corvin said that your family was silversmiths."

"A few generations back, yes. I'm afraid I don't have much skill in smithing myself."

"I'm looking for some people who would come along with me. I don't need you to unmake the blade, but I'm hoping for a few companions to go on a sort of a quest with me, to get the dwarfs in the Blue Ridge Mountains to unmake the blade."

"You're going to see dwarfs?"

"That's the idea. Yeah. I'm sure it won't be a big deal, everything will go smoothly, but I didn't want to go by myself. I was hoping that you would come along. If you know anything about dwarfs and smithing, that's a bonus. I really just want safety in numbers. A few people who can help out if things go sideways."

"When are you going?"

"We want to head out in a few hours. I know that's not much time, but Calliopia is in pretty bad shape, and the sooner we can get started, the sooner we can destroy the blade and get her on the road to healing."

"Yes… you don't want to wait too long."

"So would you be able to? I know you work in an office and all that, you have all of your responsibilities as a coven leader..."

"I think I could swing something. It's the weekend. If I just tell them I'm going to be an extra day or two due to a family emergency..."

CHAPTER 23

Reg got home and started to throw travel items into a bag. It didn't take her long to pack; she was used to traveling light and having to be ready in an instant.

Nico chased the straps of the backpack she was filling, and when that wasn't enough of a challenge, he attacked Reg's swinging skirts. She tried to chase him away, swiping at him with her hands.

"Hey! Cut that out! I don't have time to play right now."

He jumped back out of her reach immediately, but as soon as she started to pack again, he was going after her hands, biting and clawing and thoroughly enjoying fighting with her. Each time she tried to chase him away, he danced back, and then attacked as soon as she stopped advancing on him.

Unlike Starlight, he didn't seem to care about having water flicked or sprayed in his face. He took it on as just another challenge and kept doing whatever it was she was trying to stop him from.

"Get out of here!" Reg chased him out of the room, thundering after him as loudly as she could, and as soon as he was out the bedroom door, slammed it shut.

Doors were Nico's nemesis. He could climb curtains or Reg's leg, or even the walls in some cases, but he had not mastered turning doorknobs. Though she often heard him jumping at them, determined to figure it out. He sat on the other side of the closed door and howled.

"Now then, what am I going to do with you guys?" Reg asked Starlight, who was sitting in the window watching her calmly.

He cocked his head. She hadn't explained to him where she was going. And she hadn't yet figured out who she was going to get to watch them. She supposed it would have to be Francesca, even though she would have preferred to have the charmer with her on the quest. She put her phone down and used voice commands to call Francesca while she continued to pack, adding toiletries to her backpack.

But Francesca's phone rang through to voicemail.

Annoyingly, she had three different numbers, and Reg was never sure which one she was going to answer. She tried the next one, and then the next, each time expecting to hear Francesca's Haitian accent and to make arrangements for her to look after the two cats.

But Francesca did not answer at any of her numbers. Reg sat down, staring at the phone. Not Francesca, then.

Who else was she going to get to look after the cats? She didn't trust very many people to remember about them and take good care of them. Harrison loved cats, and Starlight in particular, but Reg feared that he'd forget any responsibility, or that he had to show up at particular times to feed him, and Starlight would starve waiting for him.

"What am I going to do?"

Starlight jumped from the window to the bed and sniffed around the backpack, then poked his head in through the open zipper. Reg laughed as he investigated it.

"You cats love bags, don't you? It's too bad there's more to traveling with a cat than just popping you into a backpack to take with me."

Starlight pulled his head out of the backpack and looked at her.

"I can't take you with me," Reg protested.

He sat and stared at her for a few minutes, then licked his paw and began to bathe. Reg opened the bedroom door to get a few other things she wanted to pack. Nico came flying into the room, streaking past her like a bolt of black lightning. Reg gave a little shout and jumped back, then shook her head and went on with her tasks, ignoring him. He would just have to stay out of trouble while she finished up.

She gathered her shoes and coat and other things that she might need while on the road and returned to pack them into her bag. When she opened the top of her backpack, she was immediately bitten and scratched from within.

Starlight was still sitting on the bed washing, so Reg knew who the culprit was without opening the hole to see who was inside.

"Nico! Get out of there! You are not luggage."

He didn't leave the bag.

Reg lifted the bottom to tip him out. She knew better than to stick her hand in and try to pull him out. That would be like sticking her hands into the mouth of an alligator.

"Come on. Out of there. Get out."

He must have been holding on with his claws, because even when she tipped it upside down, he still didn't tumble out.

"Nico! Bad kitty! Come on, get out of there!"

There was a knock on the front door. Reg glared at her backpack and went to answer the door.

It was Davyn, so she let him in. "I'll just be a minute. I'm trying to get the cat out of my bag."

He raised his eyebrows and didn't say anything. Reg went back to the bedroom. She looked around the room first to see if Nico had vacated the bag voluntarily, but didn't see him hiding under anything else, waiting to attack her. She poked the backpack, and it moved as he tried to claw or bite her.

"Can you get him out?" she begged Starlight. "Can you call him so that he'll come out of there?"

Starlight just stared at her as if he didn't understand what she was talking about.

"Nico." Reg poked the bag. "Come on. I need to get going. I'm not going to feed you if you don't listen to me."

He poked his head out of the bag and looked at her.

"I'm serious. You get out of there, or no more food."

He narrowed his eyes at her, but clearly didn't believe it, if he even understood the threat. He was a very smart animal, so Reg didn't doubt that he understood. Still, he didn't come out of the backpack. Reg picked it up and took it with her to the living room, where Davyn was waiting. She set it down, propped against one of the chairs. Nico popped his head out again and looked at Davyn. He hissed.

"Nico, be nice."

"Are you bringing the cats?" Davyn asked.

"Well… no. That wasn't the plan. I'm just having trouble convincing this one to do what he's told."

"Why don't you just—" Davyn reached into the bag to pull Nico out, and was instantly attacked. "Ow!"

Reg raised her brows and shook her head. "Why do you think I didn't do that?"

Davyn looked at his hand, striped with long scratches that were now starting to bleed. Reg noted to herself that he had been scratched a lot worse than she ever had. Either she was quicker to react, or Nico was nicer to her.

"Do you want me to get you something for that?"

Davyn moved over to the kitchen sink. "I'll just rinse it for a minute. It's not like it's a mortal wound."

Nico growled from within the backpack. Reg eyed it. If Nico thought that his fighting skills were being disparaged, Davyn might have more challenges than he expected.

Reg turned her attention back to the issue of what to do with the cats.

CHAPTER 24

When Corvin got there, Reg did not invite him in, but shooed Davyn out. "Damon should be here in a minute too. Do we all want to go in one vehicle, or split up? There's no point in going in four different cars."

"How many are there?"

"Me and Damon, the two of you. I don't know if Mr. Papillon or Ruan are coming along. The two cats, I guess…"

"We'll go in separate vehicles," Corvin said instantly. He did not like cats, and Reg could understand why he didn't want to be in the same vehicle as they were. It would be close quarters if they only took one vehicle, even if it were a van. Corvin had probably come in his little white compact, and she didn't know what Davyn drove. Damon's truck would be the best bet; they could throw all of their supplies in the back. Davyn and Corvin could share a vehicle. She wasn't sure where Ruan or Mr. Papillon would go. Neither of them would like the cats, so the car might end up being full.

"Okay. You guys decide between yourselves whether you are taking one or two. Let's get everything out to the front, so we're ready to load up."

Reg looked down at her backpack, still with a kitty head looking out the top. She had put Starlight into a cardboard cat carrier, which he definitely did not like. She picked the two of them up and took them out of the house. She would have preferred that Nico were in the cat carrier. She was more concerned about him making a break for it when they were outside. He was going to need some kind of leash or harness. They'd have to pick something up on the way, because she wasn't going to drive around looking for something before they left. Calliopia's situation was dire, even if she was finally sleeping peacefully.

They needed to get on their way. They had ten hours of driving through the night plus whatever time it took to track down the dwarfs and get them to unmake the dagger. Reg didn't know if they would then need to rush back to Calliopia's side, or whether she would start to heal as soon as the blade was destroyed.

She put everything down to lock the door, then she and the warlocks made their way out to the front of the house, where Damon was pulling up in his big black truck.

He raised his eyebrows when Reg lifted the backpack and cat carrier up into the truck cab and moved the seat forward so she could put them into the second row of seating. Ruan was sitting in the back, barely tall enough to see out the window.

"Sorry, you get some traveling companions."

Ruan looked at the cats and hissed. Nico, head poking out of the backpack, did the same. Reg shook her head, laughing. "Get used to it. You're going to have to sit with them. Unless you want to talk to Corvin and Davyn about going with them."

Ruan craned his head around to look at Corvin, and shook his head. "With that creature? He is worse than ten cats."

Reg thought of the nine draugrs and the Witch Doctor they had fought. "Well... I guess you're right about that."

"We are ready to go." Ruan moved restlessly, looking out the front window of the truck. "Reg Rawlins is ready to go?"

"Yes, I'm ready." Reg readjusted her seat, leaned far over to grasp the door handle and slammed the door. "Let's go!"

"Are those two ready to go?" Damon asked. "Does everybody know where we're heading?"

Reg looked in her wing mirror at Corvin and Davyn. It was a little awkward for them to be talking to each other and traveling together, considering that Davyn was Corvin's coven leader and was supposed to be shunning him. He wasn't even supposed to acknowledge Corvin's presence.

"Give them another minute; they shouldn't take too long."

"Do we have pre-set pit stops?"

"No, I'll just text Corvin when we want to stop. I don't want to have to stop any more than we have to."

She watched impatiently. But she knew that if she interrupted them to tell them to hurry up, it would just take that much longer for them to get moving. Eventually, Davyn got into Corvin's passenger seat, and everyone was set.

"You know how to get there?" Reg asked Damon. "To the place the dwarfs live?"

"Ruan does."

"Have you been there before?" Reg looked over the seat at him.

"It is in the lore of my people," Ruan said. "We know the way."

"Well, that's great. Let's get going, then."

Reg hoped that there hadn't been so much development in the mountains that Ruan would no longer be able to find the traditional path to the dwarfs. Or that they hadn't decided the highway was too close to their home and decided to move elsewhere.

How long had it been since any of the pixies or fairies had been there? Reg hoped that they had regular commerce with each other and that a pilgrimage wasn't just something they did every three or four generations and passed down in song.

* * *

A road trip with a pixie and two cats was worse than those she remembered as a kid, jammed into the back seat with other foster kids she barely knew and expected to get along until they could get to their destination. Which was invariably somewhere dead boring that Reg wished she had never been to. But turning around and going back home meant another ten-hour drive in the back seat of the car with other foster kids she barely knew, now hot and grumpy and unable to stand each other.

The cats alternately hissed and yowled their protests over having to ride along in the box on wheels, and Ruan was almost as bad. He kept hissing at the cats and complaining about them, and he wanted to drive.

"You can't drive," Reg told him, "you look ten years old."

"I am many years older than that."

"I know, but no cop is going to believe it. We'll get pulled over as soon as you hit the interstate."

"I have driven," Ruan growled. "I drove Calliopia."

"I know you did," Reg had seen them in her visions. Traveling all across the country. "And you took back roads to keep from getting caught. But we can't afford to do that; we need to get Calliopia help as soon as we can."

"Yes," Ruan admitted, dropping his eyes as he thought of his mate.

"Doesn't matter anyway," Damon growled. "It's my truck, and I'm driving. No one else drives my vehicle."

"You're not going to drive the whole way, are you?" Reg asked. "I can spell you."

"Spell me?" Damon repeated, glancing at her.

"You know, give you a break," Reg laughed. "I didn't mean... magick you."

He gave her another sidelong glance, not sure she was telling the truth.

"Spell you," Reg repeated. Had he never heard the expression before? Maybe growing up in a magical household, it had a completely different meaning for him from what it did for Reg.

"I'm driving," Damon repeated. "No one else drives my truck."

"Well, you let me know when you start getting tired because I don't want to go off the road somewhere. Driving tired is just as bad as driving drunk."

"I'm just fine. I haven't gone off the road yet."

Reg rolled her eyes and looked out her window, mentally shaking her head at him. Men could be so hard-headed sometimes. What did he think, that she wasn't capable of driving his baby? She might get into an accident or run out of gas? Or grind the gears?

"Humans and their cars," Ruan said in a tone that echoed Reg's thoughts about Damon. She looked over the seat at him. He was sitting as far into the corner of the seat as he could, with both cats watching him.

"I was surprised that pixies drive," she said. "Or are you an exception? I don't think any of the fairies drive."

"Not many piskies," Ruan admitted, "usually night, when no one can see."

"And the fairies? Not at all?"

"Horses and other animals. Coaches, not cars."

"They don't think much of technology, do they?"

Ruan shook his head. "Human technology is… automation and noise. Not better. Except cars." He looked out his window, down at the road. "Cars are good."

Reg laughed.

CHAPTER 25

After they decided they weren't going to be escaping from the car any time soon, the cats settled down. The panting and yowling stopped, though there was still a certain amount of hissing aimed at Ruan. Nico decided he didn't need to stay in Reg's backpack any longer. He squirmed out of it and started to explore the truck.

"I can't believe I had to take you with me," Reg told him. "Two cats in a truck! This is not the way to travel."

She hadn't figured out yet what she was going to do about food and water and a litter box. She was afraid that as soon as they opened their doors, the cats were going to make a break for it. Starlight was in a carrier, so he was pretty safe, but it was only cardboard and she imagined he could gnaw a hole out if he put his mind to it.

Nico jumped onto the headrest of Reg's seat.

"Hey, get down from there," Reg told him, reaching up for him. He swiped at her hands and managed to slash her once. Reg ignored the wound and grabbed him around the belly to pull him down. He started kicking with both back legs, and Reg had to hold him away from herself to avoid getting slashed by his powerful back legs.

"Cut it out! Behave yourself! You're the one who wanted to come on this trip, so you should be on your best behavior!"

He hissed at her and meowed and squirmed to be put down. Eventually, Reg set him down by her feet, on the right side, as far away from the driver as possible. Damon looked over at him.

"They shouldn't be out of their carriers. What if he gets under the pedals?"

"He's on my side; he won't."

"Isn't this the one you can't control?"

"Uh…" Reg tried to think of an excuse or diversion. "It isn't that I can't control him, he's just…"

Nico looked up at her, his yellow eyes shining.

"He's a little… ADHD," Reg tried. That was how she and Francesca had labeled him. He wasn't a bad cat, and he didn't mean to get into trouble, but he was full of energy and kitty curiosity, and his attention was attracted by every little thing. He was worse than that dog in the Pixar movie.

"I don't think cats get that," Damon said dryly.

"Have you met Nico?"

"Can you put him in the carrier, please?"

"Uh... sure."

Reg reached down to grab ahold of Nico, but that was easier said than done, especially since she was wearing a seatbelt and he was not. He slithered out of her grasp and bounded over the seat, back into the back seat where Starlight and Ruan were. Ruan let out a shout.

She wasn't sure what he was saying, and whether he was speaking in pixie or cat, but she was pretty sure it wasn't very complimentary. He was yelling and spitting at Nico, and Nico bounced off of him, not taking it very kindly. Ruan grabbed his knee, hollering louder.

"Cut it out!" Damon shouted. "I can't drive with all of the screaming! What's going on back there?"

"Bit me! Bit me!" Ruan shouted at Reg, holding his hand over his injured leg. "Unprovoked, he attacked me!"

He was making a lot bigger fuss about a little bite from a cat than he had about being cut when Reg took the dagger from him.

"You were yelling at him and he didn't like it."

"He attacked me! If he does not like riding in the truck, he should attack you! It is not my plan to bring a cat! Two cats!"

"I know it wasn't your fault. It wasn't anything to do with you. He's just not used to it. If you sit quietly and show him how to ride properly in the truck, maybe he'll calm down and get the idea." She spoke in as soothing a voice as possible. She was pretty sure she'd heard this lecture more than once from her foster mothers over the years. She must have absorbed their words, even when she was trying to block them out. And now she had all of their motherly advice in her head.

"He is a cat. They are not supposed to be riding in a truck."

"Neither are pixies," Damon said, "but we're still letting you ride."

"I am a person, not an animal. Not a dumb beast!" He aimed this last salvo at Nico.

Nico crouched low, his tail swishing back and forth as he eyed Ruan.

"Nico!" Reg warned. "You leave him alone."

"He's looking at me!" Ruan shouted.

"Nico, stop looking at Ruan!" Reg covered her face, not sure whether to laugh or cry in frustration. In another minute, she would be trying to deal with, 'Mom, he's on my side!'

"Nico. Come up here."

Nico turned his head to look at Reg. He didn't look like he was going to obey. "Nico. If you don't come up here and sit nicely with me, I'm going to stuff you back into that backpack and tie down the flap."

He glared at her, then bounded onto her headrest again without warning, making Reg shriek. Her yell startled Damon, and he swerved partway into the next lane, raising car horns from other drivers. Reg pulled Nico down and tried to hold him in her lap. He squirmed, bit, and scratched to get free. She knew she was going to have to let him go, or he was going to end up drawing blood.

Her phone started to ring. Nico made one last wild attempt and ended up on the floor beside Reg's feet again.

"You just stay there!" Reg told him sternly, and looked at her phone. Corvin. She sighed and picked it up. "Don't tell me you need a pit stop already?" she asked.

Corvin chuckled. "Is everything okay up there?"

They were following and had apparently seen the truck swerve into the other lane.

"Uh… yeah. Just Nico."

"Nico is driving now?"

Nico sat up, ears pricking up.

"No, Nico is not driving." Reg glared at Nico. "Nico is not allowed to drive."

He lay down, folding his ears back.

"So, everything is okay?" Corvin asked.

"Bringing cats on a road trip is not a good idea," Damon announced loudly, so that Corvin would be able to hear it.

Reg giggled. "It wasn't my idea. Anyway… I think things are settled down for the moment."

"Look!" Ruan insisted. "I told you he bit me!"

Reg looked into the back seat, where Ruan had pulled his tattered pants down to his ankles to inspect his knee, which was oozing blood from a couple of fang marks.

Reg looked quickly away. "I see that. But I don't think you're fatally injured. Now put your pants back on."

There was silence on the phone. Reg could just imagine what Corvin must think about the bizarre conversation.

"Nico is wearing pants now?" Corvin questioned after a few beats.

"No, Ruan. Or rather, he isn't wearing pants."

"I see." Corvin's voice was thoughtful. "You know, in all of the research I have done into the history of the magical peoples of North America, I have never been able to find out…"

"What?"

"With the state of disrepair that the pixies' clothing is usually in... do they wear undergarments? Or have they pretty much worn away to nothing at this point?"

Reg snorted. "I didn't look that closely."

"Well... a little bit of research wouldn't hurt..."

"I'm not checking."

"It would be for posterity."

"No."

Corvin sighed. "Could you tell Damon to pick up the pace? At this speed, we're not likely to get to the mountains until late tomorrow morning..."

Reg looked at the speedometer. "We're just over the speed limit."

"You could go much faster. That thing's got a hemi in it."

"And then we'll get pulled over by the highway patrol. This is good. You'll just have to deal with it. And it won't be late morning. It will still be before dawn. Unless you're planning long pit stops."

"I'm hoping for no pit stops."

"That's not going to happen. We'll need gas and I'm not peeing into a bottle."

Another sigh from the warlock.

"Why don't you talk with Davyn?" Reg suggested. "You've got someone in the car with you. Take advantage of an opportunity to catch up with an old friend."

"That's sort of difficult, when he won't acknowledge that there is anyone in the car with him."

"Really?"

"You know Davyn. He has this thing about keeping the rules."

"That's probably why they made him head of the coven. You can't put a rule-breaker in as the head warlock. You'd have all kinds of complaints."

"There are complaints anyway. Right, Davyn?"

There was no reply from Davyn.

"Davyn goes skyclad to the grocery store," Corvin prodded.

Still no answer from Davyn.

"See what I have to deal with?" Corvin asked. "Ten to twelve hours of stony silence."

"At this point, I'd be happy to trade with you. How about two cats and a pixie?"

"No, thanks."

"Yeah, that's what I thought. Why don't you give Davyn one of your lectures? I'm sure he'd appreciate it. How about the one about the comparative history of draugrs in cultures all over the world?"

"Draugar," Corvin corrected. "I've told you that the correct plural form—"

"Tell Davyn," Reg said and hung up.

She sat looking at the phone, waiting to see if it would ring again, snickering to herself.

"What did he say?" Damon asked.

"He's bored."

"Ah. He wouldn't be bored here."

"No, but he has this thing about cats."

Reg looked down at Nico, who was still crouching by her foot. But he hadn't curled up and made himself comfortable, so she was sure that he would be on the move again before long.

"Why don't you come up here and cuddle? You like it when I scratch your ears and rub your throat."

Nico looked at her but did not oblige by jumping up into her lap.

"I can't really cuddle while driving," Damon said, "but if you want to scratch my ears..." He gave his head a little wiggle.

"This is the weirdest road trip I've ever been on!"

CHAPTER 26

They did have to stop for gas eventually. Though the truck had a large gas tank, it was not a low-consumption vehicle. Damon had been driving back and forth between Reg's place and the Papillon estate before even leaving town, and he hadn't bothered to top up the gas before leaving.

"May as well drive until we can't anymore," Damon said philosophically, as Reg anxiously watched the fuel indicator dip down into the red zone. So it wasn't until Corvin called again to say that they wanted to stop for refueling that they pulled into a service station for gas, snacks, and a much-needed bathroom break. Reg managed to get out of the car without letting Nico out, but she looked around inside the service station convenience store for a leash to ensure he couldn't escape when they decided to take the cats outside to relieve themselves.

There were no leashes, which was not a big surprise. Apparently, people who took their pets on road trips with them usually planned ahead and had leashes from home. Reg found some string she hoped would do the job. She needed to be able to fashion some kind of leash or harness out of it that would hold Nico, but not choke him. And probably one for Starlight too, but she was far more confident of him not running off. Still, Starlight might decide he didn't like road travel and try to go back to the cottage on his own.

She went to the front counter with her string and put it down among a growing pile of snack foods. Reg looked at the pile, her brows drawing down.

"We only have five people. This looks like we're feeding a whole Girl Guide camp."

Corvin looked over the food and shrugged. "Looks about right. Especially when one of those people is a pixie. Have you seen the amount they eat?"

Reg thought of the waif-like faces of the pixies and wasn't sure she believed it. They always looked half-starving. She suspected that Corvin was just covering for how much he was planning to eat.

"Have you ever been to a Girl Guide camp?" Corvin asked, inching closer to her and looking her over as if trying to imagine her in one of the ugly brown uniforms.

"You might be surprised."

He snickered. She could feel the heat radiating off of him and the musky scent that she associated with him when he wasn't giving off the scent of roses. She closed her eyes, pretending that she couldn't smell it and wasn't imagining herself in his arms once again. There was no way that he could ever know how much she enjoyed his physical proximity. He already used his charms on her too often, determined to get the advantage over her and to talk her into relinquishing her powers to him.

"I can imagine little Reg Rawlins as a Girl Scout," Corvin said. "But somehow, I don't think you were the same rule follower as Davyn. I think you were probably the one toilet-papering the other cabins, leaving food out for the bears, and disappearing into the wood, forcing them to call in search and rescue."

Reg bit her lip, trying to keep herself from being drawn in by his charming smile and twinkling eyes. "Maybe two out of three of those."

"Two out of three… now I have to wonder which two…"

"You'll have to imagine, because I'm not going to tell you."

"Ah, Regina." He exhaled roses in her direction. "You and I would make such a good team."

Reg took a step back, holding her breath and building a psychic wall between the two of them. She needed to stay focused on Calliopia. She couldn't let herself be distracted by a handsome warlock who knew how to push all of her buttons.

Calliopia was what was important. Reg needed to get to the dwarfs, convince them to unmake the blade, and then… she wasn't sure of the next step, but it would be easier to heal Calliopia. Once the blade was destroyed, then Calliopia's wound would be able to knit together properly so that she could heal. With her mother's ministrations, more morphine as needed, and Reg's strengthening magic, maybe they could save her.

They <u>would</u> save her.

Reg couldn't contemplate any other outcome.

* * *

They were back in their vehicles and on their way again. Reg opened the various snacks and helped herself to a bite of this and that, though she wasn't really hungry. She needed to keep up her strength, and they had all of the food groups — pop, chips, chocolate, and jerky.

Ruan went for the jerky first, tearing open several strips and ripping at them with his long, pointed teeth. Reg looked away. The fairies and the gnomes were vegetarian. The same was not true of pixies. But then, she had already guessed that from comments made by her friends, and by the pixies themselves. Reg strongly suspected that they were not only omnivorous, but possibly even carnivorous and cannibalistic. The way that the warlike pixies had looked at her when they had fought to free Calliopia… it was unnerving. And she was pretty certain that they also ate cats.

Damon sucked down several colas. Reg didn't dare have more than a few sips, knowing that her bladder wouldn't last long if she had much to drink. But Damon didn't seem to have any such worries. She suspected that he was more interested in the caffeine than the fluid. After telling her he was going to drive all the way, he had to make sure he didn't get drowsy. He didn't want to have to concede that he needed her to drive part of the way.

Ruan had pulled the string out of one of the snack bags and was looking at it, frowning. "What for?"

"Oh. I wanted to make sure that Nico and Starlight couldn't run off when we get out…"

Ruan looked at the string thoughtfully. He stretched a length out between his fingers, rolling it between them and looping it around. He didn't say anything else about it, and Reg turned back around to face front. Nico had finally decided to sleep, but insisted on being beside her on the seat instead of on her lap, and she found she had to keep shifting to accommodate him. She closed her eyes to rest from the scenery constantly streaming past the windows. They had left the salty air behind some time ago and, while Reg was sadder than she had expected to leave the sea, she was also excited to be on the move again. After so many years of moving around, it made her anxious to stay in one place for long, and she had been in Black Sands for too long. She didn't want to leave it, but she couldn't just sit still, so an adventure was exactly what she needed. A quick trip, a few days at most, and then she would be heading back to Florida. A break in the higher, drier air of the mountains, shadowed from the sun, and then turning around and reversing the process.

She was going to turn around and ask Ruan whether he was looking forward to being in the mountains, and especially in the caverns she believed the dwarfs would inhabit. Being a pixie, it would probably be quite restorative for him.

But before she could turn to talk to him, she drifted off to sleep.

CHAPTER 27

When she awoke, it was dark. <u>Dark</u> dark. She had clearly missed the sunset. There were trees around them and no streetlights. Watching the headlights of the truck picking out the curves on the road ahead, Reg was anxious. How could they drive when they couldn't see where they were going? There should be streetlights the whole way, lighting the road for everyone to see. The blackness of the night was disconcerting. Who knew what was out there?

Nico had left her side and, when she looked around, she found him behind her, stalking around the back seat, eyes shining in the darkness. Ruan too had fallen asleep, and slumped in his seatbelt like a toddler who couldn't make it all the way home. Reg smiled and turned back to Damon.

"How are you doing? You should have woken me up."

"Why?"

"So I could keep you awake. We could talk."

"We can talk now."

"Are you getting drowsy? It's late."

"No, I'm fine. Plenty of caffeine in my system."

"I could drive partway."

"I really don't like someone else driving my truck. It's nothing personal; I just don't like anyone else to drive it."

"Because it's your baby or because of insurance?"

Damon raised his eyebrows and considered. "Can I say both?"

"Sure, why not?"

"Yeah, both then. It's just... I think it's a good policy not to let other people drive your vehicle. Unless you live together and you share it, of course. If I was married, I'd share it with my wife."

"Would you?"

Damon grinned. "Well... maybe. But I'd probably look for someone who had a vehicle of her own, and then we wouldn't have to fight over whose turn it was to drive. She could keep driving hers and I could drive mine."

Reg yawned wide and stretched her muscles the best she could while still buckled in. She felt like she was going to grow roots into the seat, she had been there for so long. "How long was I asleep?"

"A few hours. Two or three."

"Sorry. I didn't mean to fall asleep."

"No need to apologize, I've been fine. And Starlight and Nico have been keeping me company."

Reg checked on them again. Starlight seemed quiet and calm in his carrier. Nico was restless but didn't seem anxious about being in a vehicle anymore. Now he was a pro.

"Were they good? They didn't bother you?"

"Nico talked for a while. I managed to convince him not to get under my feet or on the dashboard, and other than that, he's explored everything and gone wherever he liked."

Reg could sense satisfaction from Nico. Like a kid playing king of the castle and managing to stake out the high point. Did he think he was superior to Starlight, who was still stuck in a box? Or superior to all of them?

Starlight stirred and meowed in a low tone to Reg. He scratched at the corner of his box.

"What's up?" Reg murmured to him. "Are you tired of being in that box? It can't be very comfortable."

"They might be hungry or thirsty," Damon suggested. "The air is a lot drier here, and they haven't been out."

Reg nodded. "I know you probably don't want to make a stop, but maybe we should."

"Yeah, okay. I could stand to stretch my legs for a few minutes. Why don't you call Corvin and tell him we're going to pull over at the next opportunity?"

Reg relayed the information to Corvin and, in a couple more miles, there was a place to pull over. Damon stopped and turned on the interior light of the truck. Reg started to puzzle again over how she would tie the cats securely so that they couldn't run away, but so they wouldn't choke. She turned around to get the string that Ruan had taken out of the bag.

Ruan was stirring, awakened by the cessation of motion. He looked around, his eyes glowing like that cats' in the dim light.

Reg stared. The roll of string was gone. On the seat next to Ruan lay a couple of harnesses that looked like they had been crocheted.

"Did you make those?"

Ruan looked at the harnesses and nodded. "They are fine?" he asked, picking the smaller one up and fingering it, looking over the lines critically.

"Those are amazing. How did you do that?"

Ruan looped one trace around his small finger. "It is not hard. Piskies are skilled in making use of every scrap."

She had thought that with the way they wore out the clothing that they did have until it was muddy and worn and looked like it had been used for a hundred years without being washed that they must not have any skills in textiles. They had only limited access to clothing and used it over and over again, patching and repairing, until it was tattered ribbons. If Ruan and the pixies were so skilled in in textiles, why didn't they have beautiful clothing like the fairies? Or at least clean, neat homespun?

"That is… amazing." She couldn't think of another word to describe it. "Can you show me how to put it on Nico? Or maybe you'd better show me how to put it on Starlight, and I'll do Nico myself. I don't want him to injure you any further."

"It is not hard," Ruan said. Despite his animus toward the cat, he reached over to Nico and fit the harness around him, quickly tying a couple of bows to keep it in place. He stretched out the braided leash that flowed seamlessly from the harness and looped it around his hand, showing it to Reg.

Reg couldn't believe that Nico had allowed Ruan to put it on him. Was he mellowing out? Ready for another nap?

"Okay, I'll try Starlight." She opened the box that Starlight was in and picked him up and cuddled him. "I'm sorry you've had to be in there for so long. Are you okay?"

She rubbed and kneaded his body, hoping that it felt good on his cramped muscles. He purred loudly in her arms. Reg kissed the top of his head.

Ruan made a gagging sound. "Need to season it before you eat it."

Reg laughed and was horrified at the same time, not sure whether he was serious or making a joke. She picked up the second harness, this one larger, and tried to loop it around him the same way Ruan had put Nico's on. She carefully tied bows across to keep it in place, trying not to catch Starlight's fur so that it would pull. She stretched out the leash and wrapped it around her hand.

"Okay, I think we're good to go. Do you want to take Nico, or do you want me to?"

Ruan looked at Nico for a moment, then shrugged. "I will hold him."

"Thanks." Reg opened her door and jumped down with Starlight. Ruan pushed the seat forward and jumped down at the same time as Nico. Nico made a little dash as if he were running away, and was stopped by the harness. But he didn't pull and strain against it, and Reg had a sneaking suspicion that he realized the purpose of the harness and was just checking to make sure it worked. He wasn't actually trying to escape.

Starlight liked his harness even less, and did pull on it and wriggle around as if something were running after him. He fell on his side in the dirt and lay there as if he'd been poisoned or beaten. Reg shook her head at him. "A little melodramatic, don't you think? I expected Nico to have a problem with it, not you!"

He just lay there, flicking his ears at her, looking owlish.

"Well, if you want to use the litter box, this is it. Pick your spot. And Damon has some water if you're thirsty."

Starlight looked up at her in disbelief. Reg looked at her phone. "You have five minutes. If you need to… answer a call of nature… now is the time."

Starlight continued to stare at her. Nico was sniffing around the ground with Ruan standing by holding his leash. Ruan watched with interest. Reg wondered whether he was starting to get over some of his instinctive—or learned—dislike of cats.

Neither cat seemed particularly interested in using the facilities as offered.

"Maybe water first," Damon suggested, coming closer. He moved slowly so as not to spook the cats. "How are we going to do this?"

Reg hadn't even thought about bowls or how they were going to manage the logistics of giving the cats water from the water bottles they had bought.

"Uh... I guess we can dribble it, see if they'll lick the bottles. Sometimes they drink from the taps when they're dripping. If not, maybe drip it onto the ground somewhere it won't soak in right away and isn't too dirty." Reg looked around. Somewhere that wasn't too dirty? They were in the middle of the wilderness.

"There is water nearby," Ruan said.

"Damon has water; we're just trying to figure out how to give it to them."

"Come with us."

Ruan started toward the woods. It was dark and spooky, and Reg didn't have much desire to wander around and get lost in the woods. Who knew what kind of creatures might be lurking in there, normal or magical?

But Ruan seemed surefooted and acted like he knew what he was doing. Reg followed hesitantly.

"Hey, slow down… I can't see in the dark."

Ruan turned around and looked at her, his eyes flashing. "You cannot see?"

"No. It's too dark. Let me turn on my flashlight app…"

He shook his head. "No lights. Just follow."

"Slow down, then, I can't see where I'm going. Are you sure you know what you're doing?"

"You cannot smell the water?"

Reg was starting to get irritated. "No, I can't smell the water. I can smell it sometimes, like when we're near the ocean, or after a rain, but not out here…"

Ruan shook his head. "It is a wonder humans live as long as they do."

Reg picked her way after him carefully. "I suppose it is."

Ruan went more slowly, though still too fast for Reg. She kept stubbing her toe and tripping over things. She was worried about tangling up Starlight's leash and tried to keep it short and not let it get caught on any bushes between them as they walked, but it was not easy. She bent over and picked Starlight up, and he complained and squirmed in her arms.

"Just for a minute," Reg assured him. "I'll put you down when I can see better. I know I'm being a bumbling human and you can see better than I can, but just let me try it this way for a bit."

He settled down and let her carry him, but Reg found that holding him presented another problem, in that she could no longer use her arms to balance herself, and if she tripped, she would drop him and might land on top of him. She went slowly, trying to keep Ruan in sight.

The wind in the trees brought a fresh, green, earthy smell, and she wondered a couple of times whether she could hear the trickle of water that Ruan was following.

She was just getting ready to turn back, suspecting that Ruan was leading her into an ambush so that she would either fall over a cliff or so that he could eat her, when he motioned for her to stop.

"Carefully, blind one."

Reg would have been offended, if she could see anything other than shades of darkness around her. Ruan moved forward slowly, and then changed direction. It wasn't until she was right beside the stream that Reg could smell the fresh running water and see that Ruan was scouting downstream for a good place for the cats to drink. Eventually, he stopped, and Reg made her way over to him.

There was a little bowl-shaped pool fed by a trickle of water. The water surface shimmered slightly. Ruan knelt down at the edge and scooped water to his mouth using his hand. He took a few sips.

"It is good."

Reg wasn't sure she wanted to drink water straight from the ground, with all of the bacteria and leeches and who knew what else. But Nico made his way to the edge of the little pool and, after sniffing it, started to lap the water. Reg took Starlight closer and put him down and, in a minute, he too was having a drink.

Shivering slightly in the cool night, Reg rubbed her arms and watched the cats drink.

CHAPTER 28

Reg was more confident walking back to the vehicles. She couldn't see or hear or smell them, but she had an idea what direction they were in and wanted to get out of the dark woods. Ruan still led the way, after the cats had satisfied themselves and had found a suitable place to attend to the call of nature. Reg could feel Corvin nearby before they broke out of the woods. She was tired and that meant that her defenses would not be as strong.

"Regina." She heard his voice in the darkness.

"Where are you?"

"Over here." He had moved slightly since he had spoken her name, and he was to her other side. "I was beginning to wonder if Ruan had made off with you."

"Made off with her?" Ruan repeated, offense in his tone, "She tries to heal Calliopia."

"I suppose," Corvin admitted. "Come to me, Regina, this way." He was again not where she had expected him to be.

"Quit playing hide and seek," she snapped. "Stay in one place, so I know where I'm going."

Hide and seek?

Or cat and mouse?

Reg looked to Ruan as a protector rather than a threat to her. Corvin was bigger, stronger, and was playing games with her. She didn't like it. He didn't care whether she healed Calliopia. The only thing he cared about was getting her powers.

Ruan guided her forward. "This is the way. Ignore the power-drinker."

"Okay, thanks."

Reg followed, keeping close to Ruan and, in a few more steps, they were breaking free of the trees and she saw their vehicles.

Damon was coming out of the trees farther down the road, probably answering his own call of nature. Davyn stood watching the cars, a tiny fire dancing between his hands.

Reg went to him. She kindled fire as well and was comforted by its glow and warmth.

"You can call your fire when you need it," Davyn reminded her, his voice low and comforting. "When you're in the dark. When you're cold."

"When I need to defend myself?"

She couldn't see his expression, his face shadowed by the hood of his cloak. He looked at her for a moment.

"We haven't talked about using fire in battle, but yes, of course, you can use it to defend yourself. Just beware—when your emotions are high, it will be more difficult to control your fire. It will be easier to burn things when you don't intend to. To start a fire or feed a fire far more than you would have wanted to."

Reg nodded slowly. She didn't want to be responsible for someone getting killed in a fire. She didn't know how she would live with herself after something like that.

"You remember lighting Corvin on fire when you were angry," Davyn said.

At the time she had been angry, she had wanted to stop him and to hurt him. To keep him from saying ugly things about her or from winning the tribunal over. She hadn't realized that she was the one lighting the fires, though she had found it immensely satisfying when he'd been forced to stop what he was saying to remove the flaming cloak.

Thinking back on it later, she had thought it was funny. It had been somewhat comical. But reflecting on Davyn's words, she didn't think it was so funny. Corvin hadn't been injured, his clothes had just been a little scorched. But what if she'd gone further? She didn't yet have enough control over her fire to tamp it down or extinguish it when she wanted to.

She hated what Corvin had done to her. He needed to be punished for it and to be taught how the real world worked. But she was also attracted to him and, even if she weren't, she didn't want anyone to be burned alive.

"Yeah. I'll try to be careful."

Reg's flame had flickered out. She rekindled it and let it grow slowly between her hands. Davyn was a stabilizing influence and she was able to stay focused on her flame.

"Time to hit the road, Reg," Damon called out.

Reg extinguished her flame, not sure how long she had been staring into the fire, entranced like she used to be staring into a campfire as a girl.

Starlight was sitting on his haunches, watching her, his whiskers twitching.

"What does Starlight think of your fire?" Davyn asked.

"He isn't sure yet. I don't usually do it in the house."

"He can help you control it."

Reg hadn't thought about that. "Yeah, he helps me focus with other psychic stuff."

"And he's had the fire inside him when I helped to heal him, so I think he would understand that it can be helpful and not hurt him."

"If he remembers that."

"Even if he doesn't remember, he may still know, in his body."

"Huh." Reg nodded. Maybe Starlight could feel the fire the same way as she could. At least he hadn't tried to run away when he saw her conjuring fire. "I guess we'd better get on our way. Just a few more hours and we'll be there."

Davyn nodded. He climbed into the passenger seat of Corvin's car. Reg went over to Damon's truck and put Starlight up into the cab before climbing up herself. She pulled the door shut and then undid the harness on Starlight.

"Those are really wonderful harnesses," she told Ruan, turning around to look at him. "I'm amazed that you could just make them like that, without any pattern. I didn't know what I was going to do!"

Ruan looked at the string harness he took off of Nico. "Piskies have skill with thread," he agreed. "Humans do not care for clothes."

"We don't care for them?" Reg repeated with a laugh of disbelief. "Pixies are the ones who always look like their clothes are ready to fall off. Look at you; look at how stained and worn your clothes are."

Ruan nodded, stroking the front of his shirt as he looked down at it. "Humans get one mark or tear and they throw them out," he said with affront. "They care not for what they have. They just replace it with newly-made clothes. No craftsmanship, so cheap and ill-made. Piskies make clothes well and wear them well."

Reg had just assumed that the pixies couldn't make clothes, and that was why they all looked like they'd been handed down for three generations. She thought it meant that they didn't care at all about their clothing, when maybe the opposite was true.

"I never thought of it that way."

Ruan tsked and shook his head. "Humans think they know all and are always right."

"We do at that," Reg agreed.

Damon started the engine and pulled back out onto the highway. Reg tried to see through the darkness to their destination in the mountainous peaks ahead. But she couldn't make out anything more than dark shapes.

"You make fire," Ruan commented.

Reg looked back at him again. It creeped her out how his eyes glowed in the dark like an animal's. It would be handy to be able to see in the dark like he did, but she didn't like the reflective eyes.

"I'm just learning. I didn't know before that I could do it. So Davyn is teaching me... how to use fire without hurting anyone."

"Fire is very powerful."

"Yes." Reg didn't like where the conversation was going. If the warlike little pixies had the ability to cast fire, Reg imagined it wouldn't be for the benefit of anyone's health. They wouldn't be healers like Davyn.

"You associate with dangerous beings."

Reg assumed he was including Corvin in that comment.

Ruan nodded to Damon, driving the truck. "What power has this one?"

"Nothing. He's just driving." Reg gave Damon an apologetic look. She knew that he had powers, but she didn't want to give anything away to Ruan that they didn't have to. She didn't like the way he was keeping score, tallying up the powers that each of them had. He was too small to beat them all, but that didn't mean he couldn't try. Pixies were sneaky.

Once Reg had provided her assistance in saving Calliopia, there was no guarantee he wouldn't turn on them. He probably would.

On all of them.

* * *

Reg found herself getting drowsy again, but she did her best to keep herself awake. She chewed on her lip and pinched herself and turned on the air conditioner even though it was cool enough that they didn't need it. Damon smiled at her.

"Too warm?" he teased.

"Uh. Not exactly." Reg rubbed her goosebumped arms. She had an impulse to kindle fire to make herself warm, but that would defeat the purpose of turning on the air conditioner, which was to keep her awake. Though maybe having to focus on the fire would keep her awake. Probably not. Watching a fire was hypnotic and was likely to put her right to sleep.

"There are more drinks." Damon motioned to the energy drinks in the console between them, which he had been packing away at an alarming pace.

Reg eyed them. She had been watching her liquid intake carefully, but they were getting close to their destination. It wasn't going to be much longer. It was more important that she stay awake. And she had a sneaking suspicion that once they found the dwarfs, they wouldn't be heading to bed. There would be all kinds of ceremony and negotiation and convincing them to unmake the fairy blade. Her wits had better be sharp.

"I suppose." She picked one up and popped the tab.

Ruan looked at her from the back seat, leaning forward slightly. "What is it?"

"Just a drink. Like fruit juice."

"Is it only for humans?"

"I don't know. I don't know how it would affect pixies. Do you?" Reg looked at Damon.

"I have no idea. I wouldn't want to harm anyone by testing some human potion on pixies." He turned his head slightly to speak to Ruan, but not all the way around.

"You said it is juice," Ruan argued, cocking his head at Reg.

"It is juice, but it has other... herbs in it as well."

"Ah." Ruan nodded sagely. "What herbs?"

Reg squinted at the fine lettering on the can, trying to make out the words. "One called caffeine. And guarana. And ginseng. And other... stuff."

"Ginseng," Ruan repeated. "That is good for pixies. Let me try."

Reg eyed Damon again. "Do you think...? Should I?"

"I doubt it's harmful. But just warn him. Ruan."

"Yes?"

"We don't know how pixies will react to this juice. If the herbs in it are bad for pixies, you can't blame us. It's your own choice. You are choosing for yourself, when you don't know if it will be good for you."

Ruan nodded impatiently. "Yes, yes. I will try some. Give a taste." He reached for Reg's open can. She handed it to him. Ruan tipped the can up slowly and wet his lips. He ran his quick tongue over his lips, rolling his eyes upward as he thought about it. He took a small swallow and they all waited. It at least didn't seem like it was going to kill him or make him melt into a pile of sugar. Hopefully, pixie and human physiology was close enough that it would have no worse effect on Ruan than it would a human of his size.

"You'd better give it back now," Reg advised. "See how it affects you before you have too much. It is potent."

Ruan chugged a couple more gulps down before handing the can back to Reg. He wiped his mouth with the back of his hand and belched loudly. "It is good." He declared. "Very sweet."

"They don't turn into gremlins if you feed them after midnight, do they?" Reg asked Damon.

"It's a little late to be asking that now."

Reg smiled. She looked back at Ruan to make sure that he was still okay, and then turned back to face the windshield again.

"Will you know when we are getting close to the dwarfs?" she asked. "Do you know the way from here? Or do you need to get out or look at a map?"

Reg hoped they wouldn't have to wait until it was light for him to be able to recognize landmarks and direct them there. But he'd already demonstrated his ability to see well in the dark.

"We get close," Ruan said with a nod. "Over this mountain. Down to the river. There is the entrance to the kingdom."

"What is the entrance like? Can we drive up to it? Is it guarded or hidden? Will we have to do something special to get in?"

Maybe these were questions that Reg should have asked before heading out. Maybe they should have picked up some gold coins at the bank or a sacrificial goat at the last pit stop.

Ruan looked at her. "It is guarded, of course. They are dwarfs."

"Yes. Right. What will we need to do to get in?"

"Perhaps we will not get in."

"But... isn't that the whole point? Why are we going if we are not going to get in?"

"To unmake the dagger."

Reg considered for a moment. It was true; they didn't need to be able to get into the dwarf caverns themselves. They just needed to talk to the dwarfs and to give them the dagger to be unmade. There was no reason the dwarfs had to let them into their inner sanctum.

"Right. Okay. And you think they'll do it, right?"

Ruan shrugged. "Reg Rawlins said she would have them unmake the blade."

Reg grimaced. "Yeah. I will."

She hoped.

CHAPTER 29

They drove on. Ruan began to bounce in the back seat. Reg looked back at him after a few minutes of restless bouncing up and down.

"What's up?"

Ruan scratched his arms and made a face. He bounced some more. The cats were looking at him with their ears back and kitty scowls on their furry faces.

"Too much sitting," Ruan explained. He looked out the window, then looked around them restlessly. "We are not there yet. We should be there. We need to be there."

"I know. Won't be much longer now, right?" Reg had tried to get as detailed a picture of where the dwarf kingdom was before leaving as she could in order to plot the GPS route and arrival time. Ruan wasn't the best for picking it out on Google maps, but he had grunted and pointed and Reg had zoomed and panned on her tablet as they tried to pinpoint the exact road they would take once they left the highway.

"Not much longer," Ruan agreed. He looked out the window, growling to himself.

Reg shrugged and looked back out the windshield. She could understand his restlessness after being in the vehicle for so long. He wasn't used to road trips. And she was tired of sitting in the truck herself. She was surprised that Nico had been so well-behaved. He had gotten bored and had played with Ruan for a while, and then had eventually gone to sleep. That had been a couple of hours before.

"More juice," Ruan announced suddenly. He unbuckled his seatbelt and leaned over the seat to grab a couple of cans out of the console. "Need more juice."

"Uh, wait, hang on—just one of those. And you probably shouldn't have a whole one. Just have a half. I'll share it with you. Or Damon will." Reg reached back to take one of them away from him.

Ruan bared his teeth and hissed at her, making her jump back in alarm. Nico awoke and went into fits, jumping up and arching his back and making stiff-legged jumps at Ruan. Ruan was no longer tied down by his seatbelt. He moved forward, growling and baring his teeth again. Reg was a little nervous that they might actually fight tooth and claw.

"Guys, guys, we're just about there. Calm down. Don't get into a fight now." Reg reached over the seat and grabbed Nico. "Why don't you sit up here with me?"

Nico flailed. He squirmed around, biting and scratching anything he could sink his teeth into, letting out a caterwaul that made Reg's hair stand on end. She let him go, worried he was going to tear her arm off.

"Sheesh! Calm down. No one is going to hurt you. I just don't want you guys getting into a fight. Try going back to sleep."

But she knew it was pointless. There was no way Nico was going to go back to sleep when he was spoiling for a fight with Ruan. Reg pushed Nico off of the seat into the footwell, and he promptly attacked her feet. But at least her feet were well-covered with her shoes. He could bite them all he liked. She looked back at Ruan.

"Now, you get your seatbelt back on and behave yourself," she snapped.

Ruan bared his teeth again, but he moved back to his seat and pulled the belt across himself. Reg must have managed to get that don't-mess-with-mom tone right. Ruan popped open one of the energy drinks and chugged down the contents.

"You don't think he's acting that way because of the caffeine, do you?" Damon asked.

Reg ground her fist into her forehead. "Yes, of course it is. It's got him all wound up and angry. Great idea, Reg. Give the pixie caffeine."

"We warned him."

"Yeah, we should have warned ourselves."

Damon chuckled and nodded. "Let me see if I can do something about that…"

Reg frowned. "What do you mean?"

Damon didn't say anything. He just stared straight ahead at the road. Reg looked over her shoulder at Ruan, and saw him sitting slack-jawed, eyes wide, unmoving. Then he startled and shook his head.

"Out of my head, witch!" he growled, clawing at his eyes. "You said he had no powers."

But of course, Damon did have powers, and one of them was the ability to show other people visions. He had obviously been trying to calm Ruan by showing him some vision that he thought would make Ruan happy, but Ruan had been able to figure out what he was doing. The pixies had methods of their own for mesmerizing, so he undoubtedly knew a thing or two about confusing an opponent by getting inside his brain.

"Don't hurt yourself," Reg said, worried about the way he was scratching his eyes, trying to rid himself of all vestiges of the vision.

"No powers!" Ruan whined. "You are a liar, Reg Rawlins."

Reg sighed and shrugged. "Yes, I am. In fact, I'm lying to you right now."

Ruan opened his mouth, then closed it, frowning. "What?"

"I am a liar. I am lying to you."

He shook his head. "If you be lying, then you are not a liar, but if you be not a liar, you are telling the truth."

"Yes. Exactly."

He snorted and blew his breath out his nose, scowling fiercely. With his youthful face, he just looked like a little boy who had been grounded from his favorite TV show. Not like the fierce warrior Reg knew him to be.

"You be lying or telling the truth?"

"Yes."

Ruan kicked the back of Damon's seat. "Tell me!"

Reg just laughed and looked out the window into the dark night once more. "How close are we? Do we need to start watching for our exit?"

She heard him gulping and turned in time to see him swallowing the rest of the contents of the can. More caffeine. Not just half a can this time, but a full one. And another in his hand that Reg hoped he would forget about. Maybe he would get too dizzy or buzzed to drink the other one. Ruan belched, threw down the can, and opened the next one. Reg looked at Damon and grabbed the rest of the drinks from the console and put them by her feet so that Ruan wouldn't be able to reach anymore. Nico hissed and bit her hand.

CHAPTER 30

By the time they got to the turnoff, Ruan was literally bouncing his face off of the window glass as he chanted or raved in pixie talk. Reg was leaning forward in her seat, pretending to ignore him and Damon had turned the radio up in an attempt to drown him out. The two cats were in evil tempers and Reg didn't dare pick either of them up.

"Here, here!" Ruan started to shout. He convulsed like he was trying to jump to his feet, but the seatbelt held him back. He waved his arms and kicked the back of Damon's seat. "Here, here, can't you see it? Blind humans! There! The road!"

Damon tramped on the brake pedal and they both searched for a break in the trees in the direction Ruan was pointing. Damon crept the car forward, leaving the highway and eventually finding a lightly-graveled or worn path.

"This is a road?"

Corvin's headlights were right in the back window, so Reg couldn't see Ruan when she looked back for confirmation, just his silhouette.

"Here, yes, here!"

"You're sure?"

Ruan shrieked something either incoherent or speaking pixie, as he pointed and kicked.

"Are you <u>trying</u> to get him wound up?" Reg demanded.

Damon grinned and didn't answer, which was an answer in itself.

"We don't want him to be so agitated that he ends up running us off the road or getting killed by the dwarf guards. We want to look like reasonable people coming to ask a favor, not like raving lunatics!"

"Well, we'll just leave him in the car."

Ruan screamed imprecations back at him.

"See?" Damon asked. "He doesn't mind."

Reg just shook her head, unable to find anything to say to that. "Just find the place. Don't get him more upset."

Damon drove on with a self-satisfied smirk. But he followed Ruan's directions and didn't say anything else to get Ruan upset.

Eventually, they ended up in a little clearing. There was no more road or path. There was, as Ruan had told them, a small river or large stream and a craggy mountain face. They were surrounded by trees, sentinels in the darkness around them. Reg got out of the car and looked up at the sky, where millions of stars twinkled as they only could far from the lights of civilization.

"It's beautiful."

Ruan was wrestling with his seatbelt inside the car. He had apparently forgotten how to unbuckle it and was trapped. Reg hadn't let either cat out. Damon sat inside watching Ruan with amusement.

Corvin slammed his car door and walked up to Reg. "Is this it?"

"Apparently." Reg tore her eyes away from the stars and looked at the rocky cliffs. "Somewhere in there."

"And what are we supposed to do? Knock? Speak the password? Captivate them with song?"

"I don't know. Our guide is a little... indisposed."

Corvin's eyes followed Reg's gaze back into the interior of the truck. "What happened? He looks... absolutely frantic."

"Apparently, that's what happens when pixies overdose on caffeine."

"You gave him caffeine?"

"Well... he took it. We didn't exactly encourage him."

Ruan pounded on the window for Reg to let him out of the truck.

"What do you think I should do?"

"Not a lot of choices. Either let him out and see if he can help you, or keep him in there until it's worn off. Which may be... this time tomorrow."

"Ugh. Why did he have to drink so much?" Reg went back to the truck and opened her door. She climbed up into the seat to get Nico's harness, then picked him up to put it on him. Nico was half asleep, but he turned and bit at Reg, his teeth finding purchase and sinking into the meat of her palm. "Ouch! Come on; you were good when Ruan put the harness on you!"

Nico thrashed around and Reg couldn't hold on to him without getting hurt. She dropped him. Nico jumped out of the truck and sailed to the ground. He dashed a few feet away, but then stopped, much to Reg's relief.

"Stay there! Don't run away!"

"Don't give him ideas," Corvin said out the side of his mouth.

"Yeah, you're probably right. Starlight, come here. Let's get you into your harness."

But Starlight stayed just out of reach as she tried to get ahold of him.

"Star, come on, be a good example for the kattakyn."

But he refused. Reg figured he was probably scared by Ruan's tantrum and didn't want to be touched. He would hide until things settled down, and then maybe he would come out when they made contact with the dwarfs. When things were calm. She hoped.

"Okay, Ruan." She moved into the driver's seat and reached over the back to unbuckled Ruan's seatbelt.

He too bit at her. "Hey! No biting! I'm trying to get you out! Don't you want to get out?"

He thrashed his head back and forth, chanting something. Reg tried again to reach the buckle.

"Ruan. Calm down. Just take a couple of deep breaths, and I'll get you out of there."

He breathed in, a long, strong intake of breath. Then he let it out and again snapped at Reg.

"Ruan!" Reg snapped, giving him a fierce look.

Ruan cowered. Reg took the opportunity of that instant of stillness to reach over and pop the button on his seatbelt. The latch came free and Ruan ripped it away, escaping his bonds. In an instant, he sprang out of the car.

Reg watched closely to make sure he didn't disappear or run away too fast for her to follow. If he got into the trees where he could see with his night vision and she couldn't, they would lose him.

But Ruan didn't run away. He stopped in the clearing with them and bounced around on his toes. "This is the place." He nodded vigorously.

"Good. Where is the entrance? Or do we need to call them?"

Ruan scratched his ear. "Where are they? Where are they receiving strangers?"

"This is where you directed us."

He nodded, but seemed confused. Was it because they had not been met by a delegation of dwarfs? Maybe every time he had been there before it had been a scheduled visit or a big caravan that the dwarfs couldn't help noticing.

"Do we need to knock? What should we do?" It was the middle of the night. Had Reg really thought that they would just be able to drive up and talk to someone in the middle of the night? "Is there a door or cave entrance? Should we camp out until morning? I don't want them to think that we're a threat."

Ruan cocked his head at Reg. Their little rag-tag group a threat? Reg's face warmed when she realized how egotistical that must have sounded. Just like the humans, to assume that they were any kind of threat to the dwarfs, a warlike people who probably slept with their swords. A few humans, a pixie, and two cats? Not a threat.

Ruan ran on tiptoes over to the water and balanced on the edge of the bank as if trying to decide whether to jump in. He turned to study the rocky faces of the mountain.

"Ho, the cave!" He shouted. "Anyone home?"

Reg gazed at the side of the mountain, trying to make out a cave entrance. But it was too dark for her to make anything out for sure. She didn't doubt that Ruan knew what he was doing and had the right place. But would the dwarfs come out to see them? Were they still there? How long had it been since Ruan or his people had seen them? She always heard news of species and civilizations that had been extinguished by the modern world and development. Humans were remarkably stupid, thinking that they knew everything there was to know and that it didn't matter what they did.

"Many of the native tribes across North America have legends about little people living in the mountains,"

Corvin said, making Reg jump. She hadn't realized that he had sidled up right next to her. "Usually they are said to be very fierce. Sometimes the natives left gifts for them, to appease them or allow them safe passage."

"Very fierce?" Reg repeated. "You didn't think to mention that before now?"

"Would it have stopped you from going?"

"No… but maybe… I don't know; we could have brought more people or armed ourselves, instead of just walking into it."

"I think that would be more aggressive than we want to be. We don't want to appear to be confrontational or a threat."

"Well… okay. What do you think we should do?"

"I think Ruan is doing it. Just sit back and see what happens."

They watched Ruan. He put his hands to his mouth in a megaphone shape and hollered again. "Ho, the cave! Are you all sleeping?"

This time there was a reply, a low, growling, gravelly voice. "It is the darkest hour."

Ruan laughed and ran over to a boulder. He stood perched on top of it, looking around. "We seek the ear of King Nar. We have journeyed far and are..." Ruan considered and apparently decided it was best not to claim they were tired. Not when he was so high on caffeine he couldn't even stand still. "We seek respite! Wine and story, and the ear of King Nar."

"King Nar is dead," the gravelly voice intoned. "Long live King Fraeg."

"'Tis truth?" Ruan inched forward on the boulder, leaning toward the mountain face. "When?"

"Save but a fortnight ago. The kingdom is in mourning."

"Sad news. Will King Fraeg give audience?"

"We will have to see in the day. You are the first strangers we have had since Nar's death. Who leads your company?"

Ruan turned and looked over their little group. While Corvin and Davyn were much older and more powerful and better known than she was, they hadn't been the ones to initiate the quest.

"We are led by Reg Rawlins, sorceress, who seeks to have a fairy blade unmade."

"I'm not a sorceress!" Reg protested.

Corvin put his hand on Reg's arm, giving her a mild shock. "He knows protocols better than we do. If he thinks it's best to introduce you as a sorceress, then let him."

"But I'm not! What if they expect me to do some kind of magic to prove it?"

Corvin raised his brows. "Then… let's see… you could read their minds. Speak to King Nar beyond the grave. Start breaking glasses. Light someone on fire."

"That's not…"

"You can block me, even freeze me with your power. And you still think of yourself as a normal human being without powers. I get that it's a shock, but it's time to get over it. You are magical, Reg. You have greater powers than most of the population of Black Sands.

You've fought an immortal. I know your powers, even if you don't, and they are not inconsequential."

Reg looked down at the ground, embarrassed. It wasn't like he was lying, but it did seem… exaggerated. She wasn't a powerful sorceress. She was more like a toddler on wobbly legs.

"Okay, whatever."

She turned her attention back to Ruan and the voice of the dwarf.

"What fairy blade?" the dwarf voice inquired.

Ruan let out an exaggerated sigh and turned away as if he had lost interest in the conversation. He jumped down from the boulder, stretched in a way that reminded Reg of the cats, and looked around.

"Do we have any sustenance?"

"You already drank all of the energy drinks," Reg pointed out, though he hadn't. She didn't want him thinking there were any more left and going after them. If he did, his head might just explode. Or hers.

There was a loud dragging noise, like rock being dragged over rock. Reg turned toward it, straining her eyes at the cliff face. It still seemed just as craggy and dark. Unless… there was a faint light. She could just make it out if she squinted. Then it coalesced into a single point of light that seemed to be moving toward them.

"Ruan…?" Reg tried to get his attention to show him the approaching figure.

Ruan rolled his eyes and stretched again. "Perhaps they are not interested."

It shouldn't have taken Reg that long to get the ploy. She was a consummate con artist herself. Her only excuse was she was tired.

"Oh, I guess not," she agreed. "I thought since we came all this way, they might take a look at it, but you're right. We could go back home. Or, I hear there is another colony of dwarfs in Montana..."

"Montana?" growled the dwarf marching toward her. "You are not going to Montana with a fairy blade."

Reg looked at him, arching an eyebrow. "Why not?"

"You have us!"

The dwarf got close enough for her to see him, and she examined him, trying to take everything in. The light in his hand was not a torch, but appeared to be a cell phone. He was short and had the long, graying beard of the dwarfs in fairy tales. But his clothing didn't look like anything from Disney or Tolkien. It looked instead like it had been purchased from the children's section at the local Wal-Mart. Camouflage cargo pants with big pockets, a Spiderman belt, and a SpongeBob Squarepants shirt with a rude comment on it. He had on a baseball cap turned backward so she couldn't see the logo on it, but it was black with yellow markings.

Reg swallowed her surprise and tried to continue the conversation as if she had spoken to many modern-day dwarfs in her time.

"I don't know. I'm not getting the best feeling here. Ruan said that there would be a delegation to meet us and everyone would be interested in helping with the dagger. I realize that we arrived in the middle of the night, but I would think that we might be afforded a little more consideration than... one inexperienced youth."

Ruan gasped dramatically. "Reg Rawlins…" he shook his head slowly. "Please don't put a curse on this one too."

The dwarf took a step back, eyeing her warily.

"Dwarfs will be at your service," he promised, making a brief bow. "Apologies that everyone is sleeping. We are in mourning and things are not as they should be. Very soon, I will bring you someone to examine the blade. To tell you its worth."

Why she would want to know its worth when she had brought it to be destroyed, Reg didn't know. But that was their business.

The dwarf looked at Reg, then looked at Ruan, expecting something. What did he want? A tip? Ruan's feet were tapping. He was clearly having a difficult time standing still, pretending to be cool. He cast a glance toward Reg.

"I suppose he wants to see the blade for himself before he goes back to tell his betters that we have work for them."

"Oh." Reg touched her pocket. "Should I?"

Ruan nodded, widening his eyes. "Yes, Reg Rawlins. Let's show them what they are dealing with."

Reg reached into her pocket and reluctantly pulled the dagger out. It was strange, after coming so far on the spur of the moment to have the knife destroyed that she was now not so keen to do so. She knew that it had to be done to help heal Calliopia. But what if there were another way? Maybe it could just be cleansed, like Davyn had initially said. Or Corvin could ingest its powers. Maybe it just needed to have a new master who was skilled enough to handle it. Fairy adolescents were unpredictable; they didn't have a handle on their magic. Not a good master for a dagger like that. It had come to Reg first and she should have been more careful to keep it in her possession.

It was her own fault that Calliopia was so badly injured. If Reg had done what she was supposed to, Calliopia would never have been hurt. She would still be running around the country, honeymooning with Ruan, instead of lying on her deathbed.

Everyone was watching her, weighing her reluctance to pull the dagger out of her pocket, and then to grip the ornate handle and pull it from its sheath.

The dwarf waved his phone over it to shine some light on the subject. His bushy gray eyebrows pressed close together as he studied it from inches away, as if trying to catalog every scratch or flaw in the blade. But Reg couldn't see any imperfections. It glowed in her hand.

It was practically weightless. With a knife like that, she could…

CHAPTER 31

Reg caught herself. She could what? She wasn't a fighter. She had only ever protected herself from others. She had never intentionally harmed anyone who hadn't first attacked her. She wasn't the type who walked around with a dagger, looking for someone to hurt.

She slid the sheath back on over the blade and put it quickly back in her pocket.

"Well?" she demanded. "Now, you'll go tell the king?"

The dwarf bowed again.

"This is indeed an interesting weapon, with an impressive history. How did you come to possess it?"

"I don't see how that's any of your business. What does it matter where or how I got it? I have it now, so it's mine."

He nodded again and rubbed his fingers on his pants as if he'd been eating and they might be greasy. "I will inform the king and the others in the kingdom. We will discuss the matter."

"Good. And we will be… here, I guess. How long will it be?"

"You may lay out your sleeping rolls here. You will not be disturbed in our glade. Rest while you still can and, by the time the sun is over the mountains, we will come to you."

Reg had not brought any sleeping rolls. No camping gear of any kind. She hadn't thought about lying in the damp, cold grass and the rocky ground. They had just talked about coming, getting the dwarfs to do what she needed them to, and then… she would go back home, and Calliopia would be okay. Or maybe she would need something more, but she would be better and, with the blade destroyed, they would be able to heal Calliopia completely.

Reg watched the dwarf turn and retreat into the darkness, lighting a small space in front of him with the LED on his phone. She sighed and turned to the others.

"Well? What do you think?"

"Things seem to be progressing," Corvin said with a shrug. "Now… we wait."

"Yeah… that's just what I want to do. Sit around on the cold, hard ground and wait while they sleep and then discuss whether they feel like helping or not."

"They will help," Ruan assured her. "You saw he liked the blade."

"Liked it? He hardly had anything to say about it."

"Oh, no," Ruan said, shaking his head. "He liked it very much. He called it <u>impressive</u>."

"Well, okay. He said that, but…"

"They will do it," Ruan assured her. "He will wake the dwarfs and they will discuss their strategy. You may be assured."

"And we're just supposed to sit here in the meantime? Waiting?"

"Sleep," Ruan suggested.

"Yeah, right. Are you going to sleep?"

He bounced up and down and blinked rapidly. "No... I am very awake."

"Why don't you scout the area?" Damon suggested. "Since you have the best night vision, you can make sure that everything is as it should be. Maybe let us know if there are any berries or fishing holes that might come in handy if we have to wait too long."

Ruan looked suspicious. "Why, human?"

"Because you're the best one for the job. Aside from the cats, I mean. They have night vision too. I guess maybe I'll just take them..."

"No!" Ruan made a rapid-fire spitting noise. "I will do the scouting. Cats are not needed."

"They're going to need a place to drink and to... relieve themselves, like before."

"First, I will scout for humans. Cats can fill their own needs."

Ruan turned and retreated into the trees. Reg could only keep her eyes on him for a few seconds, and then he was gone, either turning invisible or losing himself in the shadows of the trees.

"That's the pixie taken care of," Damon said cheerfully. "Now, what about the other warlocks?"

"What are you doing?"

"Trying to make things more comfortable for ourselves. If you have to be stranded in the woods for a few hours, you might as well make the best of it."

"This isn't a date."

"It could be. I have some blankets in my car. There may not be any marshmallows to toast or wine chilling, but we haven't finished all of the snacks. We can make do."

Reg looked down at the unforgiving ground. "Maybe we should just sit in the truck."

"Trust me; you will enjoy it far more if you can let yourself relax for a while. It's a magical place."

Reg looked around. "I don't see what's so special about it."

"Magic isn't always something you can see or hear. Sometimes it is only something you can feel."

"Or that you know of from school history books," Corvin said dryly, interrupting the conversation.

"Hey! Were you asked?" Damon snapped back. "I'm trying to—"

"You're trying to act like the expert. The only reason you know about this clearing is because you learned about it in school. Not something that you can sense on your own."

"I happen to be very sensitive to—"

"So <u>sensitive</u>," Corvin mocked.

"Corvin, why don't you butt out?" Damon demanded. "Before I have to take things into my own hands?"

"Take it into your own hands? You know that I'm stronger than you. Exactly what do you think you can do to me?"

Damon couldn't come up with something quickly enough. But Reg was tired of the two warlocks' jealousy.

"Both of you just shut up. Damon, get the blankets from the car, so I have something to sit on. And I will... light a fire."

"Are you sure that's wise?" Corvin challenged in a soft voice. "Do you think you have the control for something like that yet?"

"Just kindling a fire? I could do that even without a gift."

"Don't be so sure."

"I've always been great at lighting fires. At girls' camp —"

"You may have always been great at lighting fires because it has always been your gift. You just didn't know why or how until now."

Reg frowned, digging her toe into the soft dirt in front of her.

Corvin was standing too close. Reg moved away a few steps, not wanting to give him the chance to ensorcel her. Or to be tempted to do so. Walking away wouldn't stop him, but it would help if he weren't right under her nose.

Damon returned with the blankets. There were enough to make a small circle. Reg pointed to the center of the circle.

"I can kindle fire there?" she asked Davyn. "As long as I keep it under control?"

Davyn nodded slowly, shifting around to get comfortable on his blanket. Starlight and Nico decided that Reg's blanket looked more comfortable than the damp grass, and settled onto it, cuddling against her.

442

"Stay focused," Davyn reminded Reg. "I'm here to help contain it, but you need to make sure you're not distracted by... anyone else here."

Reg looked at Corvin. He raised his hands palms-up, innocent. "What?"

"That means keep yourself to yourself if you don't want to get burned."

"I think you'll find it's against the fire casters' code to threaten to light people on fire."

Reg looked at Davyn. "There's a code?"

"We'll get to that later. You need to develop your skills first."

"I'm still going to threaten him."

Davyn chuckled, looking at a loss as to what to say to that. Reg closed her eyes and felt Starlight's warmth against her leg. He would help her to focus too. He started to knead her leg with his needle-sharp claws. Reg took a few long breaths, trying to center herself and to relax.

She kindled fire in her hands first, as Davyn had taught her, then placed it in the center of the circle. They all stared at it. Reg grew it larger, like a crackling campfire, even though she had not gathered the wood for fuel. The fire was warm and soothing, and it felt good to be able to use her fire and not to be required to keep it inside.

She stared into the flames, letting herself be hypnotized. She was drifting in a meditative trance, floating out of herself as if she were in a sensory deprivation tank.

Not that she'd ever been in a sensory deprivation tank before, but she'd heard about it.

"Reg."

She tore her eyes away from the flames to look at Davyn.

"Bring it down. We don't need a bonfire."

She shrank the flames down to campfire size again. No one spoke. They were all tired, all thinking their own thoughts. Reg started to think of Damon, sitting to her left in the circle. She imagined it was just the two of them alone there, holding hands, cuddling up, staring into the fire together, with just the night noises around them and not another human being within miles. It would be so nice…

"Hey," Reg growled, making everyone jump.

Damon saw that she was looking at him. "What?"

"What did I tell you before about putting visions in my head?"

"Did I? Sorry... I guess I started sharing my daydream by accident."

She looked at him, trying to discern whether he was telling the truth. As a diviner, he was very good at catching others in a lie, but he was way too good at lying himself, and Reg had a hard time reading him. A diviner shouldn't be allowed to lie.

"Well, cut it out."

"Reg, stay focused," Davyn reminded.

Reg turned her attention back to the fire, calming the leaping flames. It was a lot harder to keep a flame under control once it had started burning on its own.

She could imagine what would happen if it got away from her, a huge wall of fire destroying everything in its path. She shivered in spite of the heat of the fire.

"I'm focusing," she told Davyn. She stared into the flames again, trying to unite with the fire so that they were one entity.

* * *

Reg wasn't sure how long they sat around the fire, and when exactly she started to drift off to sleep. Davyn was there to extinguish her fire and make sure that they were all safe while she sat there, snoring away. Everyone was tired or, at least, all of those who hadn't overloaded on caffeine on the drive there. Reg awoke in an awkward sitting position, staring up at the mountain peaks, watching the sky lightening to a pearly pink color.

"Oh, it's pretty," she commented.

Corvin gave a little groan and moved his body around stiffly. "If you've seen one sunrise, you've seen them all…"

"No way. Every one is different."

"Light in the sky. Happens every morning. Nothing new."

"Look at the pink light over the blue mountains. It's incredible."

Corvin yawned. "Hopefully, a sign that the dwarfs will be here soon to negotiate."

CHAPTER 32

Reg was more than ready for the day to proceed by the time the dwarfs got there. The guard had told them that the dwarfs would be there when the sun got over the mountains, but Reg hadn't thought about how high the sun would need to be in the sky before it topped the craggy cliffs. It was long past dawn by the time she heard the movement of the great stone gate and the marching feet of approaching dwarfs.

Ruan came out of the trees as if he'd been there the whole time watching them. How much scouting had he been doing and how much had he been spying on his own company? She didn't like to think about what could happen if one of the cats had gone off exploring on its own. She didn't feel particularly safe around the pixies herself, knowing how much stronger they were than humans and that they sometimes stole children away. She didn't know if they stole children to raise them, like the fairies did, or whether they ate them. She hadn't asked. She didn't really want to know.

Reg watched the dwarfs come out of the trees. Like the initial guard, they were not dressed in chain mail or armor like the dwarfs of the silver screen, but were a rag-tag collection of children's brand-name clothing. Lots of superheroes and cartoon characters. A few metal bands or other popular trends.

Soon the dwarfs were upon them. Their faces were old and stern, a strange contrast to the children's clothing. They formed a semi-circle and Reg's small company sat in the open end to negotiate.

"Filan reports that you have a fairy blade," one of the men said, not introducing himself.

Reg looked at him and said nothing in return.

Ruan glanced at her, but he didn't criticize her approach.

Reg kept in mind Corvin's instruction that they would want to negotiate, that they would barter to get a good deal. And Reg knew about bartering.

"Filan—" the man started again.

"Maybe Filan should be here to speak for himself," Reg snapped.

The dwarf closed his mouth and looked around at his friends. Reg was pretty sure that none of them were Filan, who she assumed was the guard from the night before. It was hard to tell them apart with the beards and facial hair, and it had been dark, but she was pretty good with faces.

"We are here to negotiate," the dwarf said.

"I am Reg Rawlins, sorceress," Reg announced. "If you want to negotiate, take me to King Fraeg."

"The king does not get involved in our trade," the dwarf started.

"You are no one. Why would the king send me such unimportant emissaries? He must think I am no one."

"I am Gwythr, son of Zim," the dwarf said importantly. "I am chief of the smithies."

"I am Reg Rawlins. And you know Davyn Smithy, I'm sure," Reg said, indicating Davyn.

The dwarf looked at the warlock. "A smithy? What smithy be thou?"

Davyn lifted his chin as if he were too proud to even talk to such a lowly dwarf. "My people smithied for generations. My great-grandsire was Harold Smithy of the South. He was greatly respected."

Gwythr nodded, making a short bow. "It is a great family," he acknowledged. "We are honored to have you here. With Reg Rawlins, the sorceress."

"If you are head of the smithies, then perhaps we can talk," Reg said. "Now that you are not a nameless nobody."

He looked properly chastised for not giving his name and lineage. That meant he was starting on the wrong foot, which put Reg in the position of power. And she had a warlock from a famed Smithy family with her.

Gwythr tried again. "I am told you have a knife of great lineage."

"Yes. It is a great knife with a grand history," Reg agreed. "It is unfortunate indeed that it must be unmade."

"May we see the blade?" This query was accompanied by a bowed head.

Reg looked at her companions. At their nods of agreement, she again removed it from her pocket and pulled it from the sheath. She knelt close to the dwarfs, laying it across her palm. Across the scar that the knife itself had made in the hands of Hawthorne-Rose.

The dwarfs pressed near and, one at a time, took a close look at the knife, squinting their eyes and furrowing their eyebrows, some of them actually sniffing it. But none of them reached out to touch it, keeping a respectful distance. When they had all had a chance to see it, Reg withdrew it and put it away again. She sat in silence, letting them deliberate.

"It is a powerful dagger," Gwythr said finally. "It has caused much hurt, has it not?"

"Yes. It is an evil blade, imbued with the blood of at least three races, and it needs to be unmade. A fairy girl lies mortally wounded on her deathbed with the poison of it. Until the blade is unmade, I fear she cannot get better."

They nodded gravely as if this were a commonly known problem. And maybe for them, it was. Magical blades, fairy blood, curses and evil inanimate objects could be common in their world.

"It will be a great work to unmake this blade," Gwythr said. "You knew when you came here that it would be stretching our skills to do so."

Reg was surprised by this admission. Was it a negotiating technique? Saying that it might be too hard for them?

"If you do not have the skills, then perhaps I should take it elsewhere."

"There is no other kingdom who has the skills," Gwythr said. "We are your only hope."

Reg didn't like the sound of that. Now he was going to drive up the price. And all they had to offer were a few 'trinkets' that Corvin had brought with him. It wouldn't be enough.

"I could help," Davyn offered.

All eyes turned to him. The dwarfs' eyes were beady and small, making them look like they were always plotting something, always thinking something else.

"You are… a fire caster?" Gwythr asked, looking interested.

"I am."

"But you have not been a smithy."

He shrugged. "I know the family lore. I am a fire caster. But… no, I haven't spent time learning and practicing the skill."

Gwythr stroked his beard thoughtfully. Reg looked at Davyn, wondering if she should tell the dwarfs that she too was a fire caster. Davyn shook his head minutely. Reg let the opportunity pass.

"What can you offer us for this great work?"

They all looked at each other.

Corvin reluctantly removed a box from his pocket. In the box was an object wrapped in a rich velvet wrap. He unfolded it reverently, and displayed it to them.

Gwythr peered at the bracelet, fine silver embedded with beautifully cut gemstones. He looked around at the other dwarfs, then motioned it away with the back of his wrist.

"Scrap metal. Pawnshop detritus. We take PayPal and Bitcoin."

Reg nearly choked. Maybe she should have been warned by their modern clothing and cellphones. A few of them even appeared to be wearing smart watches. She didn't look at Corvin, afraid of how he might react to this news.

He paused for a moment, then withdrew the bracelet and tucked it back away. "I understood that you were interested in this blade. Perhaps I misunderstood."

Gwythr looked at him, calculating, chewing the inside of his lip in a way that made his mustache wiggle in and out.

"Maybe you have… something more. Such a job will take many dwarf-hours to do properly. We have a backlog of work. It's an international market. Many orders from all over the world."

"Is it my problem that you've overbooked yourself?"

"The jobs with up-front money are the ones that will take precedence. This is a pretty blade, but we cannot let its beauty beguile us."

Corvin looked at Reg. She waited for him to bring out the next trinket. He had said that he had more than one. She should have made sure before they left that he actually had enough to negotiate with the dwarfs. They had come a long way on a whim.

Corvin put his hand in his pocket and fingered the box that he had brought out before. He looked around covertly, then reached under his cloak into some hidden pocket and drew out a knife.

It was different from Reg's dagger. Smooth and sleek with no ornamentation. The surface of the blade shimmered like oil. Almost like something alive. Corvin passed it to Reg. It was as light as paper in her hand. There was a sort of crossbar to keep the bearer's hand from sliding down onto the blade, and the handle was subtly textured to make it grippy. Reg tested it in her hand. It felt like it belonged there. She had rarely used a weapon but, like her dagger, this one made her feel like she could. Like it wanted to be used. She attempted to pass it back to Corvin.

"I don't think we should barter with that. You shouldn't give it away."

"I would hate to part with it," Corvin admitted. He didn't take it back from her. "And I don't know if the dwarfs would even consider it, given that…"

Reg found herself holding her breath, waiting for the reason the dwarfs might not want it. Given its history? Its origins? The kind of magic that Corvin had drained from it? She ran one finger down the shimmering flat surface of the blade. Beside her, Corvin radiated warmth like one of Reg's fires. She caught a whiff of roses. He wouldn't try to charm her there, right in front of the dwarfs. And in front of Davyn, whose

.

responsibility it was to ensure that Corvin didn't overstep the bounds of the law.

But he wasn't looking at her; he was looking at the dwarfs. Maybe he was trying to use his charms to soften them up. His magic didn't work as well on men as on women, and who knew what kind of effect it had on dwarfs, but she had to admire Corvin for trying. He was putting everything he had into the negotiation, when he didn't even care about the fate of Calliopia. Reg wove a protective spell around herself to keep herself from Corvin's charms.

"No, I don't think so," she agreed. "We should keep this one."

The dwarfs were definitely reacting to the knife and their words. Maybe to Corvin's charms as well. They

.

leaned forward, beady eyes quick, trying to get a better look at it.

"Let us see this new blade," Gwythr prompted. "To work on the other is tempting, but we cannot possess it. This one would not be unmade…"

"No," Reg pulled it back, holding it close to her body, "you said PayPal or Bitcoin. I don't have much money, but maybe I could crowdsource a bit more, in a few days…"

Gwythr rose to his feet and moved toward her, crouching low, so that he was still no higher than Reg's head as she sat there. "I <u>will</u> see it."

CHAPTER 33

Nico, who had been exploring the edge of the stream, chose that moment to bound back to Reg. In a black streak, he placed himself between Gwythr and Reg and screamed a warning. It was a caterwaul like Reg had never heard from him before, so primal and threatening that it made the hair on the back of her neck stand up.

Gwythr froze.

The dwarfs didn't laugh at the little cat jumping into the fray, but visibly recoiled. Did dwarfs hate cats too, like fairies and pixies did? Reg found herself unaccountably irritated that so many of the magical races seemed to harbor animosity toward the cats. Harrison liked cats. He'd been so affectionate with Starlight that it made Reg uncomfortable. But other than humans, the other races seemed to have an instinctive dislike of cats.

"You have a champion," Gwythr said, bowing his head slightly to the cat.

Reg nodded, trying to look cool and unsurprised by the turn of events. "Yes. This is Nico."

Nico drew himself up taller, a shiver running through his lithe form, and he bared his teeth in a silent snarl. Gwythr took a step back, bowing again.

"You will not approach me," Reg warned.

He nodded. "This feline is very fine." His eyes glittered.

"Yes, he is." Reg looked at Corvin, trying to read how much to tell the dwarf of Nico's origins.

Corvin let down the walls of his mind just enough for Reg to access his warning. <u>No. Don't tell them.</u>

"He comes of incomparable stock," Reg said instead, keeping his secret. "There are only a handful of his line remaining in the world. Very rare and very valuable."

Gwythr returned to the spot where he had previously been sitting. He turned his head slightly to speak with the other dwarfs, his voice a low murmur. They spoke among themselves, their words incomprehensible to Reg. She could do little to read their faces, but their auras were changing as they became more interested in what her company had to offer.

Gwythr turned back to Reg. "May we see this new knife?" he asked respectfully.

Reg looked at Nico and over at Corvin. They both seemed to leave it up to her. Reg checked both Damon and Davyn, but neither seemed to have any recommendations. Reg got to her feet as gracefully as possible and stepped closer to the dwarfs to show them Corvin's knife. Gwythr's eyes gleamed.

"So maybe this is a straight-across trade," Reg suggested. "A knife for a knife. You umake the cursed dagger, and I give you this one as payment."

Gwythr stroked his beard, considering. He looked at the other dwarfs, and they muttered back and forth.

"The assassin blade <u>and</u> the bracelet," Gwythr negotiated. "The bauble isn't worth much, but it helps to even out the trade."

"The blades are of even value," Reg pushed back. She was entirely satisfied with trading both items, especially since they were Corvin's rather than hers, but if she agreed too easily, the dwarfs would not feel like they had gotten a fair trade. They would think she had scammed them. "You can have the bracelet or the knife, not both."

More muttering between the dwarfs. Reg waited.

One of the other dwarfs shook his head adamantly. "The fairy blade has a long heritage. We should be compensated for giving that up in the destruction of the dagger."

"Who is this?" Reg demanded. "I am negotiating with Gwythr."

Gwythr's eyes were down. "Brimir is son of King Fraeg," he said respectfully.

A prince. He had stayed incognito for the first part of the negotiations and now made himself known. Reg studied him openly. He didn't look any different from any of the other dwarfs. It wasn't like he was wearing a crown. He had on red sweat pants and an oversize button-up shirt with an insignia on the pocket. Maybe a royal logo or maybe just a store brand.

"So, do you speak for the king?" Reg asked. "Who am I supposed to be talking to?"

Gwythr kept his gaze averted. Brimir appeared to have taken over as spokesman. "You may speak with me." He said. "My word is final."

There was a murmur from the other dwarfs, and Reg thought that there might be some disagreement over whether his word was the final say or not. Maybe the king would still have a veto over it. But it would appear that he at least had some cachet with the dwarfs.

"I don't know about including the bracelet and the knife," Reg said, scratching her head. "That seems like a lot. They are both very valuable."

"The bracelet is easily replicated. There are many such trinkets around."

"Then why do you want it?"

Brimir hesitated, looking to the other dwarfs for a moment. "It would be a goodly gift for my woman."

"Oooh," Reg laughed. "I see! So maybe there aren't as many similar trinkets around as you would like me to think." Reg noticed Starlight lurking at the corners of her vision and held out her hand for him. He approached, sniffed her delicately, and sat beside her. Reg watched the reaction of the dwarfs, who seemed impressed that she had not just one, but two cats. What would they have thought of all of the nine kattakyns together? Reg bent down and whispered in Starlight's ear. "What do you think? Should I give him the jewelry for his girlfriend?"

Starlight licked his paw and washed his other ear, considering it. He studied the dwarfs, sniffing the air, whiskers quivering. Then he lay down, feet bunched under him, in one compact loaf shape.

"Starlight thinks I should include the bracelet as well," Reg told Brimir magnanimously. "As a gift to your woman."

There was an appreciative murmur and some applause from the dwarfs.

Reg squared her shoulders. "Do we have a deal?"

Brimir spat on his hand. "It is agreed."

Reg hoped she wasn't expected to shake that hand. She looked at Corvin. He shrugged. Reg imitated the movement, pretending to spit into her hand. Then she nodded. "We are agreed. How soon can the blade be unmade? A life hangs in the balance." She wiped her hand on her skirt.

"We will need to test it," one of the dwarfs who had remained quiet until then informed her. "Humans think all you have to do is hit it with a hammer, and it is done. But that is not how a magical blade is unmade. It cannot merely be broken. It must be… reforged. Formed into something else. There must be experts consulted on whether its magical properties have been extinguished."

"But it will be done today, right? We're not talking about days or weeks."

He rubbed his chin. "Humans are impatient. It takes millennia for metals and jewels to form in the earth. Dwarfs are patient. Humans expect everything to be finished before dinner."

"Well… yes. That would be good. I need to get back to Calliopia, see what else can be done for her once the magic spell has been broken."

"We will do our best. But proper forging takes time."

Reg rolled her eyes, but refrained from saying anything further.

"In the meantime," Brimir said, clapping his hands together loudly. "We will provide our guests with victuals and respite."

CHAPTER 34

Reg knew about dwarf feasts. She'd seen <u>The Hobbit</u>, after all. Lots of singing, food, wine, and broken plates.

Maybe she should have guessed by their wardrobe and tech-savvy ways that things had changed. They were ushered into the mountain by the delegation, and that part, at least, was pretty much as she had expected. A huge wall of rock that swung out from the mountain to allow them all in, and then closed behind them without a crack. The inside of the cave was pitch black until the dwarfs started turning on their phone lights. A few of them had headlamps strapped to their foreheads, and one carried a huge Maglite that was almost as long as he was tall. Reg didn't have to be as careful of the low ceilings as her human companions did, but it still felt claustrophobic. Ruan seemed perfectly at home in the caves. They were an upgrade from the damp, muddy tunnels that his people lived in.

They marched through the caves at a quick pace. Reg struggled to keep up, getting out of breath. For people with such short legs, they moved quickly.

There were red-brown paintings on some of the walls, and Reg tried to make something of them as she walked by. Pictographs of people, animals, hunters with bows, boats, trees and cacti. The dwarfs didn't appear to pay any attention to them. Reg supposed they walked by them every day and probably didn't even see them anymore. Were they a history of the dwarf kingdom? Or just graffiti?

Damon fell in behind Reg as they were forced to move in single file and whispered to her as they hustled along. "Good job with the negotiations. Well done. Dwarfs are notoriously difficult to barter with."

Reg nodded. "I've done my share of bartering in the past."

"I guess it helps to be psychic. You can tell when they're bluffing and when they wouldn't go any further."

"Not really. They were all pretty closed off and their faces and body language are hard to read."

"Because they're dwarfs?"

"I guess so. The full beards don't help. You can't see half their faces."

"Right. Anyway, I think you did well."

"You don't think it's going to take a long time to get the dagger unmade, do you? The whole point of getting here was to get it done right away so that Callie has a hope of recovering."

"I don't know. They're craftsmen. It's hard to hurry craft."

"Maybe another bauble would do it?"

"You never know."

Reg looked around again to make sure that the cats were still with her. They seemed to understand that they needed to stay close and go with the group. They hadn't wandered away to explore on their own. "Keep up, guys, I don't want to lose you."

Starlight made a <u>mrrrow</u> sound. Nico didn't answer, but dashed ahead of Reg, chasing after the dwarfs.

As they moved through the tunnels, Reg expected them to keep getting narrower and deeper, leading downward toward… the Balrogs and spiders and whatever else hid in the depths of the earth. But they didn't have to go very far before Reg started to see light up ahead. Lights were strung along the ceilings, and there was fresh air flowing to them. Reg quickened her step, eager to get to wherever the air was coming from. Maybe the passages just took them through one mountain into an open valley? She had assumed that the dwarfs lived underground due to all of the fairy tales, but maybe they didn't. Maybe that was just an old tradition and it wasn't true. Or they had started to live outside, even if the older generations still lived in the mountains.

In a few minutes, the tunnels ended, and Reg found herself and the others in a vast cavern, filled with light. It wasn't an open valley, but Reg found herself looking upward to see if it were a volcano cone and they would see the sky above. But it wasn't and she couldn't. She could see the rocky ceiling of the cavern, with stalactites encrusted with thousands of lights. The air couldn't be coming from outside either, because she couldn't see any windows up above them. It had to be blown in, circulated by fans in some huge HVAC system.

She and the others in the party just stood there, looking around in interest, fascinated with the whole thing. Ruan was scowling.

"What's the matter, Ruan? You don't like the light?"

Ruan shook his head. "Why live underground with this? Better than the sun, but still…" he shaded his eyes with his hand, "too bright."

"You've been living outside in the sun, so I didn't think it would bother you anymore."

He made a coughing noise. "Not how it is supposed to be underground. All of the light and blowing air." He coughed again, like it was foul. "Not like underground at all."

"Well, I guess the dwarfs appreciate some of the things from outside and found a way to bring them in."

Ruan sniffed and didn't make any further comment on it.

"Hopefully, we won't be here too long," Reg told him. "I'm hoping that it will just take them a few hours and then we can hit the road again. Be back to see Calliopia by tomorrow morning."

Ruan looked at her, his childlike face showing grief for an instant. Then his eyes were away again, putting on a mask. "Let us hope."

"This is the great hall," Gwythr announced, making a gesture to indicate their surroundings. "We hold meetings here. Big ceremonies. Sort of a town square."

There were many dwarfs bustling about, both big and small. Or both small and smaller, depending on how one looked at it. Reg was startled by the appearance of some of the dwarfs nearby.

"Girls!" she pointed out excitedly.

The others looked at her, both from her own company and the others around her. Reg felt her face heat up. She covered her cheeks with both hands and lowered her voice, speaking to Damon beside her. "I thought that girl dwarfs were rare. Or that the women looked like the men. You never see girl dwarfs in movies. And I thought I heard somewhere... that the women had beards, just like the men, so you couldn't tell the difference."

Damon raised his eyebrows. "You can't believe everything you see on TV."

"I never thought I'd see girl dwarfs. I thought… they all were just men."

"Hard to perpetuate the species that way. There are other ways of reproducing, of course. But most humanlike species use…" he cleared his throat, "the same methods of reproduction as we do."

One of the female dwarfs approached, staring at Reg. Maybe they were just as curious about her as she was about them. Maybe the only delegations who ever came to the mountain were men.

"Hi," Reg said shyly, giving the diminutive woman a tentative smile.

The woman reached up as Reg bent over, and caught a fistful of braids. "Red hair," she said with wonder. "I have never seen human with red hair."

Reg laughed. "Well, there aren't a lot of us, but there are more than just me."

"And this weaving. What do you call it?" She picked at the skinny braids.

"They're just braids. They're called box braids. Or cornrows. Different people call them different things, I guess."

"Like this?" The woman pushed her doo rag aside to show off a couple of braids wound around her head in a circlet.

"Yes, just the same."

"Can you do that for me?"

"I'm not very good at it. My fingers are so clumsy. I can do bigger braids; they won't be tiny like these. And it takes a very long time."

Ruan looked at Reg's hair as she bent over. "That is not difficult."

"Well, it is for me…" Reg thought about the way that he had made the harnesses for the cats. "But I bet you would be good at it. You're really good with that kind of thing."

Ruan nodded. "I would be very fast," he told the dwarf woman. "Not slow and clumsy like a human."

Reg rolled her eyes.

"Come this way," Gwythr announced, motioning for the company to follow him. "Let me take you to the feast."

Reg moved eagerly. She'd had nothing but a granola bar and leftover juice for breakfast, and she wouldn't mind some coffee and some ham or sausages or whatever other breakfast meats they might have. Unless breakfast was over, and there would be ham or chicken or roast sliced up for hearty sandwiches. That would be good too. She wasn't usually up to eating much for breakfast, but a long time had passed since her last meal, and she looked forward to the feast.

The rest of the company appeared to feel the same way. They all followed Gwythr quickly, eager for the feast.

He led them through a couple of tunnels to a smaller cave, set up like a school cafeteria with long tables and rows of chairs. Reg looked around, sniffed the air for some sign of roast pig or lamb.

Gwythr strode over to a wall filled with cupboards, and opened a few doors. "Everything you could want," he announced. "Chips, fruit roll-ups, single-serve macaroni, snack cakes…" He opened a couple of refrigerated units. "Bologna, cheese, Jell-O. Everything you need."

The guests all exchanged looks. Feast? Reg could eat better at home, even on the days Sarah didn't bring over a stew or casserole for her.

"This looks… very nice…" Reg said slowly. "Is there… anything hot? Or do you leave your hot meal for the end of the day…?"

"Microwaves!" Gwythr opened another door to show off a column of microwaves at the ready. "Warm up whatever you like. If you want something you don't see, write it on the list." He gestured to a whiteboard, where various kinds of snack food had been scribbled this way and that, interspersed with runes she couldn't read.

"I don't think we're going to be here that long," Reg said. "We'll just... eat what's here, I guess."

Gwythr nodded agreeably. "And respite," he announced, "in case you would like to rest." He led them out of the cafeteria into a room filled with rows of sleeping pods like something Steve Jobs might have thought of. "You can take any pod that is green. Program your own sleep sounds or silence, heat or cold, level of darkness, and rest as long as you like."

"Okay..."

In spite of how futuristic and uncomfortable they looked, Reg was tempted. She had slept little the night before, and then only restlessly, sitting up, dreaming and trying to keep one eye open all the time. If the dwarfs were going to take a while to unmake the blade, she might as well catch up.

"What about… drinks…?" she suggested hesitantly. She hoped that dwarfs hadn't given up wine for Kool-Aid or Tang, as they had seemed to have reverted to childhood in everything else.

"Oh, back in the feast," Gwythr said with a vigorous nod. "We have everything you could want. Energy drinks, Yoo-hoo, iced tea…"

Reg saw Ruan's head go up at the mention of energy drinks. "No, you don't. You stay away from the energy drinks," she warned him. "You know how you reacted last night."

"I didn't need to sleep," Ruan said. "If one can drink instead of sleeping, one can do much more work."

"No. You still need to sleep sooner or later, and you'll crash and have to sleep even longer to catch up. Stay away from it."

Ruan scowled at this, and Reg knew very well the first thing he was going to do once she didn't have eyes on him anymore was to go for the energy drinks.

"Is that all?" Reg asked. "What about... wine, beer, mead...?"

"Of course," Gwythr boomed. "All in the feast. If you can't find something, you have only to ask."

"Good. I think I'll get a drink before going to sleep." She looked over her company, and most of them nodded in agreement. "Okay. Lead us to the grown-up drinks."

* * *

They split a couple of bottles of wine between them, and Reg even managed to find bowls for the cats, which she supplied with bottled water and tuna. The company sat down at the long tables, resting and looking around at the dwarfs who came and went sporadically.

"It's nothing like I expected," Reg said. "I know Damon said don't expect everything you see on TV to be true, but isn't any of it true? About dwarfs, I mean? They obviously haven't always lived like this."

"No," Corvin agreed. "I've done quite a bit of research into the history of the species. They certainly have not always lived like this. They have lived in darkness, more like the pixies, with heat and light from fires, cooking over a flame, traditional breads and meats and all of those things that you were expecting. This... is something new. I've never visited the dwarfs before. I had heard that they modernized, but I ... was not expecting anything like this."

"They're like some tech company," Reg marveled, shaking her head. "Like Google or Facebook or something. Everyone acting like kids. Casual dress, eating junk food, and sleeping in pods. It's bizarre."

"No more so than humans doing it."

"But I still live in a house and eat real food and sleep in a bed. We don't all live... like this."

Davyn chuckled. "Not all humans live the same way, and I don't imagine all dwarfs do either. Who knows what others outside the colony live like. Individuals who don't feel like living like teenagers. Kingdoms that have not embraced technology. Isolated civilizations that are still living the way they did a thousand years ago."

"I guess." Reg sipped at her wine. "I'm worried though... what if they've lost their smithing skills? What if they've joined the high-tech world, and they outsource all of that kind of thing on Upwork? Or they just order their daggers and swords from Amazon? They acted like they know what they're talking about, but what if they're really planning to ship the dagger to some third-world country to have some peasant unmake it?"

"Hmm." Davyn didn't laugh at this idea. "Maybe I'll have a look around while you take a nap. I know what an active forge should look like. I can see whether they are still set up to smithy here."

Reg let out her breath. "Would you? That would be fantastic. I don't want to waste our time here if they can't actually do it."

"That makes sense."

"What if they don't want to show you their forge? I kind of thought that it should have been on the tour, but it seems like all they want us to do is eat and sleep."

"They don't have to show me. I can sneak around."

Reg remembered Davyn's ability to cloak himself. He would be able to turn himself nearly invisible and to have his run of the place, provided he didn't need to get past any doors secured by optical scanners. "Right. That's perfect."

The wine was going to Reg's head and she yawned sleepily. "I think someone had better show me how to program one of those iPods and I'll knock off."

"I'll give you a hand," Corvin offered courteously, standing up and reaching out to assist Reg.

"Hunter," Damon growled. "I'll do that. You can make yourself scarce for a few hours."

Corvin eyed Damon, his eyes narrow. He looked relaxed, but Reg could feel him coiled like a spring, ready to strike. But she was too tired to worry about them scratching each other's eyes out.

"I'll figure it out myself."

"You can't let him get near you while you're sleeping," Damon insisted. "I don't know if those things have security locks. Someone had better stay with you. Someone who can protect you. Keep predators away."

Nico gave a hiss and a growl, baring his teeth at Corvin. Corvin flapped his cape at him.

"Get out of here, cat!"

"Leave him alone," Reg told him. "He's just protecting me."

"Cats are dirty and annoying."

"Cats are cleaner than you are." Reg snorted. "And less annoying."

Corvin sniffed. He held his hand out to Reg again. "Come on. I'll help you to get settled."

Reg let him help her up, enjoying the little electric buzz she got from touching his hand. She was normally more careful not to allow skin-to-skin contact. But she was feeling pleasantly at ease after the dwarf wine. With Davyn's promise to look into whether the dwarfs still had a forge, she felt like everything was under control.

With an angry yowl, Nico attached himself to Corvin's leg and, while Corvin was trying to shake and peel the black kattakyn off, Starlight darted in on his other side, nipping in at his calf and even jumping up to snap at his hamstring. Corvin danced around, trying to get them both to leave him alone. Reg giggled.

"Get them off!" Corvin snapped. "Or one of them is going to get kicked, or worse."

Still laughing, Reg bent down to try to get Nico to release Corvin's leg. He stuck there like a limpet, hanging on with all of his claws and biting Corvin whenever he got the chance.

"Nico. Come on. Be good. Come on."

Eventually, she managed to coax the kattakyn away, but not without sustaining a number of scratches and bites herself. Starlight was more careful to stay out of reach, sitting down to watch when he saw that Nico had been removed.

"I'll go find a pod." Reg mumbled. "I'm sleeping in a pod. A poddy-pod-pod."

She went back to the sleeping room with the cats and looked for a pod with a green light. The ones that did not have green lights were, she assumed, either occupied or had to be cleaned and refreshed. She found one with a green light and crawled inside.

She hadn't considered the fact that they were made for dwarfs, not humans, so it was like crawling into a crib. She could fit, curled up on her side, but the taller men were going to have problems. They'd have to sleep with their legs stuck out the end. Reg poked random controls on the touch screen until she was too tired to keep her eyes open. She laid her head down and closed her eyes. The cats cuddled up to her, and she let their rumbling purrs lull her to sleep.

CHAPTER 35

Reg didn't know how long she slept in the small white pod. It was more comfortable than it looked and, being short on sleep and having drunk some wine and filled her belly, her body turned everything off so she could regenerate.

The cats were still cuddled up against her, warm and soft, and Reg didn't want to move. But she could hear voices outside the pod. They weren't soundproof, or Reg hadn't managed to turn the sound dampening system on.

"She's sleeping. There's no need to wake her up now."

"She'll want to talk things over. She wants to get the dagger unmade so that we can return."

"And they can go ahead and do that without her input. It isn't hard. We just want it done so that she can try to heal Calliopia."

"Who made you her guardian?"

"She did."

Reg scrubbed her eyes with her fists and stretched as much as the confined space would allow. She shifted the cats and wriggled to the end of the pod where the door was. She pressed the button to open the door and sat looking out at Damon and Davyn.

"What's going on?" Reg yawned and wiped tears away from the corners of her eyes. "I was having a great sleep until you guys decided to make a racket out here. Don't you know this is a quiet zone?" Reg nodded toward a red warning sign on the wall.

"I thought you would want to hear what I have found," Davyn said.

"And I think it can wait," Damon asserted, arms folded across his chest. "I'm here to make sure that you aren't bothered by... certain warlocks."

"Yeah, by Corvin," Reg reminded him. "I don't think Davyn is here to do anything to me."

"You don't know what the hazards might be in a place like this."

Damon might have been more convincing if they were in a fire-lit cavern deep in the bowels of the earth with moisture dripping down the walls, as Reg had imagined, rather than in a room filled with shiny, high-tech sleeping chambers.

Reg shook her head irritably. "I need to hear what Davyn found out."

Davyn shot a superior look in Damon's direction. He looked around, but there wasn't anywhere to sit down and have a conversation and, as Reg had pointed out, they were supposed to take any conversations outside the sleeping chamber. "We'd better go back to the cafeteria or find somewhere private to talk."

Reg nodded and reluctantly left the warm, soft bedding of the sleeping pod. The cats yawned and stretched and followed her. She and Davyn looked around for a private meeting room. There was a series of meeting rooms down a hallway, each with a self-locking door to ensure privacy. She and Davyn entered. Damon was in the hallway, hanging around close by. The cats wandered toward the cafeteria, and there didn't seem to be anyone around who would hurt them, so Reg let them go. They knew where to find her.

"Shouldn't this be the whole company?" Damon challenged.

Reg looked at Davyn. "I don't know, should it?"

"I think we need to get things moving now, not be wasting time trying to round everyone up. You're the one heading up this quest. You can bring the others in after if you want."

Reg nodded. "Okay. Damon, you can come in if you like. Just shut the door, so no one overhears."

Damon joined them, shutting the door behind him. Reg sat on one of the squashy, oddly-shaped meeting room chairs and tried to look interested and professional as she sank into it, struggling to stay upright. Davyn did the same, sitting stiffly upright with his knees close to his chin. Damon remained standing, in his 'bouncer' pose, arms folded in front of him, looking as formidable as a brick wall.

"They do have a forge," Davyn announced without preamble. "So that part, at least, is true. They aren't sending items out to subcontractors. Or at least, not all of them. I don't know the whole operation."

"I hear a 'but' coming."

"They have a new, modern forge."

"And that's good."

"On the surface, at least. It should warm up quickly, be built professionally to safety standards, all of that. But I'm not sure that you can buy a forge off of Amazon and expect it to function the same way as a traditional forge built by generations of dwarfs."

"Unless they're the ones selling it on Amazon."

"Uh, right. But I don't think that's the case here."

"So you don't think it's any good?"

"I don't know. I don't think anyone knows. It looks brand-new. They're forging small items, jewelry and tools that they can sell..."

"On Amazon and Etsy," Reg guessed.

Davyn gave a shrug that indicated she was right. "But I don't see a lot of ironwork or larger items like swords and armor."

"Maybe they don't need a lot of that. They don't look like they're ready to go to war." Reg thought of the cartoon t-shirts and laughed. They looked like miniature geeks, not warriors.

"I wouldn't judge by the dwarfs you've seen so far. I don't think they are revealing their full force."

Reg nodded slowly. The dwarfs had been a warrior race; that didn't change in a generation because of new technology or clothing styles. A number of the dwarfs she had seen had been wearing swords, even with their casual clothes. More of them probably had weapons at home. The colony could have modernized their weapons. They could have automatic guns, grenades, even missiles.

"But to get back to the matter at hand," Davyn said, "the steel used to make weapons like the dagger has a much higher melting point than you would need for jewelry made from softer metals. They are hardened not just with alloys, but with magic. A fairy blade requires a lot more heat to craft than one you would buy at your local forge. The fairies told you that they couldn't unmake the blade at their home? That no one in the area could do it?"

Reg remembered that they had. "Yeah."

"A little forge like the one they're using, one commercially available for crafters... that's not what you need to forge fairy steel."

A knot tightened in Reg's stomach. She felt sick. "So we came all this way for nothing. They can't do it."

"They say they can. Maybe they've modified the forge, or enhanced it with dwarfen magic. They could be telling the truth. Or they might not realize that they don't have the equipment or skills that they need, because they haven't had to do anything like this lately."

"But you don't think they can. You think it's a waste of time."

Davyn stared at the wall behind Reg so intently that she turned to look at it. There was an inspirational poster mounted on the wall.

<u>There's nothing small about a dwarf.</u>

She blinked at it and turned back to Davyn. He wasn't looking at the poster. Probably didn't even know it was there. He was seeing or thinking of something else.

"Davyn."

He focused back on her and scratched his jaw. One thing the dwarfs probably didn't have on hand was razors. Davyn's nails rasped like sandpaper on his whiskery jawline.

"In the lore of my family... back when they were actually smithies, they were able to work anywhere there were blacksmith tools. They didn't need a forge for heating the metal, because..."

"Because they were fire casters. They used their own fire."

He nodded.

"Can you make your fire that hot?"

"I don't know. I've never had reason to try."

"So even if they don't have the right kind of forge, you might be able to help with your fire."

"It's possible. But I'm not a smith. I've never even attempted metalwork."

"Would you need to? Couldn't you just provide the heat, and they would do the rest? The… pounding and shaping?"

"If they were prepared to work with a human."

"They seemed pretty impressed that you were a fire caster and came from such a good line."

"Yes. I don't know whether that will translate into cooperation or not."

They might admire him but be jealous and resentful. They might declare that they had never worked with humans before and weren't about to start. There could be all kinds of racial and political factors at play that she had no idea of. Before coming to Black Sands, she'd never thought about witches and magical creatures having biases and prejudices. It never occurred to her that the peoples living a traditional lifestyle had hundreds of years of ingrained biases to be confronted. Fairies and pixies didn't mix. The long-lived races considered the shorter-lived ones inferior and inconsequential. Far from equalizing them, magic seemed to make them more divided.

"So... what do we do? Do we confront them? Negotiate? Compliment them? I don't know anything about dwarfs but what I've seen on TV and, apparently, that's all wrong."

"I think it's important that we keep good relations for as long as possible. Better to have them on our side if we can. So we'll admire their equipment, ask questions, try to stay close to the project and see if we can help."

Reg nodded. "Okay. I can do that. Should we go find Gwythr? Or the other one? The prince?"

"Brimir. No, I think… we'll try Gwythr. I don't know much about dwarfen barter, but I think that Brimir was just a figurehead. Just there to show you that you were dealing with the royal house of Fraeg."

"And Gwythr is the real expert?"

"I think he was the real negotiator. Whether he is really chief of the smithies or not remains to be seen."

"Or whether the chief of the smithies actually does the work."

"Now you're getting it," he agreed.

Reg nodded. She really didn't like politics.

Damon had remained quiet to that point. Davyn was the spy and Damon didn't have any intelligence. He had been in just one place, guarding Reg, while Davyn went off spying. Reg wondered where Corvin had disappeared to. At least he had decided to stay away while Reg was sleeping. The combination of Damon and the cats had kept him away, even if he had the power to get past them.

"So, you're the spokesman for the company now?" Damon asked Davyn.

Davyn considered, eyeing Damon thoughtfully. "I am not the spokesman. I'm not in charge. But I am the one who knows the most about dealing with dwarfs."

"Because your grandfather or great-grandfather was a smithy? That doesn't exactly make you an expert on dwarfs."

"Are you claiming that you know more?"

"No... but what about Corvin? He's been around for longer than either of us. He's studied their history. He probably knows more about negotiating with them than either of us."

"He's been helping me so far," Reg agreed.

"Corvin is occupied at the moment. He's gone off on his own and is doing whatever it is that he does."

Reg looked at Davyn in concern. She had thought that he would have a better idea of where Corvin was and what he was doing. Davyn was supposed to keep an eye on the warlock, make sure he followed the rules of the coven, even while he was being shunned. If Davyn had just let Corvin go off to do his own thing, he could be creeping around the dwarfen halls looking for people and objects he could drain the power from. He could be causing all kinds of havoc.

"You don't know where he is?"

Davyn looked at her sideways. "He's fine. What's he going to do down here?"

"I don't know. He could do all kinds of things. Don't dwarfs have powers?"

"Their magic is mostly external. Spells and secrets. Not inborn gifts."

"But still…"

"I'm sure we would have heard if he was causing issues. The dwarfs won't put up with anything. More than likely he's just watching them, learning about their ways and how they have modernized. Or he's found a library and is lost in the scrolls."

"You don't think we should check?" Reg pulled out her cell phone to get in contact with Corvin.

"I don't think that's going to work in here," Damon said.

Reg looked down at the face of her phone. No bars. "But the dwarfs have phones. They have to be able to use them down here."

"They've maybe adapted the technology. Or they have their own cell phone provider down here. Or they're just using them as glorified clocks and flashlights."

"We should go find Gwythr," Davyn repeated. "Don't worry about Corvin right now. If you want, Damon can go look for him, and you and I can deal with the smithies. Maybe that would be the best."

"No one put you in charge of me," Damon snapped. "I'm not part of your coven and you're not in charge of this company."

Davyn rolled his eyes and looked at Reg. She tried to soften the instruction and appeal to his instinct to protect the vulnerable.

"It's not your job. You're not responsible for Corvin or anything he does, and you can do whatever you want to while we're here. I just... worry about what he could be doing. He's not known for his stellar impulse control."

Damon nodded at this, his dark eyes concerned.

"If you want, you can just stay with me. I know you came here to keep an eye on things... but if Davyn and I are with the smithies, I'm pretty well-protected. But there could be others here who don't know about Corvin and how to protect themselves against him."

Damon didn't make a decision right away.

"But he could just be in the library," Reg finished lightly, with a shrug. "So, you know, it's up to you."

"I'll take a look around," Damon agreed. "If he's out making trouble, it shouldn't take too long to find out."

"Sounds good. Thanks."

CHAPTER 36

Reg let Davyn lead the way. She kept her eyes open for the cats as they cut through the cafeteria, but there was no sign of them there. Maybe they had stopped to eat, then gone on to hunt cave moles or find another place to sleep. Davyn took her through a labyrinth of tunnels that Reg didn't even try to keep straight. As they progressed, Reg could smell something hot. Something growing hotter. There was still a cool breeze, but it was doing less and less to keep her cool as they approached the room the forge was kept in. Reg could hear chattering voices, hammering, lots of activity.

Eventually, they reached the forge. They were in a large cavern, almost as big as the great hall. There were a lot of tables and workstations filled with tools and crafts in various stages of production. Looking around, Reg thought the dwarfs were mostly working independently, each making their own thing. Like a Ten Thousand Villages shop, only in the production phase rather than sales. She imagined they each had their own little storefronts on Etsy, Amazon, or eBay. Or maybe selling direct from their own websites. A few music systems blasted competing music over the hum of voices and metalwork, and some of the dwarfs had earbuds or even big over-ear noise-canceling earphones.

She and Davyn walked past the various tables, looking over the half-finished wares with interest. He was right; they were mostly jewelry or other small crafts. Which made sense commercially. Smaller products meant they didn't need to purchase as many materials, and the softer metals would be easier to manipulate. There were some tools and larger items in the mix, but she didn't see any swords or fairy daggers. Nothing that was at all similar to the blade they had brought. It was no wonder the dwarfs had been so interested in it, and in Corvin's knife which Brimir had referred to as the assassin's blade.

Had they lost their ability to work with weapons? Or was there another room with an older forge in it where armor and weaponry were still forged? In their foray into the modern world, had they decided that with the proliferation of guns, blades were no longer a profitable business?

A female dwarf strode toward them, clipboard in her arm, a stern 'you're talking too loud in the library' look on her face.

"Uh-oh," Reg intoned. "I think we're in trouble."

"It's your fault. I didn't get in any trouble when I was in here last time."

"You were invisible when you were in here last time."

He flashed a smile at her, but was again serious when he turned to look at the woman approaching them.

"Madam, you must get the one in charge here."

"Do you have time booked? You can't just come in here to work on random projects. The forge is tightly booked." She had a name tag that said 'Frida.'

"I was looking for Gwythr. Does he have time booked to work on the unmaking of our fairy blade?"

"You should be conferencing with him directly on that."

"Yes, you're right," Davyn gave her a firm nod of understanding. "I was hoping to be able to find him. We were resting after our journey, but I'm eager now to find out where we stand. Our communications don't work down here." He showed her his phone, frowned, and slid it back away into a pocket inside his cloak.

"He should have updated you on the project timeline." Frida looked over to a flat wall divided into columns, with an assortment of cards with words or runes on them. A Kanban board? Reg shook her head in amazement.

"Let's see. You would be Reg Rawlins?" Frida asked.

"I'm Reg Rawlins," Reg offered. "He is part of my company."

"Yes, it looks like Gwythr has begun work on the project." She looked down at the clipboard, which Reg realized belatedly was not a paper clipboard, but an e-ink tablet. Frida paged through several different screens with her pen, tapping in various places. "Brimir has booked the forge for later this afternoon. They should be having a team meeting right now to make sure that all of the various resources and tasks have been assigned."

"Where would that be?"

"I don't see a place listed. That probably means that they are at the palace. We don't handle palace bookings. But I wouldn't bother to go all the way over there, by the time you get there, they'll be breaking up and coming here. You might as well wait for them."

"Okay. You don't mind us having a little look around?" Reg smiled at the woman expectantly.

The dwarf woman looked around, scowling. She wasn't used to having strangers in her forge, but she had just told them they could stay there, so she wasn't sure what to do about it.

"We won't get in anyone's way," Davyn promised. "It's just so nice to see a working forge and craftsmen at work. You think that everything in the world is mechanized and faceless now, and then you see a shop like this in operation. It warms my heart."

It warmed every other part of Reg too. Despite the air conditioning, the room was very warm. She hoped they didn't have to wait there for too long. She'd be dehydrated before they even had a chance to talk to anyone.

Frida nodded, smiling thinly. "Fine," she agreed. "You make sure you stay out of the way. If I get complaints, you'll be waiting outside the room."

"Yes ma'am," Davyn agreed.

Reg nodded her agreement as well. Frida put a few more checkmarks on her virtual lists and walked away from them, head down. Reg wandered down a row of worktables, looking over the work being done. Even though she was sure that Davyn had just said what he had to talk the woman into letting him stay, she did find it pretty amazing to see all of the work that was being done by hand. It was good to see that there were still individuals who cared about their craft.

As she walked down the aisle, she became more and more aware of the forge at the end of it. The heat pouring off of the unit made it difficult to ignore and, as the workers used it, there were plenty of bangs and shouts and instructions back and forth. A working forge was not quiet.

She looked at Davyn and saw the sweat gathering at his brow. Was it the heat, or was he, like Reg, starting to feel the pull of the fire? It called to her, inviting her to play, to make her fire part of it and feel its power.

Davyn raised his brows at her. "Fun place to be," he commented.

Fun wasn't the word Reg would have chosen. Tempting. Powerful. Enchanting, even.

She couldn't get much closer to the forge without responding to it, so she turned around to retreat on the other side of the aisle. Davyn walked toward the forge. He was more experienced than she was, better at being able to keep his fire under control. If Reg got any closer to it, she was afraid the flames would be shooting up to the ceiling.

It wasn't a long time before Gwythr got there, but it wasn't the five or ten minutes Reg had hoped for either. He looked surprised to see them there, but he smiled pleasantly rather than scowling that they had intruded on his domain or that he thought they were checking up on him.

Which they were.

"Ah, Reg Rawlins and Davyn Smithy. I am honored to have you at my forge." He looked over to Brimir, who was in the company of men he had brought with him. "Our forge," he corrected, with an eye roll that Reg just barely caught. He had said that he was chief of the smithies. But obviously, Brimir, being the son of the king, felt that it was his domain as well. Reg wondered how much experience he had with smithing. Was he a smithy, or had he just nosed in on the business because there was a company of outsiders on a quest and he wanted to be in on it?

"You have had a chance to see our new forge?" Gwythr asked. He rattled off the name brand and model number, and some of the specs of the impressive unit.

Reg wasn't interested in its numbers. She was interested in its fire and how much power it had. Would they be able to unmake the fairy steel there? Or would it be beyond their capabilities?

"I was hoping for an update on the unmaking of the fairy blade," Davyn said respectfully. "I know you have been working on the project nonstop since we arrived here, so please excuse my impatience. When will you be beginning? When will you actually start firing the weapon?"

Gwythr walked toward the forge. "We're actually going to do a couple of test fires right now, to get a better idea of its composition and what magic is upon it. Would you like to stay to watch the tests? I realize that you are not a smithy yourself, but I'm sure you will be interested in seeing it at work, thinking about how your forefathers made their living."

"We would be very interested. I was hopeful that you would allow us to observe."

"Of course," Gwythr agreed. "Come this way."

Davyn followed Gwythr and his other men to the fiery forge. Reg walked part of the way there, then had to stop to stay in control of her own fire. Davyn and Gwythr looked back at her.

"You do not need to be afraid, lady," Gwythr said, "It is quite safe."

"I'm sure it is. I'm just… not comfortable getting any closer."

"You will not be able to see from there."

"I know. But… I can't. Not right now."

Davyn didn't try to talk her into it. She didn't know if he understood what she was feeling, but he respected her enough not to insist that she get closer. He knew what her abilities were, maybe better than she did.

"Well... as you wish," Gwythr said doubtfully.

There were some looks and maybe some whispered comments from his companions. She could sense their contempt. How they thought she was a weak woman or a weak human who shouldn't have been allowed into the room. Little did they know what would happen if she got any closer.

* * *

Gwythr and the others continued to the forge, and Reg listened the best she could as Gwythr showed the blade to Davyn and talked about how it had been made and his plans for testing it. Davyn didn't give away his doubts that the new forge could handle the fairy blade, and if Gwythr had any similar doubts, he too kept quiet about them.

Eventually, Gwythr laid the dagger on a workbench near the forge. He picked it up with a pair of tongs and continued to lecture, turning it this way and that. He put it into the forge, near one of the burners and Reg felt a jump of excitement. This could be it. They could unmake the blade right there and then, and then they could go back and help Calliopia. They would tell her that it had been unmade, that she could heal from the damage it had done, the poisonous spell that kept her flesh from being able to knit together properly.

Gwythr stopped talking and was quiet as he turned the knife in the heat, examining it. He kept it in for a while, then removed it and laid it on the workbench, still glowing hot. He and the other dwarfs discussed it, and Gwythr hammered on it with one of his tools, bending close to examine the effect that it had. He reached into a pot he had placed on the bench and sprinkled it with something. Some potion to counteract its magic?

Could the evil blade be destroyed?

Gwythr was speaking to his men or muttering a chant over the knife; Reg wasn't sure which. He dipped it in water to cool it, sending up clouds of steam. He examined it closely, then put it back into the forge, heating it to a glowing white.

Reg couldn't help taking another step forward. She focused on keeping her fire to herself, keeping it completely separate from the fire of the forge, no matter how much she wanted to join with it. Davyn's eyes slid over to her once and he made no comment.

Gwythr spoke to the other dwarfs, who had suggestions that they made in their native tongue rather than giving away any trade secrets to the fire caster. It would have been funny if Davyn knew dwarfish. Maybe he did. If his forefathers had been smithies, maybe they had known dwarfish and had spoken it in the home so that they could trade more easily with the dwarfs. But it had been a few generations, so probably Dave Smith didn't know any more dwarfish than anyone else in his school class.

Gwythr removed the white-hot dagger from the fire and laid it on the workbench once more. He talked under his breath as he looked at it, sprinkled a couple more potions onto the blade, and pounded and manipulated it with the tools on the bench. But Reg didn't see any change in the blade from where she stood. It didn't become soft or molten, didn't change shape under his ministrations.

She took another step closer.

"Perhaps your forge is not hot enough," Davyn suggested. "You could increase the temperature…?"

"It won't go any hotter," Gwythr said, teeth clenched. "Newfangled safety standards."

"Maybe I could help with that?"

"I don't think there's anything you can do. Once it reaches a certain temperature, there is a dampening mechanism…"

"But that can only do so much. If I increase the temperature enough, it won't be able to keep up."

Gwythr looked thoughtful. "Perhaps."

"You're okay with that, then? What if I damage the unit?"

Gwythr waved his hand. "If you destroy the temperature regulator, you will be doing us a favor."

"And if I create too much heat and the forge splits open?"

Gwythr's smile broadened. "I would like to see that."

Brimir looked offended. "The kingdom paid handsomely for that forge. It is top of the line. If you break it with your experiment..."

"If it breaks, I will recompense you," Gwythr growled. "I do have means."

Brimir didn't look too happy with that comment. "I suppose I cannot stop you," he said archly, holding his head up high so that he was taller than Gwythr. Gwythr motioned to Davyn.

"You may join me as I fire it once more," he invited. They stood close together near the opening of the forge, Gwythr putting the knife near the burner again. Davyn didn't appear to be doing anything, but Reg could feel it like a magnetic pull. She wanted desperately to join in and let her fire join his. The two of them together plus the forge's own heat... it would be spectacular, and satisfying in a way that nothing else Reg could think of would be. She tried to regulate her breathing, counting the seconds of her inhalations and exhalations.

Gwythr's face was slick with sweat. It started dripping from his brow down over his cheeks and into his beard. Reg could feel the increase in the heat from where she stood. Everyone else who was close to the forge took a few steps away, trying to escape the wall of heat.

Eventually, Gwythr pulled the knife back once more. He tried again to shape it with his tools, but Reg sensed from his grim expression that even with Davyn's help, they weren't having much success.

The dwarf men and Davyn stood there, looking at it and trying to decide what to do next. Davyn looked over at Reg. She was aching to help, but was afraid she wouldn't be able to control her fire once she got going.

Gwythr and the dwarfs spoke, shaking their heads.

"What think you?" Gwythr asked Davyn.

"I think this isn't working. We still need something more."

"More magic or more heat?"

Davyn stared down at the knife. "Maybe both."

Gwythr shook his head.

CHAPTER 37

Davyn looked over at Reg, meeting her eyes. He had to know how much the fire of the forge was pulling her, especially when he added his own fire. He raised an eyebrow.

"Want to play?" he invited.

Reg couldn't help grinning at the question. She felt exactly like a kid, bursting with energy, wanting just to run and yell to burn it off. She nodded.

Gwythr and the other dwarfs looked at Reg, puzzled. Gwythr didn't object. Reg had been introduced to them as a sorceress, so maybe he thought there was some kind of spell she could do to enhance their efforts. Reg walked slowly closer, trying to keep her fire from feeding the forge until they were ready for her. But even with Davyn standing nearby, trying to dampen it and help her to focus, the heat coming off of the forge grew noticeably.

The dwarfs wiped at sweat beading on their brows and faces. There were rings of sweat under their armpits. Davyn was the only one who seemed comfortable with the temperature. Reg understood; as she walked closer to the forge, she welcomed the heat, like walking into a warm kitchen after being out on a cold morning. It enveloped her, making her feel comforted and happy.

"Try to focus on the blade," Davyn told Reg. "You are familiar with it. I want you to think about it and feel the magic working in it before it is fired again."

Reg had a difficult time focusing her attention on the blade instead of the fire. She ran her thumb over the scar on her palm, remembering when Hawthorne-Rose had cut into her to force a confession out of her or Corvin.

The blade was her enemy as much as Hawthorne-Rose had been. Calliopia had thought that it was an ally. She had cared for it and taken it with her, protected it instead of agreeing to have it unmade. And it had responded by seeking her life. Thumb pressed over the scar, Reg stared at the blade, trying to envision the dwarfs or fairies who had forged it, the person who had cursed it. She recalled her vision of Calliopia performing the blood spell to seek her original bloodlines. The spell that had allowed the pixies to find Calliopia and steal her away.

The dagger had caused a lot of pain and trauma, physical and emotional. For the first time, she could see an aura around the knife — a sort of darkness bleeding off the edges.

"Okay," she whispered. "I see it."

"Don't get too deep," Davyn warned. "Just observe it. This is what we need to counteract in order to unmake the blade. So far, the magic has been holding, and we've been unable to affect the metal itself."

Reg nodded.

"Are you ready?" Davyn asked.

"Let's do it." Reg's fingertips were sweating. Not from the heat of the forge, but from the fire she was trying to hold within herself. Like the darkness of the blade, she couldn't stop her heat from bleeding off at the edges, feeding the fire of the forge.

Davyn motioned to Gwythr, who took the knife in the tongs again and made his way back to the forge, walking slowly as if he were pushing through deep snow to reach it. Only it wasn't cold; it was hot. Reg tried to keep control. While she needed to enhance the fire in the forge and the blade itself, she didn't want to injure any of the dwarfs standing nearby. Particularly Gwythr, who had to stand close to hold the knife inside the forge.

"Help me," she murmured to Davyn.

He nodded. Reg hoped that he understood she needed help to keep the fire from growing too large or hot, not that he needed to help her feed it.

Reg closed her eyes and focused on the blade in the fire. She started to channel her fire toward it, which her body and mind were happy to do. But it was like turning on a fire hose.

Or a flamethrower.

Reg struggled to keep control, to keep narrowly focused so that nobody would get hurt. The dagger turned white-hot in an instant, and even the tongs, treated through the craft and magic of the dwarfs to resist heat, grew white and was on the verge of melting. Reg tried to draw the heat out of the tongs into the knife. The metal the forge was constructed of started to glow red, despite the ceramic lining and heat-dampening controls that had been built into it. Reg tried to strengthen it, mindful of what Davyn had said about it splitting right open if it got too hot.

The dwarfs shielded their faces. Sweat was pouring off of Gwythr in buckets.

"Okay," Davyn said to Reg, "pull back. Let's have a look at it."

She had to physically step back from the forge several paces before the flow of energy started to slacken. There was a tug-of-war inside of Reg as she tried to pull back and at the same time to be allowed to raise the temperature yet further. Her fire fought with her knowledge that someone would be hurt if she allowed it to take over completely. Davyn was close enough to touch her. She could barely feel his hand at her elbow, but some of the fire started to bleed away.

"No."

"Reg, focus. You can do this."

Reg moaned, still fighting with herself. "Let me do this."

"Come now. Pull back."

Between his encouragement and ability to take some of her heat, and her own will fighting against the instinct to burn, she finally managed to disconnect from the forge, and she took several more steps back, breathing hard, trying to regain her perspective.

She understood what she had previously been told about adolescent fairies not being able to control their newly-found magic once they had fully blossomed into fairyhood. And Corvin not yet being in control of the magic he had sucked from the Witch Doctor. Her newly discovered fire casting ability nearly consumed her. Without Davyn's help, she didn't know if she would have been able to control it at all. It was no wonder he had warned her about not practicing on her own.

Gwythr gratefully withdrew the blade from the forge and lay in on the bench. This time, he nodded as he looked at it, and as he began to work it with his tools, it was malleable and bent and could be reshaped. The other dwarfs crowded closer, watching his skill and making suggestions. Gwythr wiped his brow with the back of his arm, and nodded appreciatively when the woman dwarf supervisor approached and put a large water bottle down on the corner of his bench. Reg watched the remaking of the blade with interest. She'd never watched a smith at work before. That was probably a good thing, because if she'd approached a forge as a child, who knew what might have happened.

Gwythr set aside his tools and took a long drag from the water bottle. He looked at Reg, respect in his eyes.

"I need to fire it again. It should not need to be as hot this time."

Reg looked at Davyn, who was looking pale and drawn. "Should I help again? Or stay back?"

"Not as close, but I think we still need you."

Reg nodded and took a few breaths. Gwythr grasped the reshaped knife in the tongs and took it back to the fire. Reg let it heat up naturally before taking a step closer. Davyn kept a close eye on her, working to moderate her fire. Reg stepped closer, and immediately her fire streamed to the forge. She held up her hands, trying to control it. The forge glowed red and the dwarfs stepped back from it. Even Gwythr pulled back with the knife, holding his other hand up to shield his face.

"Not so much, Reg Rawlins."

Davyn's strength was slackening; Reg was losing control. "Help me!"

He was trying, but didn't have much left in him.

Reg panicked. She was going to blow everything all to hell.

CHAPTER 38

"Regina."

She recognized the purr. Corvin.

Now was not the time. She couldn't deal with him while trying to control her fire casting.

She couldn't feel the usual warmth she felt when Corvin stepped into a room, already enveloped with the heat of the forge and her own magic. But when he touched her, she could still feel the electricity between them.

And behind that, she could feel his power. He still held the power from the Witch Doctor and from the magical items he had plundered at the warehouse. But like Reg with her newly-discovered gift, he was still trying to learn how to manage his new abilities.

Reg had previously been able to borrow power from him. Not just when he agreed to strengthen her, but also when she had needed it to save the little girl she had been in the past. With the passing of her powers to Corvin and him giving them back, they seemed to have opened a conduit between them which Corvin was powerless to close. Reg could do what she shouldn't have been able to do, to take power from him without his permission.

There was an immediate struggle when he touched her. Reg instinctively sought power from him to feed her fire and Corvin fought to keep it back, to steady her as Davyn was doing and prevent her from exploding the forge and sending the entire dwarf mountain up in a blast with the power of a nuclear explosion.

Reg struggled to stop herself from pulling power from him, trying to reverse the energy that flowed from him to her, into her fire in the forge. She saw in her mind a clip from a movie she had seen at school as a girl, the blinding bright explosion of a new star being created. She didn't want to turn the planet earth into a new star.

"Give it to me," Corvin urged, choking. "Regina, yield to me."

"No."

"You want to bring this whole place down around you? Do you think you would survive that? Submit to me."

Reg resisted for a few seconds, then gave in. They didn't have any idea of what could happen if she let her fire take full control. Corvin couldn't have any clue of the devastation she would cause.

"Yes, yes."

Corvin's focus sharpened. He channeled the power from her, first a trickle, and then a stronger flow, relieving the pressure that had built up, the need to burn the whole place to the ground. He transferred it to Davyn, on his other side, who needed strength to help get Reg under control.

Reg finally relaxed, letting go, able to shut off the fire. She pulled back from Corvin, but he held on to her, unwilling to sever the connection.

"Release me!" Reg ordered through gritted teeth, trying to find her balance in order to fight back against him. She had been practicing building barriers against him, in reflecting his own powers back when he tried to charm her. But it was different this time. She had surrendered to him. He would not release her until he had stolen all of her gifts away. He pulled her closer and embraced her. Reg tried to fight back, but was paralyzed. He looked down at her, face glowing, drinking in her power.

"Corvin!" It was Davyn who spoke, not Reg. She couldn't find any more words. "Corvin, no. She needed your help, not this."

Reg felt strangled. Having yielded to Corvin without being charmed this time, it felt completely different. No feeling of pleasure and safety, no physical satisfaction. Just him taking what was not his, stripping her without regard to her feelings.

There was a struggle between Davyn and Corvin. Reg wasn't sure whether there was a psychic connection between them, or if Davyn was using some power she didn't know about or understand. But she could tell that they fought each other, Corvin to remain in control, and Davyn, like the owner of a cat or dog, trying to take away its prey.

Reg tried to pull free, but he had drained too much of her strength.

"You will never be reinstated to the coven," Davyn warned Corvin. "This will mark the end to your membership in any Black Sands coven forever."

It was an effort for Corvin to pull back, reducing his grip on Reg until she was able to pull away from him physically.

At last, she succeeded in also breaking their psychic connection, and Corvin staggered, hardly able to keep his feet. His eyes were glazed.

Reg looked for somewhere to sit down. She fell onto a stool by a workbench. The three of them stayed frozen in a tableau, all drained and disoriented.

CHAPTER 39

It was some time before Reg recovered enough to be aware of what was going on around her. She heard the hammering of metalwork and the dwarfs talking and chanting in low voices. The forge still smelled smoky hot, like it was overheated and going to burst open. But when she blinked her eyes and looked around, she could see that it was no longer red hot and had subsided to its usual flame. Maybe a little warmer and brighter than usual, but not enough to be of concern.

Reg looked around. Davyn was still standing there. He looked better than he had been, having received strength from Corvin during the transfer. Instead of looking tired and dried-out, he seemed healthy and strong. He was scowling. He wasn't quite back to normal, having expended a lot of mental and psychic energy. But it wouldn't be long. He would recover before Reg.

Corvin stood too close to Reg, his black cloak billowing slightly in the air from the HVAC. He was red-faced with the heat, but looking as she had seen him before, full and glowing with new power.

She was afraid to look inside herself, to examine her own head. She remembered what it had been like before when he had stripped her of her gifts. So quiet and empty. She hadn't known what to do with herself. She didn't know how to live like a normal person, without the voices and the impulses and the magic tugging on her heart.

She had done it again.

She had yielded to Corvin once more, allowing him to take from her. She didn't even have the excuse that he had charmed her this time, that he didn't have her informed consent. This time, she had succumbed to him, knowing what was at stake, knowing he was going to take from her. But it had been the only way to stop her fire magic from taking over, to keep from destroying the cave and maybe the mountain and everyone in it.

Corvin was the first to speak. He licked dry lips and turned his head toward her. "Regina."

Reg just breathed, unable to find the words to answer him.

"Reg," he shifted slightly, a fraction of an inch closer to her. "Are you okay?"

Reg nodded. She was alive, and so was he, and that was more than she would have been able to say if he hadn't been able to stop her. But could she live like that? Was there enough of <u>her</u> left to continue?

"Reg." He stepped closer and put his arm out to touch her.

Reg jerked back. If she had anything left within her, she wasn't going to allow him to take it. Corvin looked as if she had burned him. He withdrew his hand.

Davyn stirred. He looked first toward the forge, to reassure himself that everything was still in one piece and she hadn't blown them all to kingdom come. He scratched the back of his head and looked around, a little dazed.

"It's okay, then. We're okay." He looked at Reg, shaking his head in wonder. "I had no idea."

Reg tried to ask him what he had no idea of, but the words stuck. She couldn't get anything out.

"I knew you had an instinct for fire casting," he said, "but I had no idea... of your ability. Your strength."

He had thought that he could control her. She was just a beginner who needed some mentoring and guidance. But once she had let her fire join with the forge, he had completely lost control.

She tried to tell him it was okay. At least Corvin had been there to act as a release valve. Without him, who knew how much damage she would have done.

Reg looked toward the forge, and to Gwythr, working at the bench. His face was close to the metal he was working, lost in his craft. Maybe he didn't know how close to destruction he had come. Maybe he didn't care. He was too focused on working the metal to care about the rest of the world. Corvin had saved the day; everybody was well, so why let that stop his progress?

"The magic in the blade is broken," Davyn confirmed, watching Gwythr's progress. "They have been able to unmake it."

Reg put her hand on the workbench beside her to try to stand up. But she couldn't raise the strength to go and see what he had managed to do. The blade had been unmade; their quest was successful. She didn't know what they did with the metal after it was unmade. Gwythr was busy with it, still working it somehow, but she didn't know what he would do with it.

She put her elbow on the workbench and leaned her face against her hand. She could go for another nap in the pods. This time, she would sleep for a few days, not just a few hours. The cats were still around somewhere. They could all curl up in a pod and sleep the hours away until Reg was feeling like herself again.

If she was still herself.

She felt something familiar. Reg tried to focus on the little flutter in her brain.

Her power was not all gone. There was still something there, anyway. A familiar psychic connection. She looked at Corvin out the corner of her eye, observing him without his being aware of it. Was the connection with him? A vestige of his attack on her?

But he wasn't looking at her and it didn't feel like his consciousness. She explored the feeling uncertainly, mentally and emotionally drained. She couldn't run another race after just finishing a marathon. But there was still <u>something</u> there.

She closed her eyes, focusing on the flutter of consciousness. Her thoughts began to drift. If she just rested her head on the workbench for a while, maybe she would be able to explore it further.

Reg wasn't sure how much time had passed. Conversations carried on around her in English and dwarfish. The hammers continued to tap and clink. Then there was a sound that didn't fit — a little mrrow of inquiry.

Reg opened her eyes and looked around. "Starlight?"

He picked his way down the aisle toward her, ignoring the dwarfs at work. How could she have let him wander around the mountain caverns by himself? It wasn't safe. What had she been thinking?

But he seemed none the worse for it. "Come here, boy. How are you? What happened?"

He approached her, looked at her for a moment, then leaped onto her lap. Reg cuddled him close, enjoying the warmth, the softness of his fur, the familiar compactness of him. He started to lick her hand, his rough tongue rasping across it. Reg didn't normally like him licking her, but for once she just let him do it. It felt good to be cared for. For him to be there for her, not demanding anything, just being her familiar friend and sitting with her.

"Yeah, that's my kitty, isn't it?" She petted him, taking a deep breath and letting it go, feeling the rapid beating of her heart slowing.

Corvin wrinkled his nose at the cat. He still seemed off-balance, still standing there like he didn't know where else to go. He'd done what he'd come to do, so he could leave. Go back to the feast or the sleeping chamber, or go back outside to his car and drive away.

He had once again managed to worm his way into her consciousness and to take something from her.

Starlight rubbed against Reg, purring loudly.

"I guess it's time to go home," Reg murmured to him. "We need to go home... to see how Calliopia is."

She no longer had any hope of healing Calliopia. Corvin had surely taken whatever strengthening or healing power Reg had been able to develop. Maybe the unmaking of the blade would be enough and the fairies would be able to do the rest now that the curse was broken.

＊ ＊ ＊

Reg wanted to get up and walk away. Back to the sleeping chamber. Back to Damon's car. Anywhere but in the smithy where she was. She didn't have the strength to do anything, even with help.

Davyn walked over to her, looking much steadier on his feet than Reg felt. "Reg. What can I do? What do you need?"

"I just... I just want to sleep, I think."

"Do you want me to help you? Take you somewhere you can rest?"

Reg nodded her heavy head. She would probably fall back asleep at the workbench. It wasn't comfortable, but at least she didn't have to move from there. It wasn't so hard to just let go of consciousness and let darkness take her away.

Davyn moved to Reg's side, lifted one of her hands and wound it around his neck to hold it on the other side, and put his arm around Reg's waist to steady her, and helped her to her feet. Starlight jumped down and followed.

Reg leaned on Davyn for balance and did the best she could to move her feet to keep up with him. Davyn took her out of the smithy cavern and back through the passages to the cafeteria.

"You need anything to eat?" Davyn asked. "Get your strength back?"

"No. Can't eat."

"Okay." He looked into her face searchingly. "Are you… are you okay?"

Reg closed her eyes, shutting him out. She knew what he was asking; whether Corvin had stolen all of her powers. But she didn't have the strength to sort it all out yet. She shook her head.

"I can't think. I don't know."

He didn't say anything. Reg tried to take her own weight but was still too jelly-legged and tired to manage on her own. Davyn took her through the cafeteria. It was busier than it had been when they had been there before. She could feel the eyes of the dwarfs on her as Davyn escorted her through to the quiet room. She looked around for Starlight and saw that he was still with her.

But where was Nico? She hoped that he wasn't lost, or getting into trouble, or maybe hurt. She hadn't been taking very good care of him, focused too much on the unmaking of Calliopia's blade. Francesca had trusted Reg to look after Nico. She was supposed to be mentoring him, helping him to understand how he needed to behave so that they could find him a proper home with a practitioner. So he could be someone's familiar instead of a pain in the neck.

"Where is he?" she asked Davyn.

He looked at her and didn't answer. What did that mean? That Nico was hurt? That he wasn't coming back? That she should know?

Reg just shook her head, unable to focus on the problem. Davyn found an empty sleeping chamber and helped point her to the doorway so that she could crawl inside. Reg didn't even push any of the controls on the touch screen, she just curled up, waited for Starlight to settle in beside her, and went straight to sleep.

CHAPTER 40

Reg felt like she was swimming. Like she was floating in the middle of a dark lake, the water warm around her, but dark as midnight. She floated there, waiting for something to happen. Waiting for awareness to take over. She thought she needed to go somewhere or to do something but, waiting there in the darkness, she didn't know what it was. Someone would come and tell her, sooner or later.

She awoke several times from restless dreams. The kind of dreams she had when she was overtired, sleeping in an unfamiliar place and hypervigilant about the dangers around her.

Nothing seemed right.

It was a long time before she woke up and thought fuzzily that it was probably time to get up. She wasn't supposed to be asleep. She had a job to do.

She sat up slowly, cramped in the egg-shaped pod. There wasn't room to sit up all the way. Maybe there was room for a dwarf, but not for a human adult. Starlight moved beside her and made a noise of protest. If he wanted to sleep, then it was probably the middle of the day. She had slept through the rest of the day and the night and it was day again. Reg rubbed her face, trying to recall all that had happened the day before. She didn't know whether to be happy that her quest had succeeded and they had been able to unmake Calliopia's blade, or to be mourning the powers she had lost to Corvin. She wasn't even sure yet what she had lost. She still retained some of her gifts. Her head didn't have that echoing silence that she'd experienced when he had taken all of her powers away the first time. There were still voices there—noises, impressions, impulses. All of the stuff that she normally had to block out in order to focus on just one thing.

"What's in my head?" she muttered to herself or to Starlight. "What's still in there?"

Starlight stood and stretched, arched his back sharply and shivered all over. He made a squeaking yawn and closed his mouth again, licking his lips.

"Time for something to eat?" Reg asked.

He pawed at the exit to the pod and managed to trigger some sensor so that the door opened. Reg followed him out and looked around.

The sleeping chamber looked just the same as it had before—no way to tell whether it was day or night. Reg pulled her phone out to look at it, but the screen remained blank. She had let it run out of power. She would have to ask the dwarfs about a charging station. With all of the technology they had, they were bound to have something available.

There was no one else around.

Reg felt slightly disgruntled. What if she had needed someone from her company? Why wasn't there someone around to keep an eye on her, at least?

She supposed it didn't matter anymore. If Corvin had taken her powers, then they no longer had to protect her from him. And he would no longer be hanging around looking for the opportunity. It was the perfect solution to her problems with him. Just let him have what he wanted.

Reg wandered into the cafeteria. She might be hungry or thirsty. She hadn't been sweating as profusely as the dwarfs near the forge, but she had probably lost a good amount of water and should drink if she wanted to feel better. She took a couple of wrong doors before she found the right one. It might help if the dwarfs had English signs instead of dwarf runes to mark the routes.

She found the cafeteria again and walked in.

The conversations in the room stopped. Reg looked around. There were no dwarfs this time. The only people there were her company. All of the humans and Ruan too, whom she hadn't seen since they got there.

He smiled at her tentatively. Reg couldn't help smiling back at the childish, cheerful face. She couldn't resist it. People were programmed to respond to children's faces. Ruan waved her over, as if Reg might not know where they were. When Reg got there, he greeted her in his clear, prepubescent voice.

"Reg Rawlins, great sorceress, unmaker of the evil blade!"

Reg rolled her eyes. "I wasn't the one who unmade it. That was Gwythr."

"He could not unmake it without you. Even with Davyn Smithy. They needed the great Reg Rawlins for the unmaking."

"And then I nearly blew up the forge. You're lucky I didn't detonate this whole mountain."

"A great sorceress!" Ruan agreed.

"No, that's not a good thing!"

But Ruan was delighted with the results and wouldn't accept her attempts to play down her accomplishment.

Reg slid into one of the empty seats. She rubbed her temples. "I could really use some water."

Damon got up and went to one of the cupboards. Reg hadn't been able to memorize where everything was, but he went directly to the refrigerator that held the water.

He pulled out a couple of bottles and gave them both to her. "How are you feeling?" he asked tentatively.

Reg ignored the question for the moment. She cracked open one of the bottles and took a long drag on it. The water was so cold it was almost freezing, and it felt good going down. She really was thirsty.

She looked at Davyn, the hood of his cloak down, looking casual and relaxed. No sign he knew how close he had come to destruction. Reg dropped her eyes to her water bottle, not looking at Corvin.

"Regina…" he started.

She ignored him.

"Why don't you just leave her alone?" Damon snapped. "Haven't you done enough?"

"I didn't take all of her gifts," Corvin said in an overly-patient voice, sounding like he had probably explained this a dozen times already while she was asleep. "I only took some of her power, and most of that I funneled to Davyn, so he could help stabilize her. It was the only way to keep her from destroying the forge."

Damon made a noise of disgust and disbelief.

"She asked for my help. She gave permission."

Reg took several more gulps of her icy water.

"Ask Reg. Tell him, won't you? They think I took advantage of you."

Reg glanced in his direction, but didn't look at his face. She could feel him trying to assess her, sneaking in at the corners of her brain, trying to get a glimpse of how she was.

"My head hurts too much. I don't know what he did or didn't take," Reg said. "I can barely put two thoughts together. I don't have the strength for... anything else."

"You see?" Damon demanded, his comment directed to Davyn. "He did more than help her out. He took for himself. He went totally against the rules of the community—"

"I was there," Davyn said. "I don't know where _you_ were, but I was right there. She did yield to him. I heard it with my own ears. There is nothing I can do about it."

"She was in dire straits. And she didn't give him permission to take her gifts, just to help her control them."

"There wasn't any distinction made. And that isn't the way it works. She yielded to him, knowing full well that he could take everything. Yes, she was in dire straits, but it doesn't matter <u>why</u> she said yes. She made a contract with him. She wanted him to drain her power."

Damon opened his mouth to argue.

"I was there. She made a contract. Of her own free will. He didn't charm her. He didn't influence her."

Corvin smirked and folded his arms across his chest. Reg took another swallow of her water.

"How are you feeling?" Davyn asked Reg, focusing his attention on her. "You're pretty pale."

"That's my natural complexion. Redheads."

"You're not answering the question."

"I don't know. Honestly. I'm still too muddled to answer that."

Davyn accepted this. "You really did an amazing job."

"Yeah. Just about exploding everything."

"You're still a toddler in your fire casting experience. I should have foreseen that you wouldn't be able to control it at the forge. I was... arrogant to think that I would be able to direct your abilities."

Reg rolled her eyes. Ever since she had gotten to Black Sands, she had been hearing about how unusual her powers were. She had never even known that she had powers, had suppressed them all her life in order to be able to get along in her foster homes; then suddenly everyone was telling her how powerful she was.

She was starting to think that maybe it wasn't such a good thing.

Maybe it would have been better if all she had was a little bit of psychic ability. Then she could earn a living doing readings and acting as a medium, and wouldn't keep getting mixed up in magic that was so much bigger than she could handle.

So it was a good thing that Corvin had taken whatever he did. As long as he left her enough ability to eke out a living, that was all she cared about. Corvin wouldn't keep chasing her. She wouldn't have to perform magic beyond her ability. She could settle below the radar and not have any magical beings or objects seeking her out.

She held her head, thinking morose thoughts and sipping her water.

Ruan leaned close to Reg, looking into her face, his eyes wide. "When go we home?"

"Yeah... home. As soon as we can, I guess. No need to stick around here."

"We will need to talk to Gwythr before we leave," Davyn advised. "Get the reforged blade from him."

"We need it?"

"No telling. Might need to have it to heal Calliopia fully."

Reg sighed.

"And it is protocol to see that it has been remade and to thank them for the work."

"It isn't like I don't know it's been remade." Reg had been able to see and feel the shift when her fire had overcome the evil spell over the dagger.

"That's the way it's done."

Reg nodded her acceptance. "Do we have to wait? Is he sleeping?"

"I'll find out." Davyn pushed himself up from the table. "We should get an early start if we can."

"Is it early?" Reg looked at the blank face of her phone again.

"Well, relatively speaking. Better to leave earlier rather than later." Davyn looked closely at each member of the company before walking away. Reg closed her eyes, still feeling drained and burned out.

"Burned out?" Corvin said with a chuckle.

"Get out of my head, Hunter."

He didn't look embarrassed to have been caught where he shouldn't have been. He just shook his head, smiling.

CHAPTER 41

There was to be a ceremony. Pomp and all that. Reg just wanted to leave without worrying about all of the formalities. She offered to sit in the car while the rest of the company stayed behind to finish the necessary tasks. But apparently, that was not an option.

So she ate and drank what she could to get her physical strength back. Then she sat in a comfy chair in the main hall, quickly falling back asleep or into a trance while the preparations went on around her. Maybe when she woke up again, she would be better. Everything would be back to normal, or as normal as they could be for her.

Reg opened her eyes and looked around. "Nico! Does anyone know where Nico is?"

Davyn was close by. He looked around, shaking his head. "I keep forgetting about the cats. They seem like they can take care of themselves well enough."

Corvin snorted.

Reg blinked sleepily and looked at him. "What?"

"They can look after themselves? Down here? You really don't know anything about dwarfs, do you?"

Reg rubbed her eyes. "No. I think I made that pretty clear. I don't know anything about them. That's why you and the others are here. What does that have to do with the cats?"

"Dwarfs are not exactly vegetarian."

"Not…" Reg trailed off. She was accustomed to the fairies and the gnomes, who would not eat flesh, and came to think that all of the friendlier magical races

587

were the same. Not pixies, sirens, or mermaids, of course; they made it pretty clear that they were carnivores.

But she had seen the dwarfs' kitchen. Lots of junk food and convenience stuff. It was an omnivorous diet, to be sure, but it wasn't like they were hunting. They just ordered in what they wanted and kept it in the fridges. "I guess I know that, but… that doesn't mean they would do anything to the cats, does it? They're not exactly hunter-gatherers anymore."

"Don't assume a race's nature can be changed as quickly as all this," Corvin motioned to the electric lights and other modern conveniences. "A hundred years ago, they would still steal away the children of unprepared travelers."

And she knew that he didn't mean that they would steal them to keep as their own, like the fairies.

Reg gulped. "Why didn't you say something? You knew we were bringing the cats here, why didn't you tell me they might be in danger?"

Corvin shrugged. "I didn't care."

Reg pulled Starlight closer to her. "Star? Do you know where Nico is? I thought you guys would stay together. Did... something happen?"

Starlight rubbed against her, purring. Despite her concern over what Corvin had said, she didn't get anything other than calm, reassuring feelings from Starlight. He was doing the best he could to tell her that there was nothing to worry about. Reg held him close.

"Okay. He's okay. Everything is fine."

"You see?" Corvin nodded toward Reg as he spoke to Davyn. "I told you I didn't take all of her powers. She can still communicate with the cat."

Reg looked down at Starlight. She could feel his feelings. She wasn't just empathetic; she could feel him. And she had been able to even right after Corvin had siphoned off her powers. She'd felt him close by before she had seen him.

"Yeah. I guess I can."

Davyn nodded, his eyes serious. He was worried about her, but he refrained from asking her again if she was okay or was able to tell him how much Corvin had stolen from her.

Just thinking about it made Reg's head throb more. She closed her eyes and leaned back into the comfy chair again and tried to make it all go away. But of course, it didn't.

Even as she dozed there waiting, she could hear more and more people gathering in the great hall. That was what it was for. A big gathering place for a lot of people when they wanted to make an announcement or start a celebration. Maybe that was where they had assembled for the old king's funeral or the new king's coronation.

Reg opened her eyes, rubbed them tiredly, and looked around.

Something was different about the dwarfs.

There were still more men than there were women and children. And they still seemed to be the same, looking strangely outdated in their geekwear. But something about the women had changed. Reg studied them, trying to get her brain working. What had changed?

"The braids," she said finally, with dawning comprehension. She looked around. Every one of the dwarf women she could see had a head full of box braids. Tiny braids hung around the head of every dwarf woman and girl child in the place. Reg looked around at her company and singled out Ruan.

"Did you teach them how to do that?"

Ruan shook his head. His eyes were wide and innocent. Why would a boy be teaching women how to braid their hair like that? But Reg sensed something else beneath his bland expression. A certain amount of pride and humor.

She narrowed her eyes at him. "What?"

"I did not teach them," he asserted. "I did all of the braids."

"You...!" Reg looked around her in wonder. She knew how long it took to do a full head of the tiny braids. She'd had it done a few times, and it had meant sitting for hours, even if she had more than one woman working on it at a time. "How could you have done all of these braids in the time we've been here?"

"Piskies have nimble fingers."

"Wow!" Reg blew out her breath. "Do they ever. Why don't you guys make your own clothing, or sell crafts at bazaars? Or open up a hairdressing shop? You could make all kinds of money with your weaving and braiding."

Ruan made a face. "Piskies do not work for humans," he said, shaking his head. "Piskies work for no one."

"You could make a lot of money."

"Not need human money. And we do make clothing," he added, stroking the front of his worn and patched shirt. "We make all clothing. But we treat it with respect. Not like humans, who throw them out when they get wet."

"Well, not when they get wet," Reg corrected. "Not if it's just water. Unless you're talking silk or suede. But when it gets stained or torn…"

Ruan shook his head in disgust. "You should treat with respect. Always."

"We just… see things differently. We want to keep our clothes looking nice. For them to be bright and clean and not torn or patched. Pixies… want to make them last for a long time."

"Yes."

Reg let her eyes wander over the crowd again. So many women with braids. Ruan couldn't have had time to eat or sleep. He must have been braiding the whole time they had been there.

The dwarfs were beginning to assemble on the dais in the center of the hall. Reg had begged out of sitting there herself, not wanting to be the center of attention. They could do their little ceremony, and she would participate, but she didn't want to be up there on display the whole time.

Gwythr had a seat of honor. So did Brimir. She saw another dwarf with an emblem on his shirt and assumed that he was part of the royal household. The dwarfs all looked old, in the same way that the pixies all looked young, and it had the same effect of masking their true age and relationships. The other dwarf with Brimir might have been his brother or his father. Reg assumed that if it were the king, he would be wearing a crown of some kind. Even if they didn't wear the heavy iron crown that a dwarf on TV might wear, they were such lovers of metalwork that he would be bound to have some kind of crown.

There were a few other dwarfs who Reg thought had been with the initial negotiating party. A couple that she might have seen in the smithy.

Brimir stood up, raising his hands, and the room went immediately silent.

"People of the mountain," Brimir called out. His voice was amplified and came from speakers mounted all through the great hall. There were cameras on him as well, broadcasting his face onto several screens high up on the cavern walls. Reg shook her head. They did like their toys!

"People of the mountain. It has been a great day for our kingdom."

A cheer went up from the spectators.

"We have been graced with the presence of Reg Rawlins, the great sorceress."

Another cheer. A few of the dwarfs turned toward her, some of them pointing. Reg rolled her eyes and stared at a spot high up the wall opposite, trying to ignore the stares and whispers. Reg Rawlins, the great sorceress. They would think differently if they knew how her head was feeling. Reg Rawlins the great fake. The great uncontrollable toddler. The great threat to their survival.

"The great Reg Rawlins brought us a dagger beyond compare. A dagger forged centuries ago and imbued with magic that is no longer known. We, of ourselves, have lost the knowledge of how to unmake such a great blade. Many generations ago, we had the knowledge; we had the dwarfs and the forges deep in the earth that could have unmade it. But today, many of these things have been lost."

A murmur went through the crowd.

"We must take care not to lose any more of our legacy. Without the aid of Davyn Smithy, son of Harold Smithy, and of Reg Rawlins herself, we would not have been able to molten the blade and to remove the evil that had been done to it."

There were a few shouts out from the audience. Reg couldn't tell what they were saying. She gathered that Brimir was making a political statement about their education system or about their foray into the modern world of electronic conveniences. And not everyone agreed with him.

"But with the great power of Davyn and Reg, we were able to unmake the evil blade, and to reforge it into something magnificent."

Reg watched him with interest. No one had told her yet what they had done with the metal from the dagger. She had seen Gwythr reshape it and work over it intently, but she hadn't been close enough or been able to see from the angle she watched from in the smithy what he had made. Another knife? Reg shuddered. She didn't want to take it from him if it was another knife. She couldn't go home with a weapon, back to Calliopia's home. She couldn't take a new weapon into that house and give it to the fairy girl in hopes that it would heal her instead of hurting her this time. She didn't trust it.

"Would Reg Rawlins please come to the stand," Brimir called out.

His voice echoed around the cavern. His face watched Reg expectantly from all of the screens. Reg reluctantly got to her feet. She was still shaky. She didn't want to ask any of the men to escort her, but she worried whether she would be able to make it to Brimir on her own.

She had walked from her pod to the feast on her own. And from the cafeteria to the great hall. She could make it the short distance to the dais and up the few steps to Brimir.

There was thunderous applause as she walked to the dais. Even if it did go on for far too long because of her slow, tired pace. Reg climbed the stairs with care, trying to take them a full step at a time instead of in half-steps like an old woman. She used the rail and dragged herself to the top. She looked around, a forced smile pasted on her face, knowing that the cameras would broadcast it in all of its fifty feet of glory across all of the screens.

"Thank you, Brimir, son of King Fraeg," Reg said formally, and then wondered what else she should say. Most ceremonies required lots of compliments, over the top. "It has been a great honor to be here with you… to see the skill of your smithies…"

He scowled at that. Reg tried to recover. "And the beauty of your home, your people, the majesty of your royalty."

That was laying it on thick, and Brimir brightened, nodding his agreement.

"I have never been anywhere so remarkable," Reg went on. "Your kingdom here is so… beautiful, modern, and enchanting."

There was more applause from the audience, people even shouting out to her.

Reg looked at Brimir expectantly. It was his turn. Time for whatever was next on the agenda. She wasn't big on making speeches.

"Reg Rawlins," Brimir announced, pointing to her. More applause. It was getting irritating.

Reg made a gesture toward her seat, raising her eyebrows. Brimir shook his head.

"We need to present you with the reforged blade."

"Oh. Great, yeah. I mean, thanks."

There was a musical interlude, during which a small parade of dwarfs marched across the hall, a small chest held by one of the dwarfs in the middle. They arranged themselves on the dais, which was now becoming rather crowded, and the chest was presented to Brimir.

Brimir made eyes at the cameras, nodding and smiling, lapping up all of the adulation. He reached over and opened the chest. Reg could see that it was lined with red satin. Brimir made another motion, encouraging more clapping, then finally reached into the chest and removed the bit of metal that he was to present to Reg.

Reg looked at her company, worried about doing the wrong thing. Corvin made a small downward motion with his hands, and Reg clearly felt his message in her head.

<u>Kneel</u>.

Reg was tired of standing, but wasn't sure kneeling would be any better. And getting back up was going to be an issue. She looked at Brimir. He waited. Reg sighed and lowered herself down to her knees in front of Brimir.

She didn't like it. Her ego rebelled at the act of kneeling before someone, especially someone who had little discernible magic and only seemed to be a figurehead to the people. Or worse yet, only the son of a figurehead. She tried to close these thoughts out of her mind. She didn't want them to show in her expression as her face was blown up on the big screens. She bowed her head to hide her face from the cameras and the crowd.

Brimir opened his arms wider and reached around her neck. At first she was afraid he was going to hug her. Then she realized that he had a pendant on a chain and was fastening it around her neck. She looked down at the pendant.

It was in the shape of a cat. A heavy, solid piece of silver pounded into shape and painstakingly carved in great detail.

"Oh, it's beautiful," Reg said, admiring it. She wanted to hold it in her hand and turn it around for a closer look, but she was afraid they wouldn't like her touching it. Even if it was meant to be hers, this was a carefully orchestrated show, and she didn't want to do anything to mess it up. "I've never seen anything like it."

Brimir raised his hands, and the dwarfs clapped and clapped. When the applause finally petered out, Reg thought that was the end of it. They would sing some closing song and she could go sit down again. Or better yet, get into Damon's truck, and he would drive her home.

But there was another marching song. Reg looked around tiredly to see what was going on. Was the party carrying the box just going to march out again? But they stayed where they were, with no indication that they were going anywhere.

There was movement at the other end of the chamber. Reg watched, trying to see what was going on. It seemed to be another escort, this one pulling a child in a wagon.

She watched the wagon get closer and closer, everyone pressing close to get a look at it. Reg blinked a few times, but couldn't see through the crowds that thronged him.

Eventually, the group wound their way up to the dais. Reg could see a small, misshapen dwarf on the wagon. Some kind of royalty? But they already had Brimir and his brother or father on the stand. Was there some kind of deformed crown prince? The people kept cheering.

"Reg Rawlins, great sorceress, brought us more than a priceless blade to be unmade," Brimir announced.

Reg looked over at Corvin and the others, raising an eyebrow, widening her eyes.

She had brought them something else? She hadn't brought them anything. Or did they mean the assassin's blade and the bracelet they had referred to as a bauble? Reg should have known that it was worth more than anyone had let on. Corvin should have told her what its real value was. But she had been left in the dark once more.

The dark shape on the wagon leapt off, its movements vaguely familiar. Reg couldn't get a good look through all of the spectators. Then the black shape was making its way to her. Reg prepared to bow lower. She'd seen <u>The King and I</u>. She knew that her head shouldn't be higher than the royalty. And the new visitor was clearly as royal as Brimir.

CHAPTER 42

And then she saw him clearly for the first time.

Not a misshapen dwarf. Not even close. Four legs and a long tail. Much of his form hidden in metal plates of armor. A pure black cat.

"Nico!"

Nico made a soft meow of greeting as he hopped up the stairs to her. Reg looked the armor over. It had clearly been custom made. Large spikes were extending from his back like a dinosaur.

He made his way over to Reg and sat down, head lifted regally.

Reg didn't bow down to him. Her first instinct was to scold him, but that wouldn't be a good thing to do in front of Brimir and the audience, who apparently thought he was some kind of Egyptian god.

"Nico. Wow. Look at that armor," Reg said lamely.

"There is a helmet too," Brimir advised. "But he doesn't like it when we put it on."

"Uh… yeah. Cats don't normally like it when you put something on their heads. Mind you… I've never seen one who wore armor, either."

"You like it? It is specially made for him."

"Yes, I can see that. It's a perfect fit. Although… he's going to grow, and I don't know how big he'll get…"

"We will make him a new suit whenever he outgrows it."

"Uh… okay." Reg didn't tell him that she hadn't been planning to return, and she doubted any of the dwarfs wanted to travel all the way to Florida to find her and put a new suit of armor on a cat.

Brimir beamed at Reg proudly. Then she remembered his words. That Reg had brought him something of great value. Nico. They thought that she was giving them Nico.

Reg's head whirled. She tried to keep her head steady with her hand braced against her temple. "Uh... we need to talk. We have to talk; I didn't..."

There were more trumpets, more marching music, and the dwarfs who had brought out the pendant lined back up and marched out again. Reg closed her eyes, trying to figure out how to talk to them.

* * *

She wasn't sure how she got back to her feet, got off the dais, or reached her company again. She was driven to do what she had to do, but her head spun dizzily, and she didn't know what she was going to do. Start a war by insisting that Nico wasn't for them and taking him away?

When she was reunited with the company, Reg turned immediately on Corvin, angry.

"They're going to eat him?" she demanded. "Isn't that what you told me? It's not safe for the cats because they'll get eaten? What the heck is happening here?"

"It would appear... that I misjudged."

"I would say so!" Reg snapped. She didn't know why she was angry at him. Maybe she was just looking for a place to vent her emotion, and it didn't have anything to do with Corvin. "You got me all worried about what might have happened to Nico, and it's like... they've made him an object of worship."

"I can't say I'm aware of any lore that would indicate that dwarfs worship cats. Or venerate them in any way. This is a first for me. And I've made quite a broad study of the culture."

"What am I going to do? They think that I brought him as a gift for them. Or maybe they think that as long as they claim I brought him as a gift, I won't be able to fight back and they can have whatever they want. But I can't just leave Nico here."

"Why not?"

"Because! He's my cat!" After she said it, Reg pressed her lips tightly together. In fact, he wasn't her cat. She couldn't even say that he was Francesca's cat and she needed to get him back for her or to get her permission. Francesca had taken it upon herself to see that the kattakyns found suitable homes around the world, but she had never intended to keep any of them.

Reg had grown attached to Nico, but she had never meant to keep him. Just to train him up so that he would behave himself and could find a home where they wouldn't immediately kick him out or send him to the pound.

And she had found a new home for him. Or a new home had found him. Nico was still sitting regally up on the dais as various people approached him to admire him or speak a few words to him. Every now and then he would change his position, stretching or yawning or arching his back. He would bare his teeth or raise his chin when someone new approached, giving them a pose so that they could take pictures with their phones.

He was lapping up all of the attention.

But how would they like him when he decided to act up? The first time that he climbed the curtains or attacked someone's feet?

Of course... there were no windows, so there were no curtains to climb. She was sure he could find something equally annoying to do in the dwarf kingdom, though she wasn't sure what it would be.

One of the dwarfs approached Nico and thrust a sword toward him. Reg started forward with a cry. But Nico was instantly in the air and avoided it. He skittered around the dais at a breakneck pace, startling everyone who was still there, and ended up jumping at the face of the dwarf who had poked at him with the sword. The dwarf let out a bellow and jumped back, ending up sprawled on his back. He landed with a crash and for a minute lay there stunned. Then he started to yell in dwarfish.

There was wild clapping from the audience. Cheers. Encouragement for Nico to do more. One of the other dwarfs bent down and plucked up the first one's sword, and took a slicing swipe toward Nico. Reg was sure he was going to be hurt this time, but Nico crouched below the blade, then leaped in the air, and then after a complicated ballet, jumped on the dwarf. More cheering, more clapping.

"What a warrior!" bellowed Gwythr, who had come over to talk to the company and was standing close to Reg. "It is very rare to breed a warrior cat. They are very difficult to find."

"A warrior cat?"

"Is he not wonderful?" Gwythr said admiringly. "He embodies all of the qualities of a true dwarf warrior. Tough, light on his feet, graceful, with an instinct for attack. He is very vigilant. Very smart."

"Well, yes, he is." Reg thought of the numerous times that he had attacked her feet when she had walked past him. Was the dwarf really comparing her naughty kattakyn to a warrior?

Could it be that his bad attitude and unwillingness to listen was just a warrior nature? Something that the dwarfs saw as good?

"He is, indeed," Reg repeated, nodding.

And what about Reg? She too had been the bad kid, hypervigilant, always getting into trouble for the things that she did and the things that she didn't do. Was she just a bad fit for the society she had been raised in?

Maybe if she had grown up in a community that was more like the dwarfs', that would have been a good thing. They would have admired her and thought she was exceptional, instead thinking there was something wrong with her, something that they had to train or beat out of her.

"What are you going to do?" Corvin asked.

"I… don't know. I guess… I need to find out what Nico wants."

CHAPTER 43

It was time to go, and although Reg had been impatient to go home and to see Calliopia, to see that she was improving and would be able to heal from her injury, she didn't want to go. Mostly, she couldn't believe that she was going to leave Nico there. How could she even be considering leaving her kitten there with the dwarfs? A people that Corvin claimed might even eat him?

That was nonsense. They weren't going to eat him. Maybe they had preyed at one time on human children and stragglers, but cats seemed to be another story altogether. They had made Nico his own armor.

You didn't do that for your dinner.

Nico himself had reassured Reg that he'd found his place with the dwarfs and fully intended to stay there.

She had tried to talk him out of it, to remind him how much fun he'd had with the humans and to tell him about the loving home that he could go to if he went back with her, but he was not interested. He had lived the first part of his kattakyn life with the humans, and they did not give him the stimulation and veneration that the dwarfs did.

While some humans would wrestle with him for a minute or two, they were always jumping away or getting after him when he deployed his teeth and claws, the natural weapons he was intended to use. They always acted like he was a bad cat for biting or clawing. How could it be wrong for him to use the weapons he had been born with? Humans and even dwarfs were not born with weapons, but had to fashion their own. A warrior cat was different. And Nico was a warrior cat.

He loved the armor that the dwarfs had made with him. They would play with him and train him to be a better fighter. Maybe someday, they would go to war with another dwarf kingdom or another race of magical creatures, and he would go to war with them, marching side-by-side with the dwarfs to battle.

He didn't have any desire to go back to the humans and be coddled and sleep away long days in a sunny window. That wasn't in his nature. He would still need some time in the sun or cuddling up to a warm body at night, but the dwarfs would make sure he got that too. They knew how to take proper care of a warrior cat.

Reg didn't want to hurt Nico's dignity by too much cuddling or a teary goodbye, so she did her best to stay stoic and not give her feelings away. She scratched his ears, avoiding his claws when he decided he'd had enough of that. She told him a dignified goodbye. It wasn't until after Damon had driven the truck away that she allowed the sniffles and tears to appear. Not too much. She didn't want to appear to be a total wuss, but she couldn't help a few teardrops.

Starlight cuddled up to her, rubbing her face and making little murmuring meows to comfort her. She gave him all of the cuddles that she'd wanted to give Nico on her departure, closing her eyes and trying to figure out how she was going to explain it all to Francesca.

"He'll be okay there," Damon assured Reg. "Forget about what Hunter said. He's always trying to stir the pot. He doesn't know half of what he would have you think he knows about dwarfs. Obviously. I mean, how could he not know their tradition of warrior cats?"

Reg rolled her eyes and dabbed at them with a fuzzy tissue pulled out of her purse. "I know… it's just… I'm going to miss Nico. He was always a pain in the neck. Or in the legs. But he had his own little personality and he was a lot of fun to have around. If he was chasing something other than me. Cats are so cute when they hunt and play…"

"If he's a warrior cat, then he never would have settled down enough for a human home. You wouldn't want him to be miserable."

"No. But… I thought that I'd be able to train him to get along and be useful to a practitioner. I thought he'd be going to a home where I could write and see how he was doing, at least."

"Didn't you get Gwythr's email address?"

Reg nodded. "Yeah," she admitted. "I just hope he answers it. The dwarfs do seem a little… scattered sometimes."

"They have the technology. I'm sure he'll be happy to answer emails from outside the kingdom."

Reg blew her nose. "I hope so. I'd like to be able to keep track of Nico and know how he's doing."

"He'll be much happier there than he would have been with a witch or warlock."

"Yeah. I guess so."

Reg sniffled and tried to stop the tears. Of course everything Damon said was true, but that didn't stop her from feeling sad at their separation.

"Is it time?" Ruan asked from the back seat.

"Time for what?" Reg asked, looking over the seat into the back of the truck's cab.

"Time for juice," Ruan said, eyes glittering.

"We're not having energy drinks this time."

Damon looked sideways at Reg. "Not yet, maybe," he said. "But I'm going to need something to keep me awake when you pass out."

"Then have a conversation with Ruan. He'll keep you awake."

"Juice! Juice!" Ruan insisted, kicking the back of the seat like a fractious toddler.

"Not now. Maybe later."

"Piskies like energy drink juice."

"Yeah, they sure do," Reg agreed. "But you're only getting half a can this time. Pixies on caffeine are not fun!"

"They are!" Ruan disagreed. "Caffeine is a good herb for piskies."

Reg rolled her eyes at Damon and laughed.

CHAPTER 44

The trip back to Black Sands seemed to go faster than the journey to the dwarf mountain. Maybe because they knew where they were going and were not driving in the pitch black toward an unknown destination. They left on the faint gravel track in the daylight, so they were long past it when the sun went down. Damon turned on some loud music in the hopes of improving Reg's spirits and, despite the volume and the heavy beat, she quickly fell asleep. She was still recovering from the energy she had expended at the forge and all that Corvin had taken. The ceremony in the great hall had not been long, but it had still been tiring, and she needed more rest than she had gotten in the sleeping pod and dozing in her chair waiting for the pomp to begin.

She awoke several times along the way, mostly when they made a quick pit stop to load up on more snacks or to eliminate the drinks already consumed. Reg had a few bites to eat, but she needed sleep more than food and didn't want the caffeine. She welcomed the chance to sleep and, between energy drinks and Ruan, Damon was doing just fine staying awake during the nighttime portion of their trip.

Eventually, they made it back to Black Sands and the fairy mansion. It was the early hours of the morning before dawn, the sky not yet lightening. Reg dragged herself out of the truck and rubbed her eyes and face, trying to wake herself up completely. She would be expected to be awake and look like she knew what she was doing. Calliopia's parents would want details of what had happened when they went to see the dwarfs, the details of the unmaking and the ceremony that followed.

Or maybe they wouldn't. Maybe all they would care about was seeing their daughter on the road to recovery, and they wouldn't ask any questions about how it had all worked out.

Corvin's car pulled in behind Damon's truck. Reg hadn't expected them to come to the mansion. Corvin certainly wouldn't be allowed inside. It was surprising that the fairies hadn't placed some kind of ward to keep him off of the property altogether. But she supposed all they had to do was keep him out of the house.

"What's up?" Reg asked. "I don't think they'll let you in."

"I'm sure they won't," Corvin agreed dryly. "I'm not trying to get in. I just thought… you might need some help with the fairy girl." He rolled his eyes. "Not that I'm exactly onboard with healing other magical creatures who are only going to cause further problems, but…"

"How can you help?"

"I can do this," he offered, lifting his hands and aiming a warm flow of energy toward her.

Reg had to admit that it felt good. She needed all of the strength she could get if she were to be able to do anything for Calliopia. And she just wasn't sure what she was going to be able to do. Maybe she had already accomplished everything she could, and the rest would be up to Calliopia and her parents and their fairy magic.

Corvin gave her strength for a few minutes, then dropped his hands and shrugged. "Time for you to see what you can do."

They went to the door and rang the bell. No butler was waiting for them at the door in the middle of the night. They had not called to say what time they would be arriving. Better to let everyone sleep while they could, Reg thought. Though whether Mrs. Papillon would actually sleep while her daughter was in such a dire situation, Reg didn't know.

The butler eventually appeared at the door, not yawning in their faces, but blinking owlishly, definitely having been awakened by the bell. He was not in pajamas or a dressing gown, but he might have had some magical help to look so well-groomed when he had just gotten out of bed.

Reg began to lead the way to Calliopia's room, but Ruan dashed ahead of her, bouncing quickly up the stairs and out of sight. Reg supposed it was fitting that he should be the first one back at her side.

Reg trudged up the stairs, not in a hurry to get out of breath or to feel Calliopia's pain. Maybe with what Corvin had taken from her, she would no longer be able to feel the fairy's pain or to enter her mind. Reg had been worrying over what she would or wouldn't be able to do once she got there. What good would it do if she had broken the spell on the fairy blade, if she couldn't follow up with the healing that Calliopia needed?

The strength that Corvin had given her made it easy to get up the stairs. She didn't have to struggle.

And she didn't need to worry about not being able to feel Calliopia's pain anymore. If that were a prerequisite to being able to heal her, then Reg didn't have to worry. She wasn't halfway up the stairs, and the ache in her side began. They still had her on painkillers, so it wasn't the excruciating pain that Reg had felt before, the blinding pain that made it almost impossible for her to concentrate. But it still hurt. Reg took a few steadying breaths as she went up the stairs.

"Okay?" Damon asked.

Reg breathed out slowly. "Yeah, okay so far."

He followed her without bothering her further for details. There if she needed him, if she found she couldn't get up the stairs on her own. Out of the way so that she could concentrate and not be distracted by him at the critical moment.

Reg finally made it to Calliopia's room. Mr. and Mrs. Papillon were both awake, keeping vigil by her side. Ruan had climbed up on the bed. He bent over Calliopia, whispering to her, touching her face and hair as he gazed into her face. It was, at least, peaceful and serene rather than a grimace of pain. He looked at Reg as she came into the room.

"Come see. What think you?" he asked.

"Give me a minute."

He waited impatiently, saying nothing but clearly on tenterhooks as he watched her. Reg sat down on the chair Mrs. Papillon vacated, trying to settle and focus herself. Ruan withdrew, moving out of the way. Reg had left Starlight in the truck, but she wished that she had him in her lap to boost whatever remained of her abilities.

She took Calliopia's hand and reached out with her mind.

"Callie... Calliopia. Remember me?"

It was more difficult than it should have been. Reg had shared thoughts with Calliopia many times in the past, sometimes over great distances. It should have been easy to slip back into her consciousness. Reg didn't know whether the drugs were blocking her ability to communicate with Calliopia, or whether Corvin had taken some of those powers from her and she was operating on only a fraction of what she used to have.

"Callie. Please. Make place for me. How are you? Can you hear me?"

The answer was slow and sluggish, but it was there, at least. "Where have you been?"

"I went to the dwarf mountain. To unmake the blade."

There was a flash of anger. "It is my blade."

"It was the blade that hurt you. It had to be unmade if you are going to get better."

"But it was mine." A keen, poignant feeling of loss washed over Reg. She was startled by the strength of it. How could a possession, a weapon, mean so much to Calliopia? Especially one that had already betrayed her, nearly ending her life?

"Here," Reg reached up and lifted the necklace over her head. It was large enough that she didn't need to undo the clasp. She reached over Calliopia's head with it and slid the chain down behind her head, settling the necklace into place. She centered the cat pendant and kept her hand over it for a moment. "Here is what was remade. You can keep it with you, but it can no longer harm you."

Calliopia made a noise. An audible noise. Reg felt her twitch, and braced herself. She had no idea what was coming. A seizure? Death throes? Had she just sealed Calliopia's fate? The dwarfs had promised that the evil influence on the metal had been broken. They said there was no more danger now that the blade had been remade into something that was not a weapon. Had they been wrong?

Calliopia made a couple more noises, but did not seem to be in the grasp of something evil. Reg stroked her hair, sinking deeper once more.

"You see? You can still have it with you. But it cannot harm you any longer."

There was no response. Reg put her hand over the bandage on Calliopia's side. She concentrated, trying to push her heat into the wound. She was not going to light a fire, but Davyn had said that it might do some good. Reg's hand became uncomfortably hot. She eased back a little.

"Heal, Calliopia. Now that the evil is gone, you can heal. Knit the flesh back together. Use your fairy strength to overcome it. You can wake up and see Ruan and your parents. See what the dwarfs made of your knife."

The warmth on her hand felt good. The pain in her side eased. Calliopia's thoughts still came slowly, but maybe that was the effect of the painkillers.

"My boy."

"Yes. Ruan is here. He's waiting for you. When you wake up, you can see him."

Calliopia's head turned slightly. Her eyelids fluttered. Reg watched her. She hadn't wanted to order Calliopia to wake up in case she wasn't ready.

"Where is he?" The words were still inside Calliopia's head, not out loud. Reg motioned to Ruan.

"Come closer. She wants you."

Ruan moved closer to Calliopia. All of his caffeine-induced bounciness was gone. He was very still and quiet.

"Callie. My love." He put his hand in hers, stroking the back of her hand with his thumb. "I am here."

Her eyelids fluttered again, and she was looking at him. Reg choked up at the rush of emotion Calliopia felt for him. She tried to breathe through it and not tear up. The two young lovers gazed at each other, saying nothing, just looking at each other.

Reg withdrew her hand from Calliopia's side. It was feeling good. Still sore, but not as much. Not the blinding pain that it had been the first time Reg had felt it.

She got up off of the chair to give Ruan and Calliopia some space, and looked at Mr. and Mrs. Papillon.

Mrs. Papillon nodded at Reg. "She will heal," she said softly.

"Yes," Reg agreed. "She's on the mend."

"We did not dare hope."

Reg nodded. She was tired. It had been a long, arduous process, but Calliopia was finally on her way to getting better. They had told her that there was no chance of recovery, but she and Ruan and the others had made it happen.

"You'll let him stay with her?" she asked, turning to look back at Ruan, who had climbed onto the bed again in order to embrace Calliopia and hold her close.

"She loves him," Mrs. Papillon observed. And said nothing more. Reg took that to mean that they would let Ruan stay with her until she had recovered.

"Great. I'm going to go now."

They both bowed their heads graciously, and Reg took her leave. Damon followed her out.

"Home?" he asked as they descended the stairs.

"Home," Reg agreed.

EPILOGUE

The next day, Sarah was back from her getaway with the other witches. She looked rested and well, her gray hair a shade lighter than usual, or her face a shade darker. She was dressed as usual in a pastel pantsuit and white sandals, a slightly-overweight, grandmotherly woman Reg had come to rely on.

"Reg!" Sarah looked up from Reg's datebook on the kitchen island when she shuffled out of her bedroom, still in pajamas and cuddling Starlight. "You're a sight for sore eyes. I feel like I've been away for a month instead of just a few days. How are you?"

Sarah studied Reg, her lips compressing into a slight frown.

"You look tired. Haven't you been sleeping well?"

"Just got back from a road trip myself. Things were a little... crazy around here."

"Well, they always are," Sarah pointed out, patting Reg on the shoulder.

Reg didn't know if she meant that life was always crazy, or Reg's life in particular. She suspected the latter.

"What would you like for breakfast? Do you want me to make you some eggs?"

"Oh, you don't have to do that, Sarah," Reg protested, and smothered a yawn. "I can get my own breakfast. There are leftovers in the fridge that I should eat."

"Breakfast is the most important meal of the day. Eggs?"

Starlight gave a vigorous meow, which Sarah took as agreement. "Eggs it is."

Sarah had already started a pot of coffee, which was probably what had brought Reg out of her coma. Reg poured herself a cup. She sat down on the wicker couch, cuddling Starlight while she sipped coffee and tapped on her phone.

Sarah put a plate of eggs and toast on the table for Reg and a bowl of eggs on the floor for Starlight, just as there was a loud knock on the front door of the cottage.

"You eat," Sarah insisted. "I'll see who it is and tell them to go away."

Reg sat down at the table, where she rarely sat to eat, shaking her head. It was nice to have someone looking after her sometimes. She liked Sarah running interference for her. Some of the time.

Despite her words, Sarah would probably let in whoever was at the door. Unless it was Corvin.

"A delivery man," Sarah announced, returning to the table. Reg looked at the box that Sarah set down. "Not Amazon," Sarah commented. "Were you expecting something?"

Not unless it was Nico, having worn out his welcome with the dwarfs, but the box didn't look quite big enough to hold him.

Reg took a couple of bites of the cheesy scrambled eggs Sarah had prepared for her—heavenly—and then used her dinner knife to slice the tape at the top of the box. Starlight left his bowl to jump up on one of the kitchen chairs. He put his paws up on the table, nose quivering as he sniffed to see what had been brought into the house.

He didn't yowl at her or bite her ankles, which was a good sign. It must not be some cursed item or anything that would harm her.

Reg unfolded the flaps of the cardboard box and found another box inside. Wooden, carved with flowers and insects and polished to a shine. It rattled when Reg picked it up. She unlatched the lid and opened it. The chest was filled with glass gemstones. Reg stirred them around.

"I didn't order these."

Sarah bent down to look at them, eyes wide. "I don't think that's something you <u>can</u> order on Amazon."

Thinking of everything the dwarfs had bought off of the online retailer, Reg had her doubts. It seemed like

Amazon had pretty much everything. No reason they wouldn't have crafting supplies.

"Regina," Sarah said seriously. "These are real."

"Real what?"

"These are real gemstones."

Reg frowned, looking at them. They were sparkly and shiny, but she didn't think someone could tell just by glancing at them that they were not glass or even some semi-precious lookalike.

Sarah clearly guessed what Reg was thinking. "I know gemstones, Reg. And I can feel these. I can feel their power."

Reg looked down at the small chest of gems again, baffled. "But how... why...?"

"Who are they from? There must be some card or return address."

Reg stirred the gems around again, then looked inside the shipping box. There wasn't anything else, not even a waybill.

"In the lid." Sarah pointed to the underside of the lid of the wooden box. Reg pulled a thick cream-colored card out of the lid, where it was wedged in tightly. She tried to make out the swooping curves of the elegant cursive letters, but she'd never been good at reading and cursive was something she had not been able to master. She showed it to Sarah.

"The House of Papillon," Sarah read. She sat down abruptly in one of the other chairs. "Maybe you'd better tell me what happened while I was gone."

PREVIEW OF WEB OF NIGHTMARES

Reg looked at the glossy new business cards with satisfaction.

Reg Rawlins

Psychic, Medium, Spiritual Advisor

The cards were thick cardstock with a rich texture and brilliant swirls of color. Nothing like the flimsy black-on-white cards she had first had printed when she arrived in Black Sands. Then she had been destitute, as she always was, on the edge of homelessness, with just a few items of value that she could pawn to survive for the first month or two after getting settled. She'd expected to have to pay first and last month's rent and a damage deposit, and that took a good outlay of cash to start out with. But Bill, the bartender at The Crystal Bowl, had introduced her to Sarah Bishop, an older witch who was looking for a tenant in her guest cottage, and things had fallen nicely into place. The rent was cheap, it was furnished, and Sarah had taken it upon herself to make sure that there was food in the fridge and that Reg had a steady stream of clients for her new psychic services business.

Even then, Reg had needed to scrimp and save, putting money away for the future when she might have to leave town in a hurry. She never knew how long a gig was going to last before everything imploded and she was on the run again.

But Black Sands had been a good find. She had made friends and had a good business going, arguably legitimate. While all of her business literature still stated 'for entertainment purposes only' to avoid accusations of fraud, she had found herself more suited for psychic work than she had ever imagined.

Life in Black Sands was unsettled as she discovered new powers, real-life witches and fairies; a whole new world, both exciting and disturbing.

But for the first time, she had money and could afford to spend a little bit on luxuries. She had taken a couple of the glittery gemstones the fairies had given her to a jeweller to confirm what Sarah had told her—that they were real gemstones and not glass or semiprecious imitations. Real diamonds, emeralds, rubies, and sapphires, and some stones that she hadn't even heard of before. A rich reward for having helped save adolescent fairy Calliopia Papillon from certain death.

Reg ran her fingers through her red box-braids. She still couldn't help feeling like it was all a big mistake. She had been the only one who had believed that she could do something to save Calliopia. The fairies themselves had given up hope. Calliopia's mate had been prepared to dispatch her with the pixie version of euthanasia. All of Reg's friends had said that it was impossible, but in the end, they had helped her out anyway. And she had succeeded.

She supposed that she should probably offer those who had accompanied her to the dwarf mountain a few gems as payment for their part in the quest. She hadn't told anyone about the small chest of jewels she had received, and Sarah had promised to keep it quiet. She didn't want the cottage or the big house getting broken into by someone out to steal the treasure. If Reg's companions ever heard that she had been paid for the trip to the forge, they would probably not be too impressed that she hadn't given them at least some token payment.

She didn't have to tell them how much she had received. She could make it seem like she was dividing it evenly between the members of the company. They wouldn't know the true extent of her newfound wealth.

* * *

There was a crash from across the room, and Reg's first thought was that Nico had knocked something over. It only took her a split-second to remember that they had left the boisterous little cat back with the dwarfs, who had exalted him as a warrior cat.

It was a relief to have Nico out of the house and no longer knocking things over or attacking her with unexpected vigor, but she couldn't help missing the mischievous kattakyn a little and wondering how he was doing in his new home.

She looked across the cottage instead at her own cat, Starlight, who had just crashed into the legs of a side table in the living room. The black and white tuxedo cat was intent on something out of Reg's sight and she knew he was on the hunt. His whole manner had changed from that of a languid, lazy daytime cat to the feral intensity of the nighttime hunter. She moved carefully closer to him to get a glimpse of what he was chasing. Hopefully, just a shadow or a leaf blown in from outside.

A dark, hairy shape scuttled under the wicker couch and Starlight went rocketing after it. Reg couldn't help letting out a little shriek.

"What was that? Get it, Starlight!"

She felt his irritation at her shout. Like he didn't know what he was doing. She could see that he was already on the job.

"What is it?"

Starlight pounced, and Reg heard a crunch.

"Ugh."

Starlight backed out from under the couch and turned toward her. Multiple legs hung from his mouth.

Reg covered her eyes. "Good kitty. Just don't show it to me. Is it dead?" She didn't want to look closely enough to find out, especially if it wasn't and jumped at her when Starlight put it down. "You just go... eat it or whatever and don't make me look at it."

She had an impulse to let Starlight out of the cottage so that he couldn't let whatever it was loose or leave some dead thing in the middle of the floor. But he was an inside cat, and she didn't want to lose him. Anything could happen to him outside. Instead, she retreated. "I'm going to have a bath. Let me know when you're... finished with it."

* * *

In the bathtub, Reg soaked in steaming hot water and thick bubbles, another indulgence that she would never have considered before. She closed her eyes and thought about what else she could do with her newfound wealth. She could afford to move somewhere else and get her own house if she didn't want to live in the little cottage under Sarah's dominion any longer. But it was a comfortable situation —at least most of the time—so she wasn't really tempted to do that. She could travel. Not a road trip like usual, sitting in a cramped car for hours, but an actual cruise or an airplane to Europe or even Australia. She could go places she'd never even dreamed of.

She could visit Erin, her former foster sister, in Tennessee, and show Erin that she'd had actually made good. She'd made more than either of them could ever have expected with her skills. Erin wasn't the only one who could make a living running a small business.

Reg's phone buzzed on the floor beside the tub. Reg picked it up and swiped without looking to see who the caller was.

"Hello?" She felt totally relaxed for once.

"Hello, Regina."

Corvin. Her favorite not-favorite warlock. Even over the phone, his voice sent a shiver down her spine. Nothing like the electricity when they touched or the ability he had to charm or ensorcel his prey, but it was still disconcerting. His voice was smooth and intimate, and the way that he said her name (correctly pronouncing it Reh-JEE-nah, not ree-JI-nah) made her wish—just for an instant—that he was there with her.

"Corvin. What do you want?"

"Is that any way to greet the warlock who helped you to heal Calliopia?"

"You didn't heal her."

"Without me giving you strength when you needed it, and taking it when you were ready to blow up the forge, would she have survived? Would you have?"

He had a point there. Reg might have done most of the work, but he had been there when she had called on him and had stepped in at critical moments to save the day.

"Fine. Did I tell you thank you?" She said it sarcastically, then realized with a pang of guilt that she probably hadn't. She'd been focused on her losses and healing Calliopia. She hadn't expressed much appreciation to anyone in her company. Least of all

Corvin.

He had been only too happy to feed off of her powers, and he had taken more from her than she had intended. She still felt off-balance and wasn't sure how much of her power he had taken from her and what abilities he had left her with. It was hard enough trying to understand and manage the skills she had newly discovered in Black Sands. Having them taken away or altered was like taking a blow to the face; she was stunned, hurt, and didn't know how much damage had actually been done.

"It would be nice to hear a thank you," Corvin agreed. "Even better to hear that you remember what you promised me back in the beginning."

Reg frowned and ran her fingers through the bubbles. "What do you mean, what I promised? You mean back when you stole my gifts?"

"I didn't steal them; I contracted for them. And no, I didn't mean <u>that</u> beginning. I meant when you first got the foolish notion to help Calliopia."

"It wasn't foolish. It worked, didn't it?"

"That doesn't make it less foolish. Just a better-than-expected outcome."

"What are you talking about?"

"When you asked for strength so that you could go back and help her."

"I didn't..." Reg trailed off, remembering. He was right. She had made a deal. She had agreed to go out on a date with him.

Again.

Because all of the others hadn't ended disastrously enough.

"Oh."

"Yes." Corvin agreed. "So do you want to pick the restaurant this time, or shall I? You can start working on that thank you speech and tell me over wine how much you appreciate my help."

"I do appreciate what you did. But I don't think I'm up for a date right now."

"Why not? It would seem to me to be the best time. You don't have any big jobs to do right now. You don't have a dying cat or fairy on your hands. No supernatural parents coming out of the woodwork. So why not?"

She didn't want to tell him that she wasn't strong enough to withstand him anymore. Maybe she was, she hadn't tested herself to find out. If Corvin still wanted to see her, then he still wanted to take more of her powers. And she didn't even know what she had left.

"It's just not a good time."

"Then when would be? We can set up a time now. At least put a pin in the date."

"No... I might be going on a trip. I'm not sure when I'll be here."

"You're going on a trip? You just got back from your quest to the Blue Ridge Mountains. I would think you would want to relax at home for a while."

"I haven't decided yet. Arrangements are up in the air. So we'll have to see."

"I have a sneaking suspicion you're just trying to put

me off."

"Now you're the psychic? I wouldn't put out your shingle quite yet."

"I think there are enough psychics in this town to go around." Corvin's voice held a bite that Reg didn't normally hear from him, and it stung a little. There was no reason she should be offended that he thought there were enough psychics around. He desired her powers, even if he said he wouldn't want to be a psychic. She rolled her eyes and sank a little deeper into the water.

Corvin eventually broke the silence, his tone less acid. "Well, Regina, even if it is just for a cup of coffee... I look forward to seeing you again. Don't be a stranger."

* * *

When Reg got tired of soaking in the tub, she toweled

off and opened the door a crack for a peek at what was going on in the cottage. She didn't hear any more chasing, pouncing, or crunching going on. She didn't hear or see anything out of the ordinary. But she also didn't see Starlight. She hoped he wasn't hiding, waiting for her to come out so that he could present her with the prize.

But then, what would be worse? Seeing it? Or not seeing it and stepping on it or coming across pieces here and there throughout the house over the next few days.

Maybe it would be better if Starlight brought it to her. Whatever it was.

She entertained the fantasy for a few seconds that maybe he had just picked up a twig or a piece of yarn or something equally innocuous, and she had only imagined that it was something worse.

But she knew in her heart that it wasn't true. There had definitely been legs. And something had run across the floor before Starlight had pounced.

"Starlight? Hey, where are you, Star?"

There was no answering meow or patter of soft paws. Reg stepped out of the bathroom and looked around, hoping to spot him. No sign of him in the kitchen or living room, unless he was hiding behind or under something. Reg looked around the kitchen island to be sure, then went to her bedroom.

Starlight was sleeping on the bed as if nothing had happened.

Reg looked around on the floor, stepping carefully to make sure she didn't put her foot onto anything.

"Where did you put it? I don't want to find it around here later…"

Starlight opened one eye, his blue one, and looked at her without expression. Reg scowled and pointed at him.

"You know what I'm talking about. Where is it? Where is the… whatever it was you caught?"

Starlight curled his head under, closing his eye again and beginning to purr. Reg reached over to pet him, looking around him carefully to make sure that the thing wasn't on the bed. If he were laying on it…

But there wasn't anything on the bed but the cat himself. And Reg's messy blankets. She always meant to make the bed as soon as she got up in the morning. She knew that other people managed it. But somehow, she never quite got around to it. And when she walked by later in the day, and it was still messy, she wanted to straighten it, but it seemed like a waste of time and energy when it would only be made for a few more hours and then she would be sleeping again.

She was a terrible housekeeper. It was a good thing she had Sarah looking after her.

She turned toward the big house at the front of the lot, reaching out mentally to sense whether Sarah was there or not. She sensed someone and wondered at first whether it was an intruder, but when she took a few steps toward the house, the feeling resolved, and she knew that one of the people who had just arrived home was Sarah. But she wasn't sure who the other was.

It wasn't fair that Corvin had taken so much, making her feel half-blind, like she was bumbling around in the dark or without glasses. Not that she needed glasses.

But some psychic goggles might be helpful.

The thought drew Reg out of the bedroom and into the living room, where she took her crystal ball down off the shelf. She had initially bought it as a prop, to make herself look more legitimate, but it had ended up being a tool that she used frequently, helping her to focus her thoughts and to clarify her vision.

She placed it on the coffee table and sat down in her favorite chair. Starlight often came out when he knew she was looking into the crystal, but he didn't this time. Getting his energy back after the chase or sleeping off a stomach full of something nasty. Reg made herself as comfortable as possible in the wicker chair and stared into its depths, looking beyond the shiny surface and a few bubbles in the glass, into the heart of the crystal.

But she didn't see anything. Just glass. A sea of glass.

No shapes to indicate who was there or things to come or to pinpoint the location of some lost object.

Reg sighed and decided to go up to the house for a look. Sarah always said she was welcome at any time.

* * *

Web of Nightmares, Book #7 of the Reg Rawlins, Psychic Investigator series by P.D. Workman can be purchased at pdworkman.com

ABOUT THE AUTHOR

Award-winning and USA Today bestselling author P.D. (Pamela) Workman writes riveting mystery/suspense and young adult books dealing with mental illness, addiction, abuse, and other real-life issues. For as long as she can remember, the blank page has held an incredible allure and from a very young age she was trying to write her own books.

Workman wrote her first complete novel at the age of twelve and continued to write as a hobby for many years. She started publishing in 2013. She has won several literary awards from Library Services for Youth in Custody for her young adult fiction. She currently has over 50 published titles and can be found at pdworkman.com.

Born and raised in Alberta, Workman has been married

for over 25 years and has one son.

* * *

Please visit P.D. Workman at pdworkman.com to see what else she is working on, to join her mailing list, and to link to her social networks.

* * *

If you enjoyed this book, please take the time to recommend it to other purchasers with a review or star rating and share it with your friends!

CPSIA information can be obtained
at www.ICGtesting.com
Printed in the USA
LVHW100827100920
665516LV00025B/402